MURDER IN THE VALLEYS

A cozy Welsh crime mystery full of twists

PIPPA McCATHIE

Paperback published by The Book Folks

London, 2018

© Pippa McCathie

ISBN 978-1-7310-8002-8

www.thebookfolks.com

To Nino

Prologue

She shouldn't have come. She never should have come. The stinging blow made her head ring and brought her to her knees. She felt the rough stones of the bridge at her back and pushed against them, tried to stand up, but only managed to stagger sideways. Oh god, she must get up. But before she could try again, her hair was grabbed. Pain shot through her scalp as she was pulled to her feet. Someone screamed, she realised it was her. The next moment, hands came from behind and grabbed her neck, strong, hard fingers pressing, locking the breath in her throat.

She was already dead when her body hit the water, unaware that an earring was torn from her ear as she fell, unaware that her bicycle followed her down, just missing her lifeless body. Someone stumbled down the muddy path at the side of the bridge. A moment later, footsteps retreated at a pounding run as the deep, rapid waters of the river Gwyn began to carry her away.

Chapter 1

The sound of agitated voices, reverberating eerily from somewhere above her head, stopped Fabia Havard in her progress towards the High Street. She listened, wondering where the sound was coming from. She was just below Pontygwyn bridge. Narrow and very old, it curved up and over the tumbling water of the river Gwyn. In parts its dank, damp stones were lichen covered, and here and there were signs of patchy restoration. The volume of traffic it had to deal with now was way beyond the carts, carriages and flocks of sheep it had carried in centuries past, and it had had to be reinforced more than once in the many hundred years of its long life.

Fabia leant back and looked up, shading her eyes against the morning sun as she did so. She could see someone sitting on the parapet above. She recognised familiar jet-black hair, and the leather jacket with its splashes of garish colour. Amber Morgan. But who on earth was she lashing out at? It certainly sounded like one hell of a confrontation. Fabia was desperate to get home. She didn't want to get involved in someone else's quarrel, she had enough problems of her own. But it was no good, she had to investigate. Once a policewoman, always a policewoman, she thought bitterly.

Turning, she began to trudge up the short but steep pathway carved into the bank. It would take her up the side of the bridge and on to the road above. Slipping and sliding on the ground, soft and muddy from all the rain they'd endured recently, she finally made it to the pavement. Once there, the two voices could be heard more clearly.

Halfway across the bridge, Amber Morgan sat swinging her booted feet back and forth – thump, thump – against the stones. Her voluptuous figure threatened to burst out of the tight, plunging T-shirt and minute skirt she wore under the jacket. A contemptuous sneer twisted her full young mouth as she stared at the woman standing before her.

Rhona Griffiths could not have been more of a contrast. Her birdlike figure was encased from mid-calf to neck in a coat of neat grey tweed, the only touch of colour a pink chiffon scarf tucked into the neck and the blue eyeshadow she always wore. Her cheeks were flushed and her improbably brown curls trembled, while her mouth worked as if she nibbled at the words before letting them out.

"There's a disgrace, you are!" Nibble, nibble, went her lips. "I have to say, Amber dear, I would expect better behaviour from a girl with your background."

"I'm not your dear." Amber drew the word out sneeringly. "And what background's that then?"

"You know very well what I mean. I'm sure your parents would be ashamed of you."

"Shut up! Shut up!" Amber shouted, jumping down from the parapet. For a moment Fabia thought Amber was going to lash out. She took a step forward. All her police training told her she should intervene. But she'd worked so hard over the last two years to get out of that mindset. It wasn't up to her to break up fights and pour oil on troubled waters any more.

But it was no good, she couldn't simply stand back and watch. "Come on you two," she said as she stepped forward quietly, "this won't do."

"I'll thank you not to interfere, Fabia," Rhona snapped, without taking her eyes off the girl in front of her. "Your behaviour, Amber, must be particularly upsetting to your dear father."

Amber, who seemed not to have noticed Fabia, thrust her face inches from the other woman's. "My father's dead, do you hear? Don't you even dare mention him!"

"Dear Murray–" but Rhona got no further.

"Murray's my step-father, you stupid bitch," Amber shouted, "and I don't care a fuck what he thinks. So why don't you just bugger off?"

"Amber–" Fabia began again, but this time they both ignored her.

"I know the things you get up to," Rhona spat out. "Don't think I haven't seen you and your disgusting friends. Hanging round smoking and drinking, and the good Lord knows what other lascivious activities." Spittle sprayed from her mouth with the force of the words and her pearl-drop earrings shook as if they were as enraged as their owner. "A disgrace, you are! A disgrace! I shall be speaking to your mother about this."

"You go near my mother and I'll kill you!" Any minute now Amber would hit her tormentor. Fabia stepped forward, about to intervene, but it didn't happen. Rhona took a step back, stumbled on the edge of the pavement, teetered then recovered herself. A second later she'd pushed past Fabia and was walking rapidly away.

Amber's parting shot followed after the retreating back. "Why don't you find yourself a man, you old bag? A good screw would make a new woman of you. Bye Felicia."

At last Fabia managed to make her presence felt. "Amber," she said wearily, "do you have to talk to her like that? You know it's asking for trouble. What's that about Felicia anyway?"

"Means she's a nothing, a non-person."

"Amber! And what on earth was all that about?"

Amber turned her dark, fiery eyes on Fabia and said blithely, "Hiya, how's tricks? Didn't see you there."

"Don't give me that," Fabia said.

Amber grinned at her. "Well, I was so bloody angry with the poisonous old crone."

"Why?" Fabia asked.

Amber shrugged, assuming a nonchalance Fabia didn't believe in for one moment. "She's so bloody nosy," she said, "objected to me sitting on the parapet, said I was damaging the bridge. And it's not the first time she's had a go at me. God, I hate her."

"I know she can be difficult, but you really shouldn't be so rude to her."

The girl gave her a sulky glance. "Why? She asked for it. She'll regret it, I'll see to that." She glared in the direction Rhona had taken. "And if she goes and bothers Mum I'll – I'll bloody scrag her."

"Nonsense," Fabia said briskly, perturbed by Amber's tone. Trying to sound convincing, she added, "And I doubt very much she will."

Fabia decided to change the subject. She knew from past experience there'd be no mileage in pursuing it now. Best save it for another time when Amber had calmed down. "Shouldn't you be getting ready for that interview in Cardiff?" she asked.

At this, the girl's expression changed completely. Her eyes lit up with enthusiasm and a smile totally transformed her face. "Oh Fabia, I'm so looking forward to it, but dreading it too. I've got to be there at two this afternoon. I just can't wait to show them my portfolio, but I'm really, like, nervous as well. I'd better go and get my stuff together." Like quicksilver her mood changed again, doubt swept in. "You do think, you know, that I can do it, don't you?"

"Amber love, you're a very talented artist, all you need is to be taught how to channel that talent. Go for it."

Amber grinned and flung her arms round Fabia, all her anger forgotten. "You're the best. Thanks for all your help."

There was the roar of a motorbike and Amber turned to look in its direction. The bike drew up beside them. "Here's my lift," she told Fabia. It was young Craig Evans, son of the local publican, astride the machine.

"Hello, Miss Havard," he said, his voice muffled by his helmet. He handed Amber one and she put it on, then she turned back to Fabia.

"I'll remember everything you've told me, everything."

"You do that, and behave yourself."

"Wouldn't know how, but I'm a pussycat really," Amber said, giving Fabia another twisted grin.

"Yes, one of the wild variety."

The girl laughed and waved as they headed off down the High Street.

Fabia followed slowly in their wake, still disturbed by what she'd seen, but unable to think of anything to do about it.

* * *

It was half an hour later that Fabia had her second shock of the day. She was coming out on to Pontygwyn High Street from Reynold's Cheese Shop when she looked up and there, on the opposite pavement, was a tall, loose-limbed man walking rapidly along. His glossy hair, the same shade as a newly born conker, blew back from his face as he walked, hands deep in his pockets. His eyes – clear grey, Fabia remembered, with thick, curling lashes – gazed straight ahead. Matt Lambert. She was utterly taken aback by her reaction. She felt it as a blow to the stomach, which, for a moment, deprived her of breath.

For what felt like an age, she hesitated. Should she duck back into Reynold's? Should she turn and go home; forget she'd seen him? Or call out his name and cross the road to speak to him? This was so stupid. Being indecisive was completely foreign to her nature, and yet still she stood there hesitating. And as she did so, as if he felt her eyes on him, he stopped in his tracks and looked round, straight at her. Recognition dawned, and Fabia watched as he too hesitated, made a small, uncertain gesture with his hand, then began to make his way rapidly across the street towards her.

* * *

Chief Inspector Matt Lambert had endured a boring meeting in Abergavenny about the new regional data protection policy. His mood was not good as he got into his car and began the journey back to his own station in Newport. What a bloody awful waste of time. Still, with luck he'd be back in his office under the hour.

Three-quarters of an hour later he realised this had been wildly optimistic. Resurfacing work on the motorway had reduced traffic to a crawl and forced him to try smaller country roads. That was why he now found himself passing a road sign which welcomed him to Pontygwyn, and told him it was twinned with Brescia in Italy and Ploubalay in France. He did not want to be here. It brought back far too many memories. But he was also aware he wouldn't get much further without petrol. What was more, he'd missed breakfast and was now hungry and thirsty. Like it or not, he'd have to stop.

Having filled up the car, and rejected the dried-up apologies for sandwiches in the garage cool cabinet, he made his way down the High Street in search of more appetising fare. It was at this point he had that crawling feeling down his back that he was being watched. He stopped, looked round, and to his consternation, there she was. Just as he was now, she was standing stock still. Her mass of dark gold hair was whipped by the breeze and her wide grey eyes stared across at him. Nearly as tall as he was, he noticed that she'd lost some weight, although this didn't detract in any way from her figure. He found himself lifting a hand, ready to wave, then, on impulse, made his way across the road without even checking the traffic, causing a screech of brakes from a passing lorry.

"Fabia." The air around them crackled with embarrassment and things left unsaid.

"Matt," was all she said in reply.

"Long – long time no see." For God's sake, he thought, couldn't he have found something more original to say?

"Yes. Two years in fact." Her tone was chilly. She obviously wasn't going to make this easy for him. He wished he'd kept walking, then called himself a coward.

"How are you?" he asked lamely.

"Fine." A meaningless word. He could tell she was no such thing. She went on, "I've finally retired now, just last week in fact."

He was taken aback by the wave of regret her words caused. What an awful waste. But all he said was, "I didn't know. No more... um... sick leave then?" He saw a flash of anger in her eyes and could have kicked himself for putting it so badly.

"No more so-called sick leave," she spat it out. "I'm shot of it. No more Superintendent Havard either. Just Fabia Havard, artist and illustrator now."

"I'm sorry, that you've left the force, I mean." He really was. She'd been one of the best police officers he'd ever known and there was a time they'd worked very closely together. And they'd been close in other ways too. He owed her a lot, he had to acknowledge that at least.

Silence descended and stretched out, neither knowing what to say. Matt found it difficult to meet those penetrating eyes and glanced up and down the street, looking for a way to escape. Fabia just stood there, and he knew she wasn't about to help him out of his predicament. He glanced at his watch. "Well, I should get going. It was good to see you."

She didn't respond to this. Feeling a fool, Matt lifted a hand in farewell and made his way back up the High Street to his car without looking back, his need for food and drink completely forgotten.

* * *

Fabia watched him go, her heart beating fast, a lump in her throat; then she shrugged, turned, and continued on her way, along the High Street towards home.

What a wasted opportunity. Why hadn't she grabbed it, tried to repair the rift between them? Stupid woman. It'd take a lot more than one chance meeting to do that. What's more, a small voice in the back of her mind told her it was up to Matt to make the first move. After all, he was the one who'd deserted her. And what a lie, to tell him she was fine when she so patently wasn't.

The last two years she'd been in limbo. She'd thought there'd be a sense of relief once the end came. But the finality of her retirement after the years of uncertainty had hit her much harder than she'd expected. And the anger over the way she'd been treated by her erstwhile bosses still gnawed away inside her. It wasn't that she didn't enjoy illustrating books, she did, and she was very lucky to have had a hobby that could so easily earn her a living, just about, at any rate. No, that wasn't it. It was all that unfinished business, and not just between her and Matt. Although she didn't miss the routine and the hard slog of police work, nor the politics or the many frustrations, she did miss the intellectual battle, pitting your wits against the criminal, solving the puzzle, the companionship of like-minded people, and the occasional satisfaction of a good result.

What a hell of a morning! First that row between Amber and Rhona and now this encounter with Matt.

As she walked she thought back to Rhona and Amber. She knew Rhona well, not only because she was her next-door neighbour, but also because she was well known in Pontygwyn for snooping around in other people's affairs. Fabia herself had been the subject of Rhona's gossiping in the past and knew getting on the wrong side of her could make life difficult. Although she felt quite capable of looking after herself, she doubted the same would apply to Amber's mother, Cecily, who was a gentle, timid woman. She'd be deeply upset if Rhona tackled her. Once she'd sorted out the shopping she'd done for her dinner party this evening, Fabia decided she'd give Cecily a ring, try to reassure her should Rhona have complained about Amber.

By the time she got home a sense of foreboding had settled deep inside her, and she knew from experience it would be very hard to shift.

* * *

Amber was in a good mood. The interview had gone well, she was sure they'd offer her a place. It hadn't taken as long as she'd thought it would and she'd managed to get a lift home from Cardiff. Bit of luck that. As a result, it was only half past six when she was dropped off at the end of her road, at least an hour earlier than she'd expected. He'd refused to take her as far as the house, but she didn't mind. It was hardly surprising.

She grinned to herself. He hadn't seemed too happy to see her at first, but she'd soon made it worth his while. At least he'd been driving himself. She was pretty sure if anyone else had been with him, that chauffeur or whatever the man's job was, they'd have sailed straight past without a glance. For a second, a lurch of apprehension hit her. Would he find out what she'd done? Did she care if he did? No, sod it, she thought, defiant.

This brought Rhona Griffiths back into Amber's mind. Her mood darkened. As for her, she deserved all she got, lousy bitch. And if she'd phoned Mum and ranted on – Amber's hands balled into fists at her side and she began to run. She must get home and find out. Anxiety mounted inside her. Please God, don't let Rhona have phoned. Stupid, stupid to have wound her up like that. Fabia was right. But it was too late now.

Nearly home. She clenched her teeth as she got to the front door. And please God, don't let Mum be in one of her stresses.

Chapter 2

"Registered package," the postman said when Fabia opened the door. She squinted in the bright morning light, her head throbbing as she signed for the large padded envelope. What an idiot to have drunk so much last night.

She was about to go back inside when a high-pitched voice called, "Good morning, Fabia! God has blessed us with sun at last."

Rhona Griffiths was standing on her side of the low fence, her small eyes and pointed nose making her look like some malevolent Beatrix Potter character. Fabia considered mentioning the confrontation she'd witnessed the day before, try to smooth things over for Amber, but decided against it. A hangover and Rhona were not a happy combination, and she was reluctant to appear as much of a snoop as Rhona herself.

"So he has," Fabia said, trying not to sound too unfriendly.

"Interesting post?" Rhona went on, avid for confidences.

"Nothing much. Some work from my agent and probably a pile of junk mail."

"And what's the present project then?"

"Illustrations for what will probably be a series of children's picture books."

"There's lovely. I used to adore picture books, all those little animals and fairies. My dearest Da used to read to us every evening when we were children, never mind how busy he was."

"That must have been nice for you," Fabia said, then added maliciously. "But they're a bit different nowadays. The ones I'm illustrating are all about learning the facts of life, you know, sex, reproduction, that sort of thing."

Rhona's thin lips tightened and an ugly flush crept up her neck and spread over her cheeks. "It's my opinion the young know far too much about that sort of thing. Disgusting I call it. Really Fabia, I don't know how you could involve yourself in such a thing."

"Oh, I don't know, the sooner they learn the facts the better, and anyway, it helps pay my bills."

"My dearest Da, who was a pastor as you know, would not have approved, and nor do I." She could have sworn Rhona's nose was actually twitching, any minute now she'd sprout whiskers as she gripped the top of the fence and leant further over it. Rhona lowered her voice to a sibilant whisper. "I could tell you such things about certain people in this town. Lewd behaviour, disgraceful language. As you saw yesterday, that daughter of—"

"Yes, I'm sure," Fabia interrupted, regretting her impulse to bait her next-door neighbour. All she really wanted to do was retreat to her kitchen for a cup of coffee and two paracetamols. "But I really have to go now. Work to do."

"Well, I do think someone like you shouldn't lower themselves to such work. You used to have some standing in the community, after all. But perhaps your standards aren't quite as high as they used to be." And with this parting shot Rhona swung round and disappeared back inside, slamming her front door behind her.

Fabia no longer felt guilty about baiting her, and she was beginning to think Amber had had every reason to lash out. Poisonous little trout was about right. She behaves like a geriatric witch and she's barely fifty, and as for that much-quoted dearest Da of hers, thank God I never met him, she thought.

* * *

There were definitely gaps in Fabia's memory of the evening before, although leftover snatches of conversation kept bubbling up in her mind. She was a good cook and had given her erstwhile colleagues a meal to remember, and the wine had flowed, followed by several malt whiskies. If she wasn't careful she'd turn into a forty-year-old lush, not a happy prospect.

She hadn't told them she'd seen Matt that morning, although she wasn't entirely sure why not, but she did seem to remember asking them about his promotion. And hadn't she said something about his having been like a brother to her? God, she'd been that drunk! Alun Richards had given a snort of laughter. She remembered telling him, with as much dignity as she could muster, that she was no baby snatcher. He'd grinned and winked at her; bastard!

But all in all, it had been a good enough evening with that small group of friends from the force who'd stood by her. Part of her had enjoyed catching up on all the police gossip, in spite of the growing feeling she had now of being an outsider. Such a pity so few of her old colleagues kept in touch, but hardly surprising.

She put the kettle on and rummaged in one of the kitchen cupboards for the packet of paracetamol, pressed two into her palm and went to the sink for some water. While she waited for the kettle to boil, Fabia opened the window and leant on the sill, breathing in the clear crisp Welsh air. She always found this view calming, and calm was exactly what she needed. For Fabia nothing could match up to the landscape of her homeland. Her spirits crept up. Through the tangled branches of the old apple tree she could see the fields stretching away from the bottom of her garden in a gradual upward slope, a patchwork of greens and browns interrupted, at this time of year, by the bright yellow of daffodils. Dotted here and there were sheep, cream and occasionally black bundles of wool moving lazily about, cropping at the grass. In the far distance, the fields gave way to a more severe landscape as the lower slopes of the Black Mountains began to rise, and here the colours changed to misty blue, grey and mauve. And there, in the far distance, was the distinctive shape of the Sugar Loaf mountain. Matt had once decided they should hike up that peak, but Fabia had chickened out, opting for the much easier Little Skirrid. He'd teased her over it for days, calling her a lazy wimp.

But all this daydreaming would get her nowhere. Quickly she made the coffee, then leant across and closed the window. It was time to get to work, headache or no headache. But still her mind drifted. How strange, she thought, to be thinking of the painting as work. It didn't feel right. Sort of theoretical rather than actual. She knew, deep down, it would take a long time before she'd stop feeling like a police officer, but there was little point in dwelling on it. At least, she told herself briskly, she was lucky enough to have this second string to her bow. How many people could say that? And there were similarities, if you thought about it. In both professions you had to study faces, and body language mattered. You had to have an eye for place and position, for detail, and a good memory. Not so very different really, she told herself.

Feeling better for the coffee, she stuffed her wild hair into a scrunchy and made her way down the hall to the dining room, but before she got there the phone rang. She picked up the receiver and wandered with it into the dining room, which doubled as her study.

It was her agent, Sheena. She wanted to know if the manuscript had arrived. Fabia told her it had. Had Fabia looked at it yet? No, she hadn't had the chance yet. When would she do so? Well, now, actually. And how soon would she be able to send the first sketches? Fabia sighed, her head throbbed as she promised to get some work sent off by the beginning of next week. It was the best she could do. There was a clicking sound of irritation from the other end of the line.

"Give me a chance," Fabia protested. "Quite apart from anything else, I've got a bloody hangover."

"Self-inflicted injury," was the unsympathetic comment.

"Okay, okay. Look, I promise I'll get the first drafts to you as soon as I possibly can."

Feeling hounded, Fabia put the phone down quickly before her tormentor could say anything else. But she knew she'd have to get some serious work done as soon as possible. This could turn out to be a really lucrative commission and she couldn't afford to lose it. She pulled the padded envelope from the elastic band that bound it to the rest of the post and headed for the dining room and her desk.

* * *

The work wasn't going well. However hard she tried, Fabia couldn't concentrate, and it seemed the weather had caught her unsettled mood. The sun had gone and grey clouds were rolling in, sombre and glowering. Rain was threatening yet again. Let's face it, she had plenty to worry about – Matt, Amber, her work. It was hopeless. She'd never produce anything useful in this frame of mind. Sod the weather, maybe some fresh air would help get rid of the gremlins. It'd turned chilly but it wasn't actually raining yet. A walk across Gwiddon Park would do her good. She pulled on her boots and threw on a waterproof jacket just in case. Hunched in her coat, hands deep in the pockets, she made her way down the road and into the park.

There was no-one else about — all too sensible, back inside having their lunch and avoiding the threatening weather. But she was glad of the solitude, and she loved it down by the river in almost any weather. She liked to watch out for occasional bubbles rising as fish went about their business just below the surface. And she loved the colours, the soft greeny brown of the water, the rich brown of the earth on the banks, and the varied shades of branches bending low, mud-spattered and glistening where they'd been splashed by the passing river. All this had been one of the main attractions when she'd moved into the house her aunt had left her. But it wasn't having its usual effect. The gloom that had settled inside her refused to be shifted.

Fabia trudged on. Since the grass was so wet, she kept to the path that curved down and then turned along the river's edge. If she got nearer to the water maybe she'd be able to spot a trout or two in the pools and eddies just above the pond. She glanced up at the sky. Slate grey clouds were gathering and even the colour of a bright orange lifebelt hooked to a post on the bank seemed suddenly dulled. She shivered and hugged her arms round her body. The first raindrops began to spatter down. Maybe this hadn't been such a good idea after all. It was time to give in and go home. Perhaps she'd heat up a bowl of soup to take the chill out of her bones.

Fabia looked up at the cloudy sky and a large drop of rain hit her in the eye. At the same moment, her foot slipped and she had to grab a branch to steady herself, but still she slithered down towards the fast-flowing water. She was relieved when, with a jolt, a protruding root arrested her fall, but as she turned to make her way back up the bank something caught her eye. Just below her, in a bend of the river, where reeds were tangled in the branches of a fallen tree trunk, came a glint and gleam of silver. Slowly it glittered back and forth with the motion of the water.

She stared down, trying to make out what it was, then picked up a stick and, stepping carefully on the soft mud of the bank, edged closer. Stretching out precariously, she tried to hook out the silver object with the end of the stick, but all she came up with were long, thin black reeds. Black reeds? No. No. Black hair!

Stock still, frozen for a moment in disbelief, she gazed down at the rushing water, then threw the stick violently away from her. What she was looking at was so repugnant that at first her mind rejected it. But not for long. There was no getting away from the grisly truth as the swirl of the current cleared the hair away from a blue-white moon face. There was the glint of silver from a long earring, black sodden clothing, hair swirling in a grotesque dance, and worst of all, two open eyes staring up at her from under the water. Amber Morgan's eyes.

Chapter 3

The shock was an icy blast stinging her whole body. Fabia felt nausea rising. She clamped it down, refusing to give in to the urge. For God's sake, she'd seen enough bodies in her time, some twisted and mutilated, others who'd died with terror imprinted on their faces glaring out at her. But this was different. This had taken her completely by surprise. It was out of context. She wasn't prepared.

Anchored by her clothes, which had wrapped round some tree roots, one pale arm above the head in a macabre wave, Amber's body shifted with the current. For a second, the urge to stumble down and drag her out was almost overwhelming, but it only lasted for a second. Mustn't get too close. This could be a crime scene. She must avoid any more contamination of the area. But why should she think of it like that? It was far more likely to have been a tragic accident. That was irrelevant. It was obvious Amber was dead. There was nothing to be done to save her. This had to be handed over to the police, and that did not mean her, ex-Superintendent Fabia Havard.

With infinite care she climbed back up the bank and looked around. There was no-one in sight. Not another soul, and she hadn't got her mobile with her, hadn't thought to bring it. No choice, she'd have to get back to the house as fast as she could and phone from there. Covered in mud, dripping and cold, she broke into a stumbling run.

. She felt sick at the thought of a vibrant young life cut brutally short. And Amber had been a friend, Fabia had cared about her. But in spite of this, as she ran, her training took over. Her mind began methodically sifting through what she'd seen, analysing it, filing away each and every detail.

* * *

It was raining hard now, but Fabia barely noticed as she pounded along the tarmac path and across the road, her breath rasping cold down her throat. A horn blared as a car swerved to avoid her. The motorist shouted obscenities, but she hardly noticed. She turned into Morwydden Lane and through her own gate, up the path, scrabbling for the key in one pocket, then another. At last she found it.

Slamming the door behind her, for a second she bent, hands on knees, trying to get her breath, then she grabbed the phone and dialled 999. She gave the details with practised efficiency, hardly faltering at all. Only when she'd been assured there would be someone along very soon, did she slump down on a chair and rub at her face with soiled hands. She thought again of the blue-white skin, the long strands of black hair, and rushed upstairs to splash cold water on her face. The shock of it helped, and so did stripping off her mud-soaked boots and sodden socks. As she did so, her mind was working away.

How long had the poor child been in the river? When had she last seen her? Of course, on the bridge yesterday, that row with Rhona, and then the poor girl had gone off to her interview in Cardiff, so full of enthusiasm she could hardly contain herself. Christ! This was a nightmare.

As Fabia changed into dry clothes, the policewoman in her began to pick over the possibilities. Could it have been an accident when Amber was drunk or high on something or other? She knew Amber had dabbled in drugs; not class As, but it didn't take much as she well knew. Maybe the interview had gone really well and she'd been celebrating. On the other hand, what if it had been a total disaster? Amber was a girl of extremes. If the whole thing had fallen through, could she have decided to end it all? She wasn't the most stable person, and she'd had enough grief in her life. But somehow Fabia didn't think suicide would be Amber's way. Wouldn't she be more likely to lash out at someone else than kill herself?

It was pointless speculating. Soon enough the police machine would get underway and Fabia would be out of it. But only in an official capacity. For the first time, it occurred to her: she'd never been involved in such a tragedy from a personal point of view. Apart from when she'd had to help Matt through that awful business with his sister, Bethan, but that had so obviously been suicide.

And what about Amber's family? Poor, poor Cecily. This could destroy her. And her stepfather, so conventional, but also so caring. He'd tried hard to do the right thing for his stepdaughter. They just won't know what's hit them, Fabia thought. Even as she told herself she would have to try and help Cecily through this, her mind flinched from the idea. What could she do? She'd never had children. How could she know how a mother would feel?

The knock on the door came just as Fabia walked down the stairs again. Two uniformed police officers stood on the doorstep.

"Miss Havard? You reported an incident."

"Yes. And you are?"

His eyebrows raised at her tone of voice. "Sergeant Pryce," the older of the two said. "This is Police Constable Roberts. Now would you tell us what this is about?"

She closed the door behind her and said briskly, "Come on. I'll show you. We'll go in your car. The park gates are open, so you'll be able to drive down there."

The one whose name was Roberts looked as if he was about to protest but, after a sharp glance from his older colleague, he changed his mind. Fabia was relieved. The last thing she wanted to do was drag in her past connections in order to pull rank. As she climbed into the car Fabia noticed Rhona's sharp face staring out at them from a downstairs window next door.

Roberts, who was driving, manoeuvred carefully through the gates of the park and drove along the tarmac path. Leaning forward in her seat, Fabia gave them a brief account of what she'd found. After a few minutes, he parked at the point where the tarmac met the towpath and Fabia led the way to the bend in the river. In spite of a murmured protest from the sergeant, she stepped closer, part of her wondering if the body was still there. Stupid. Of course it was. She looked down at the pathetic shape in the water. The white face with its staring eyes gazed back at her, the black hair swirled, the pale arm waved. She felt pity, and revulsion grip at her stomach once again.

"Excuse me, Miss Havard," Sergeant Pryce's voice was brisk, "would you mind?"

"Yes, of course," said Fabia. "Sorry. Force of habit."

He gave her a sharp look but didn't comment as she stepped back up the bank. She stood watching while the policemen clambered down, talking in low voices as they went. One of them lifted his radio and muttered into it. The other, hanging on to a dangling branch, leant precariously out over the water and stayed there for some time, but it wasn't very long before they trudged back up again. Like Fabia had been, they were both spattered with mud and their shoes were caked in the stuff.

"I know who it is," Fabia told them.

"You do?"

"Her mother and stepfather live on the other side of the village, up at Well House, by St Madoc's School. He's the deputy head. Cecily and Murray Cole."

"Rightio. A sad business. We'll just keep an eye, like, until the team arrive. You'd best get back home now." It was a polite dismissal. "Roberts can drive you back."

"No, I'll walk." But she didn't move.

"The SOCO team's on its way." Part of her was pleased at his use of the term to her. At least he'd acknowledged she'd know what he was talking about, maybe he'd recognised her. "And Chief Inspector Lambert will be here soon enough," Pryce added.

"Oh no!" It was out before she could stop it.

He gave her a sharp glance. "Sorry?"

"Never mind." It just hadn't occurred to her he'd be in charge, but it should have; after all this was his patch since his promotion. Poor Matt, how awful for him. Most policemen learnt how to deal with death in all its forms, but, with his history, this case would be very difficult for him to cope with. And, on top of that, to be faced with her as well. Fate was in a truly malicious mood today.

"I expect he'll be calling on you later," Pryce said, his eyes still curious.

"I know DCI Lambert. I used to work with him."

It was obvious it had finally dawned on him exactly who she was. He looked embarrassed and wouldn't meet her eye, but his back straightened, as if he'd been about to stand to attention.

"Ah yes, of course, ma'am. I'm sorry." He gave her a slightly apologetic smile.

"Not to worry," Fabia said briskly. At least there was no tinge of contempt in his voice. "More important things for you to think about. I'll leave you to it."

Slowly, feeling weary and miserable, Fabia trudged up the road towards home. It seemed an age since she'd woken that morning. She glanced at her watch. Only two o'clock. As she closed her gate behind her she hoped the squeak of its hinge wouldn't attract Rhona's attention. But even so, when Rhona didn't appear to ask what was going on, Fabia wondered why.

* * *

Matt arrived at his office late that morning. He'd spent a restless night, unable to get thoughts of yesterday's encounter with Fabia out of his mind. As a result, he'd overslept and it wasn't until half past eight that he finally came to. Dragging himself out of bed, cursing as he did so, he threw on his clothes and slammed out of the flat. The journey from his flat to the station was short but frustrating, the usual early morning crawl not yet over.

Once there, he left his car in the car park round the back, looking up at the building as he did so. Not for the first time he thought what a pity it was such an ugly structure. Built in the 1950s when money was short, it was a utilitarian four stories of concrete, discoloured now by rain and wind. An attempt had been made to brighten the place up by painting the window frames a once vivid green, but this had faded to an unpleasant slime colour, and the whole place was in sore need of several gallons of paint, preferably not the dirty grey colour it was at present. Even daffodils that someone had planted along the front of the building did little to cheer it, only looking, with their bowed heads, rather lonely and out of place. Still, nothing he could do about any of that now. Chief Superintendent Rees-Jones was hardly going to agree to money being spent on sprucing the place up, not when the force was understrength and stretched to its limits.

Matt strode along the corridor to his office, took off his jacket, flung it over the back of his chair, and sat down to plough through the mountain of paperwork piled on his desk.

By lunchtime he felt he was more or less on top of it all. The clear-up rate looked better than usual and, just so long as they didn't have some big case come in, this month's figures would be pretty good. But his optimism was short-lived. The phone rang.

Matt picked up the receiver. His eyes widened and his fingers tightened as he listened. He slammed the phone down, then picked it up again almost immediately. After a couple of quick, curt conversations, he opened his door and called out, "Dilys, I need you."

* * *

Sergeant Dilys Bevan, sitting at her desk in the main office, jumped up. She recognised that tone of voice. Something was up. The boss was definitely not happy. He'd been in a strange mood ever since he got back, late, from that meeting at Regional HQ yesterday, and then he'd been late again this morning. She wondered what was going on and hoped she'd find out now as she sat down in the chair opposite his desk. Glancing across at him she was shocked to see the look on his face, tight-lipped, his brows almost meeting above the bridge of his nose, his dark eyes bleak. What on earth was going on? But she didn't ask, that wasn't her way. She just waited for him to tell her.

"I've just had a call from the local sergeant in charge of the Pontygwyn area. Do you know him?"

"Glyn Pryce," Dilys said, on safe ground now. She had a brain like a computer and always remembered every little detail. "Came to Gwent from the Rhondda force. Valleys boy, good bloke, keen but not that ambitious; keeps his ear to the ground, methodical and pretty efficient, I'd say."

Her boss nearly smiled, but not quite. "A man after your own heart," he said.

"You could say that."

Chief Inspector Lambert didn't go on immediately. He pulled at his mouth with his long fingers, staring straight at her but not, she thought, really seeing her. Then suddenly he sat forward, as if he realised action was needed.

"A body's been discovered in the river Gwyn. Young girl, eighteen or thereabouts. Pryce was called in by the woman who found her." He took a deep breath and Dilys wondered what was coming next. "She's an ex police superintendent, Fabia Havard. I used to work with her, bit of a coincidence really. I bumped into her only yesterday on my way back from HQ."

There was something in his voice, his whole demeanour, that Dilys couldn't fathom. A wariness, but more than that. She had the distinct impression he was deeply disturbed but couldn't fathom why. A body in the river wasn't that unusual, whether it was the Gwyn or the Usk, both were running high and that spelt danger. People went fishing, slipped, or got drunk and fell in. Perhaps it was to do with this Havard woman. Dilys remembered she'd been given extended sick leave, something to do with a fraud case that went pear-shaped. Perhaps that was it, maybe he didn't want to have anything more to do with a policewoman with a murky past. There was no point speculating. He'd tell her what it was all about when he was ready.

"Did Pryce say if they know who the girl was?"

"Yes. A youngster called Amber Morgan."

"That rings a bell, but I can't remember why."

"Her stepfather's deputy head of St Madoc's school, that expensive place for the kids of the rich just outside Pontygwyn. Anyway, the SOCO unit's on its way. I've told Pryce we'll be there as soon as we can, and I've had a word with the team, Pat Curtis included."

His tone said it all. Dilys grimaced. Dr Curtis, the regional pathologist, wasn't known for her accommodating nature. But Matt didn't elaborate. "Let's go," he said as he pushed himself up out of his chair with none of his usual enthusiasm for the start of a new case.

What the hell's the matter with him? Dilys wondered. The sooner I find out what the hell's going on, the better.

Chapter 4

"I remember now why Amber Morgan's name sounded familiar," Dilys said as she pulled out into the traffic.

Matt's thoughts had been miles away, years back, in a place he'd prefer not to be. Her tone pulled him back to the present. It was a relief.

"That drugs investigation at the Golden Monkey, she was one of the youngsters on the list to be interviewed, along with Craig Evans whose parents run The Oaks pub in Pontygwyn, and Vanessa Breverton, you know, the MP's daughter."

"I remember now. Weren't we due to interview all three of them? The community team was going to talk to Amber Morgan and Craig Evans, but the chief put a block on seeing the Breverton girl. Neville Breverton, a junior minister now, by the way, is a pal of his it seems." Matt gave a derisive snort. "Usual story."

"This rather concentrates the mind, doesn't it? Do you think there could be a connection?"

"God knows. We'll have to wait and see. But it does rather bring the drugs aspect into sharp relief."

"Or it could have nothing whatever to do with it," Dilys said. "Anyway, what else have we got?"

"She was found dead in the River Gwyn, probably drowned, could be a suicide. Fabia Havard found the body."

Dilys gave him a sharp enquiring look. "Wasn't she that Superintendent who had to be given so-called sick leave?"

Matt felt his teeth clench, this was all so unbelievable. "Yes, and it wasn't 'so-called' sick leave."

"I thought she was tied up with some corruption scandal."

"You thought wrong," he snapped.

"Sorry, sir." She sounded offended, but he didn't care. He was having a hard enough time dealing with this situation as it was. How he dreaded the next few hours! Too many memories to be dredged up, too many similarities. Usually he managed to detach himself. You had to. Self-preservation. But there were times when he couldn't. The drowning of a young woman brought it all back, his sister, Bethan, cold and waxy, dragged out of the Usk. Identifying her body like an automaton, don't cry, don't break down. Do it. Get it over. And on top of that, there was Fabia who'd been there for him all through that terrible time; Fabia, whom he'd not spoken to for two years until yesterday.

Matt dragged himself back to the present. "I gather the girl is… was a bit of a rebel. As Pryce said, she's come to our attention, but nothing serious, and nothing proved. Usual business with that Golden Monkey crowd." He paused and gazed miserably out at the passing traffic.

"And the SOCO team's meeting us down there?"

"Yes. They'll have everything set up by the time we arrive, and Dr Curtis, she should be there by now. She says she'll perform the post-mortem this evening if needs be."

"There's quick," Dilys said, giving him a curious glance.

But all he said was, "I persuaded her."

They drove the rest of the way in silence and, ten minutes later, were pulling up on the grass above the now busy scene. A police van and two other cars were already there and the area had been cordoned off with plastic tape. Matt pulled a pair of Wellingtons out of the boot of the car and noticed, as he did so, a small crowd of people standing a few yards away. They were avidly stretching and staring for a good view, but were being kept back by two uniformed constables. His mouth twisted in disgust and a wave of anger churned in his stomach.

"What is it with these ghouls? Haven't they got anything better to do?"

"No different from the usual, sir. It's human nature."

"One of its less attractive aspects."

Having identified themselves to the PC on guard, they ducked under the tape and made their way down to the river bank. A stocky uniformed sergeant turned and saw them, then made his way towards them.

"Chief Inspector Lambert? Sergeant Pryce, sir. "Nasty one this. Always is, mind, when it's a youngster."

Matt nearly snapped that this was a statement of the obvious, but bit it back. Instead he said, "We've got some of the info. Go through it again, would you?"

With admirable brevity, Pryce gave them all the salient facts and finished off with a quick update. "We've got the body out. Dr Curtis says she definitely didn't go into the water here, must have been further up, maybe off the bridge if she was a jumper. With all this rain, the river's running fast so the distance fits. The SOCOs are on the bank over by there at the moment."

Just ahead of them was an enclosure of plastic sheeting. After struggling into regulation overalls, they made their way towards it, pulling on surgical gloves as they did so.

As he elbowed the flap aside and went into the claustrophobic little tent, Matt had a desperate urge to turn and run. In the enclosed space, the dank smell of the river hit him, and something less pleasant. He stopped dead just inside, unable for a moment to go further. But he had to pull himself together. This wasn't Bethan. This was some unknown girl. And there was no way it could be avoided. He steeled himself, his lips in a tight line, the muscles in his cheeks taut over his clenched teeth.

* * *

Inside the enclosure, two people in identical paper overalls were bending over the body which lay on a plastic sheet on the muddy grass. One of them looked up, a woman with short blonde hair and a sharp, intelligent face.

"You took your time getting here," Pat Curtis snapped. Not for the first time Matt wondered why she was so abrupt. Maybe it was the nature of her job, although there was a theory at the station that she'd been disappointed in love, but he didn't subscribe to that idea. That'd hardly make her into the human version of a hornet. Having her on the case would just add to his dislike of it, but there was nothing to be done about it. He took a deep breath and refused to rise to the bait, just nodded and said, "Afternoon, Dr Curtis."

She stood aside so that he could come closer, and he bent to get his first clear view of the body.

Black clothes clung damply to shiny skin. The girl's face – glassy pale, blue-tinged – was streaked with mud, slimy weed, and strands of black hair. On one side, a long silver earring was still in place, the other was missing, and there was a tear in the lobe. Matt felt a churn of anger and revulsion. Another young life cut brutally short. For a moment he bent closer and, with one long finger, gently lifted a clinging strand of hair away from the dead cheek. "What's this?"

"Bruising," Pat Curtis said, her tone implying the question was stupid, "possibly caused before she went into the water. There's bruising on the neck as well."

Matt looked up at her with a sharp frown. "You don't usually proffer information so early."

"That may well be true, but this is very clear."

"D'you mean someone hit her? Or tried to strangle her?"

"Good Lord, how can I tell yet? You'll just have to wait until I've completed the PM before I can give you any more."

"Anything else to indicate how she ended up here?"

"Not yet." She scowled at him. "Like I said, you'll just have to wait."

"Okay." Matt risked just one more question. "But you think perhaps not a jumper?"

Pat gave an irritated sigh. "I don't know yet, okay?"

Knowing it would be just as well to have her on his side, he made an effort to contain his impatience. No good pushing too hard. She'd just dig her heels in, and that was the last thing he wanted. "Thanks for saying you'll get the PM done so soon. It'll be a great help. What time?"

"As soon as we get through here. Have you sorted identification?"

"We're about to. Anyway, thank you," he said, still trying his best to be conciliatory. He got up and turned to Dilys who was standing quietly waiting for him.

"Where's Pryce?"

Before she could answer, "Here sir," came a voice from just outside, and a second later his face appeared round the flap of the tent.

"Get them searching for the pair to that earring, would you? It's important we find it, could tell us where she went into the water."

"Will do. Anything else?"

"Not at the moment." He turned to Dilys. "We'd better go and see the parents now. Ghastly job, hate it; let's get it over with."

As they left the park a car passed them and was stopped at the gate by the policeman on duty. Matt recognised a reporter and photographer from the Newport Evening News. "The vultures are here already," he said sourly.

"Nothing we can do about that, sir."

"No. But it won't make our job on the drugs aspect any easier – if there's a connection."

Dilys gave him a sharp look. "You think there may be?"

"No idea, but it's a possibility if she was part of that crowd." He sat in brooding silence for a moment. "Maybe she didn't pay up on time, or perhaps she threatened to turn them in."

As Dilys came up to the junction and prepared to turn right into the High Street, he straightened.

"Turn left here," he said suddenly.

Dilys jammed on the brakes. "Why left?"

"I want to go and have a look at that bridge."

She did as she was told without argument and, just before they got to the bridge itself, turned off on to a grass verge.

Matt got out of the car and gazed back across the river and Gwiddon Park to the houses beyond. Through the trees he could just see glimpses of the police vehicles and the plastic tent, signs of movement and activity. Carefully he leant over the parapet of the bridge and looked down at the rushing water. It was definitely running fast, and it was deep here, the water clearer, with few rocks or branches for anything to get snagged on. It wasn't until the river neared the bend which took it down to the pond that there were a few rocky inlets, traps waiting to catch anything the water brought along. Turning, he walked back across the bridge, head down, searching.

Dilys followed him. "What are you looking for?"

"I don't know. Anything that might help."

"Shouldn't we leave it to the SOCOs–" Dilys's voice tailed off as his head snapped round to look at her. Matt stopped himself just in time. It wouldn't be fair to take things out on Dilys, particularly as she was right. Still, he told himself, a quick look would do no harm.

"Just having a preliminary look," he said shortly. A moment later he turned and walked slowly back, this time studying the parapet on the park side of the bridge. Inch by inch he ran his eye over the ancient brickwork, looking for he knew not what. He was nearly across when he gave a little exclamation, bent down, and studied the parapet more closely.

"Look at this, Dilys."

She did as he asked. Just where his finger was pointing there were some scuff marks on the granite, blackish, and above them, a piece of fabric caught under a jagged lip of stone. It moved sluggishly in the breeze. It was nearly free and would detach itself and fly off in the wind any minute. Matt rummaged in his pockets. He knew that somewhere he had one of those small polythene bags with a self-seal strip at the top. He gave a satisfied grunt as he found it.

"Have you got a pair of scissors or tweezers?" he asked Dilys. After a moment she handed him a pair of nail scissors. Trust Dilys to have what he needed.

With infinite care he prised the material clear and put it in the bag. Pressing the seal shut, he put the bag in his trouser pocket. "Radio across and get some of those SOCOs up here now," he told Dilys. "I don't want anything disappearing before they think to go over the bridge. And tell them down there to be damn careful with the girl's shoes." Dilys spoke into her mobile as he walked the rest of the way.

As the bridge ended there was a rough path curving down to the water's edge. Matt stared at it but didn't attempt to go down. There were fresh marks in the mud, hard to identify, deep groves, as if someone had slithered rather than walked down. It could have been anyone, Matt told himself. He walked slowly back to join Dilys.

"Looks as if someone sat up here."

"The kids often do," she said. "It's a regular meeting place."

"How do you know that?"

"I've got friends who live round here. I've often seen groups of youngsters sitting on the parapet."

"Damn! Ah well, still might be something. There're some marks down the side there. Looks as if someone's been down to the water's edge quite recently."

"Wouldn't be that unusual, would it?"

"Maybe not, but I still want it checked," he snapped, "and with a fine-tooth comb."

A police car arrived and parked beside them on the grass verge. Two of the SOCO team got out, and Matt spoke to them. Leaving them to it, he and Dilys resumed their journey up through the town, Matt silently steeling himself to face the girl's parents.

* * *

Rhona, unable to see enough from her lounge window, had decided to go up to her attic room. She'd get a much better view from there, especially if she used Da's telescope. Excitement mounting inside her, she made her way up the two flights of stairs and, with a trembling hand, unlocked the small door at the top. Locking it behind her, she made her way across the dusty, dark room, put up a hand and, with trembling fingers, touched a framed photograph that hung on the wall. A small shelf below it held fresh flowers in a cut glass vase. She touched it again and smiled at the stern, thin-lipped face so like her own. "Such excitement, Da. I've come to use your telescope."

In the recess made by the glass-sided dormer window stood a magnificent telescope, polished, pristine, not a speck of dust on it. Rhona put her eye to the lens. With an expert touch she adjusted the focus, moved the instrument slightly, and the activity in the park leapt up at her, clear and so near she felt she could reach out and touch the scurrying figures. As she watched, moving the instrument very slightly once or twice, never taking her eye from the lens, she talked in a breathy whisper.

"Oh Da, there's an ambulance just arrived. Yes. Yes. There's more movement now, over by there, near that white and yellow tent. The ambulance people are carrying something. It looks like a stretcher. Yes, it is a stretcher, Da. Of course it would be, wouldn't it? I wonder if that's her – her body. Such a tragedy in our midst. But then, she was a bad girl, wasn't she? Really wicked, and so rude to me, Da. I told you what she said. So wicked. Perhaps God had to punish her. Do you think that was it, Da? That must be it. I mustn't interfere then, must I? I've done my duty, just as you would have wished."

She watched in silence for a while, then straightened and looked at the photograph. Her father's face stared straight back at her with a reflection of her own superimposed upon it. She was smiling, just one side of her mouth lifted, and her small eyes were bright with anticipation and excitement.

"He'll have to take notice of me now, won't he, Da? He won't be able to be nasty to me again, because I know, don't I, Da? I do know." She clasped her hands against her chest. "I must write him a note, mustn't I? This is going to be so exciting, so very exciting." And then, once more, she placed her eye to the lens.

Chapter 5

Fabia had been unable to get back to work, she just couldn't concentrate. Restlessly she prowled about the house, brought some washing down, then forgot to switch on the machine, tidied the kitchen, but ignored the sink full of dirty dishes. She wandered into the dining room and stood gazing down at the sketches on the drawing board. And all the time thoughts of Amber and how she came to be in the river plagued her.

Fabia would never have put her down as suicidal. Yes, she was a strange child. No, child was the wrong word, woman. In spite of her age she had a mature earthiness, a sort of primitive sex appeal way beyond her years. Voluptuous was the word that came to mind – full of life. She enjoyed the effect she had on men, revelled in it. Okay, she'd been frustrated by the restrictions of village life, and angry, yes there'd been a lot of anger bottled up inside her, but she'd not been unhappy exactly. And she'd been incredibly talented, and so looking forward to her interview in Cardiff. Fabia was sure she'd had another one lined up at St Martin's in London. Now all that talent would be unfulfilled. She felt an overwhelming regret at the thought.

Pacing uselessly up and down from the dining room, down the hall to the kitchen and back again, she felt frustration mounting. She wanted to become involved in the investigation, be in control and not dependent on Matt coming to her. What was taking him so long? And yet, part of her dreaded his arrival. She still felt so very angry with him. Two years had made little difference to that. The anger burned as strong as ever, the hurt was still as raw, and no amount of telling herself to get over it, to put it all behind her, had had any effect. Perhaps when you cared that much about a person, detaching yourself completely just wasn't an option. It was a glue designed to hold on, come what may and, if it was torn off, it took a piece of you with it. But brooding was a pointless occupation. To distract herself she rummaged in a drawer and, finding a pad and pencil, began to make notes about Amber, just as she would have if this had been a case she was working on.

* * *

The light was failing and Fabia was thinking longingly of a glass of wine when she finally heard a car draw up outside. Her heart beat hard in her chest as, through the lounge window, she saw Matt unfolding himself from the driver's seat. With him was a short, stocky woman, neatly dressed in yellow shirt and navy-blue suit, her mouse brown hair cropped short and spiky on her head. By the time they arrived at the front door, Fabia had it open.

Covertly she studied his face. He was pale and looked cold, his hair was in a mess and his tall body stooped with fatigue. His high cheekbones seemed more prominent than she remembered, making his face look gaunt and older than his thirty-five years. She had an overwhelming urge to reach out and touch him, comfort him, but she forced herself not to do so. Quite apart from anything else, it'd hardly be appropriate at a time like this.

He was studying her just as closely, but his face was expressionless, except for one raised eyebrow. Not a good sign. This wasn't going to be easy.

Fabia took a deep breath and said, "Hallo Matt, I hardly expected to see you again so soon." She was pleased at how neutral her voice sounded. "Come in. We'll go through to the kitchen. I expect you two could do with a cup of coffee or something." She didn't wait for them to comment and, without a word, they followed her along the hall. "Sit down, do," she said as she filled the kettle.

"This is DS Dilys Bevan." At least Matt's voice sounded normal enough, but when she turned to look at him he wouldn't meet her eyes. His sergeant did, and Fabia could sense curiosity and something else in her. She wondered if Dilys knew their history. Almost certainly, given the police force's propensity for gossip.

The silence dragged on and Fabia was relieved when the kettle clicked off and she was able to occupy herself with making the coffee. She placed steaming mugs in front of them, pushed the sugar bowl across, and sat down. "So," she said, "you want to ask me about finding the body."

"Yes." Matt seemed to find it difficult to continue and Dilys, after an awkward pause, glanced at him and plunged in.

"We'd like your account of that, ma'am, but we also gather you knew the girl. Perhaps you could give us some background. Anything you think relevant. The more information we have, the better."

"I realise that," Fabia said, her voice cool, then regretted it as she saw a flush creep into Dilys's cheeks. It was hardly fair to take out her feelings on the poor woman. She smiled at her. "As you might know, I used to be in the force, so all this is pretty familiar stuff for me."

"Yes, ma'am."

"For God's sake, don't bother with all that. I'm no longer a police superintendent." She didn't bother to keep the edge out of her voice. Matt shot her a look she found hard to decipher, but obviously decided not to comment. She was relieved, but also cross with herself for bringing up the subject. The last thing she wanted was a confrontation with Matt while his sergeant sat there, an unwilling audience.

"Okay," he said, tight-lipped, "take us through everything, from when you left the house to finding the body, and then through to phoning us. Why where you in the park in the first place?" His tone was abrupt and cold. Fabia could feel her hackles rise, but she took a deep breath and begun her account, step by step, in minute detail. When it came to describing Amber's body under the water, she faltered, then grabbed a piece of paper and a pencil and made a rough sketch. The scene came alive under her fingers and, when she'd finished, she thrust the paper across the table towards them. Only then did she notice Matt's jaw was clenched tight, and the pain in his eyes made her stomach lurch.

"Matt, I'm so–"

The look he gave her silenced her. "So. You didn't try to pull her out?" His voice sounded accusing.

"It did occur to me, but I'm afraid my training got in the way. And it was so obvious it was too late to help her, there would have been no point. For goodness sake, Matt, imagine your reaction if I'd trampled all over the site like some brainless idiot. Do you think, because I'm no longer in the force, I've forgotten all the rules?"

His pale skin flushed a little and his lips twisted in what looked, to her, like contempt. Sitting back in his chair, he said curtly, "Go on."

Fabia, trying to ignore the mounting fury inside herself, went on with her account without further interruption. "And so," she ended, "I went with Sergeant Pryce and the constable to show them where the body was, and they took over. Then I came back here and waited for you to arrive. That's about it."

"You say you knew the girl."

"Yes."

"How well?"

She shrugged. "Quite well."

"Was she into drugs?"

"Probably. Most of that crowd is."

"And you didn't think to do anything about it?"

"Don't be stupid, Matt! What could I do? Anyway, that wasn't the sort of thing we talked about. She wanted to go to art school and she used to come round to talk about painting mostly, that was all."

"And when was the last time you saw her?"

Fabia was just about to tell him about the incident on the bridge, when something came into her mind. It was like a piece of film, blurred at first but clearing. Something about last night as she stood on the doorstep saying goodbye to Alun and the others.

"What is it?" Matt's voice was sharp.

"Hang on a minute," she waved a hand at him then pressed it to her forehead. Why had she drunk so much? Oh Christ, she had to remember. Someone had clattered past her, on a bicycle, head down, pedalling frantically, so fast that she felt the draft of their passing. She'd stopped to look at the disappearing figure, saw the black hair streaming out behind, and the glint of long silver earrings swinging frantically from side to side. Amber. It'd been Amber, and she'd been in a desperate hurry.

* * *

"Why didn't you remember this before?" Matt asked furiously once she'd told them what she'd seen.

"Probably because I had a hangover."

"Oh, for fuck's sake, talk about irresponsible."

"Don't be a hypocrite. I seem to remember you've put a few away in your time."

"That's rich! I'm not the one who withheld information."

40

"Now you're being ridiculous. Anyway, I've told you now, haven't I?"

"Excuse me, but–" Dilys's precise voice cut cleanly through the pointless argument. Fabia caught Matt's eye, saw what she thought was a glint of laughter and couldn't help giving him a twisted little smile. "Bit like old times, eh?"

But he wasn't having any of that. The laughter died, may never have been there, and the official tone returned as he looked at her coldly. "So, you saw Amber Morgan cycling past last night. She seemed to be in the devil of a hurry. Now, exactly what time was this – if you can remember, that is."

Fabia no longer had any desire to smile. She placed her elbows firmly on the table and crossed her arms, gave him the kind of look she would have reserved for a cocky recruit in the old days. "I had some friends to dinner. Some of the old crowd, Matt, including Alun Richards. You remember him?"

Matt nodded curtly, making it clear he didn't think this a time for reminiscing. Fabia clenched her teeth for a second, then went on.

"It was as they were leaving, about half-past eleven it must have been."

"At the speed you say she was going," Matt said, "it would have taken her, what? Five minutes to get to the bridge? So somewhere between 11.30 and when you found her today, she went into the river."

"The traffic over the bridge is pretty heavy from about 7.00 in the morning onwards," Dilys said. "I doubt it would've been after that, someone would have seen her. I'd guess it was between 11.00 and first light."

"Yes. I agree," said Fabia. "But I don't think she committed suicide."

Matt looked at her sharply, frowning. "What makes you say that?"

"Instinct."

"Oh, come on," he said scornfully.

"I knew the girl, Matt. She wasn't a jumper."

"Here we go again. Facts are what we need. Okay, so you knew her, but how can you be so sure?"

Fabia didn't answer immediately but picked up her coffee mug and walked to the kettle, switched it on again. They'd always parted company on the value of instinct as against facts. Matt's inclination was to think along straight lines, rely on what he knew to be true rather than what he simply believed to be so. But Fabia had always relied on gut reaction. Her hunches had always been a source of teasing and scorn, not only from Matt but from others as well, no matter how often she was proved right. Just luck, they'd insist, that's all. So, now it was hard to answer Matt's question in terms of facts. But come on, this wasn't just instinct, she told herself. It was also a feeling based on her knowledge of the girl. Now, thinking back to the times Amber had come to visit her, she remembered again the sense of energy that had oozed from every pore of the girl's body, as if she was hard put to contain all the life bubbling away inside herself. She'd been obsessed with her art, desperately keen to do well at art school, and had talked incessantly about her plans for a future away from Pontygwyn.

"Oh Fabia, I just can't wait. There are so many ideas I want to get going on, but I need someone to help me, like, organise them in my head. You know, control them and get them from my head on to paper, or moulded into clay, whatever. It's all very well having the ideas and the talent, but I need to learn the craft part. You do see what I mean, don't you?"

And Fabia had, very well. Amber had shown her some of her work. Raw splashes of colour, collages using anything she had to hand, thick oil paint daubed like butter onto bread. There'd been a primitive force about them, and there'd undoubtedly been a great deal of talent there.

Fabia felt a renewed stab of anger at the thought that now all that would come to nothing.

"Fabia?" Matt's impatient voice broke into her thoughts.

"It's hard to put into words that you won't sneer at," she snapped at him.

"Oh, for goodness sake!"

"Sorry." She felt angry with herself now. That really had sounded pathetic. "What I mean is, she was so full of life and enthusiasm, and she had such plans – we talked about them a lot – and she had the most enormous talent, the best I've come across in years. With guidance and some good teaching, she really could have gone far. She was absolutely determined to go to art school, and well on the way to being offered a place at one of the best, in fact she had an interview in Cardiff only yesterday, and another at St Martin's in London next week. I really can't see her throwing all that away. No," she shook her head, "she'd never have killed herself."

"You seem very sure about all this." At last, he appeared to be impressed by what she was saying.

"I am."

"Okay. Just for the sake of argument, let's assume you're right."

"It may have been an accident," Dilys pointed out.

"Possibly," Fabia said, "but another thing I know about Amber is that she was a very strong swimmer. She used to win medals at it. So, say she was sitting on the parapet, perhaps with her legs dangling on the riverside, and she fell off, the water's deep there, no rocks or anything. She could have swum for it."

"Maybe she hit her head before she went into the water," Matt said, frowning. "Pat Curtis found some bruising on the side of her head."

"So, Pat's on the case, is she? Still as disagreeable?"

He nearly smiled. "Worse, if anything," he said shortly. "Okay, if we assume for the moment it was

43

murder, can you think of anyone who'd want to see her dead?"

"Are you asking me to speculate, Matt?"

He gave her a black look and snapped, "You knew her, and you live in the village. You probably know what crowd she went around with and, knowing you, you'll be well up on all the gossip."

"Thanks a bunch!"

"Well, I seem to remember it was always you and not me who knew who'd been sleeping with whom, whose marriage was disintegrating."

Fabia felt as if he was implying she'd spent her whole time gossiping about her colleagues. "I just kept my eyes open, Matt. It's one of the things someone in our... your profession is meant to do, wouldn't you say?" She watched a slight flush rise up his cheeks.

Once again Dilys intervened. "Is there anything else you think may be relevant?"

Fabia, suddenly conscious of the fact that Dilys had had to sit there and listen to them bicker, gave her an apologetic smile. Fabia thought Matt was still looking haggard, suddenly she felt sorry for him. This case was far too near to home for Matt, he must be finding it very difficult, quite apart from having to face her. How many years had it been since Bethan died? Eight, maybe, though it probably seemed like yesterday to him. The sound of a mobile ringing broke the silence. Matt rummaged in his coat pocket, glanced at the screen. "Hallo doctor."

Fabia could hear the staccato notes of Pat Curtis's voice but couldn't decipher what she was saying.

"You're sure?" Matt asked a moment later. "Okay. Are you ready for the identification? Right. We'll pick him up since we're in the area. He's already agreed to do it. We'll see you there."

He returned the phone to his pocket. "She says it looks like murder, the girl was dead before she went in the water, so here we go. We'd better go and pick up her stepfather." Matt turned to Dilys. "And we'll have to get a search of her room underway. Organise it, would you."

As they stood up to go, Fabia thought of something else. "I suggest you tell them to look out for her diary."

"She kept a diary?"

"Yes. A handwritten one. She mentioned it to me recently, maybe a couple of weeks ago, said it was half diary, half artwork." Fabia frowned and pressed fingers to her forehead, remembering the look on Amber's face as she'd talked about it, remembering that it had rung alarm bells. It had been as if the girl had a delightful secret she wasn't going to share, and what she'd said had reinforced that feeling.

"We'd been talking about Paul Vaughan," she went on, "you know, the music promoter chap who bought Bryn-y-Mor Lodge at the end of St Madoc's Road. She said something about him wanting to read her diary and that he'd have got a hell of a shock if he had. You should interview him."

"We'll be doing so." Matt's voice was icy, and Fabia guessed he hadn't known about Paul Vaughan before now, but she ignored the tone.

"Yes, obviously, you'll be contacting everyone who knew her," she said with patience. "What I mean is, I think he knew her rather well. I wouldn't mind betting she was sleeping with him, at least up until Christmas. After that, I got the impression the relationship changed."

"Christ almighty, Fabia!" Matt snapped angrily. "This is what I mean! You know perfectly well that's just the sort of information I need, and you wait until now to tell me."

"Well of course I know," she retorted, equally angry. "But even I can't think of everything at once. I've been going over and over things this afternoon, jotting them down as I think of them while I waited for you to turn up. I'll get my notes sorted as quickly as I can and let you have them. I'm just as anxious as you to find out what happened to Amber. More so, she was a friend of mine."

He glared at her, opened his mouth to speak, but Fabia wasn't going to give ground yet.

"I'll be giving you all the information I can, don't you worry, instinct, hunches, the lot. But you haven't got time now. You'll have to come back later," she said.

"If I can. Look, you'd better have my mobile number."

"I've still got it," Fabia said shortly, "unless you've changed it in the last two years."

"I haven't," he snapped. "If you think of anything you feel I should know, ring me immediately. Do not, for God's sake, go snooping around of your own accord. You're no longer in the force, you know."

A blaze of anger burst inside Fabia. How dare he?

"Fabia, I …"

"Leave it," she said, and hated the fact that her voice shook as she spoke. This was definitely not the time to tackle him, not with his sergeant looking on, taking it all in. She marched down the hall ahead of them and at the door she didn't even say goodbye, but just stopped herself clipping Matt's heels as she slammed the door on his back. It was as she returned to the kitchen she realised she hadn't told him about Amber and Rhona's confrontation on the bridge. Damn! It could be important. But by the time she got back to the front door and flung it open, his car was gone.

Chapter 6

"I think we've got plenty of time, sir."

Dilys's quiet comment broke into the turmoil of Matt's thoughts. He glanced down at the speedometer, then jammed his foot on the brakes and forced himself to relax his hands on the steering wheel. Out of the corner of his eye he saw Dilys glance at him and decided he owed her some kind of explanation.

"We've known each other a long time, Fabia and I," he said stiffly.

"Yes, sir." Her voice was totally expressionless. "I think I picked that up, sir."

There was a pause, then Matt said. "You know I snapped your head off when you suggested Fabia had been chucked out of the force? Well–"

"You don't have to explain, sir."

"Sod it, Dilys! What's this 'sir' at the end of every sentence?"

"Sorry, sir."

"Dilys!"

She grinned at him and he gave a bark of laughter. "No, I'm sorry. The thing is, I used to work very closely with her, although, as you can probably tell, our methods varied somewhat. I suppose she was my mentor when I first got into the CID, but it was more than that, she was a bit like ... an elder sister." Well, wasn't that what she'd said she wanted? "We were friends as well as colleagues. Anyway, when she was implicated in that fraud case, I just could not believe it. I tackled her, but she didn't actually deny anything. That was what was so strange. Of course, by this time the knives were out for her, whatever the reality was, but I thought she'd be upfront with me of all people. Instead, she clammed up, wouldn't tell me anything. I sort of assumed it was because she had something to hide. Of course, our friendship couldn't survive that." He shrugged. "As you've just seen, it didn't."

"And was she implicated?"

"That's the bugger, I'm still not sure. Some of the old hands always refused to believe it. But, well," he glanced at Dilys and gave her a mirthless smile, "I had my promotion to think of, didn't I?"

"I wouldn't have thought that'd weigh very heavily with you."

"Wouldn't you?" Matt grimaced. "I think that's a compliment, but maybe you don't know me as well as you think you do."

"Maybe," she said, turning away from him to look out of the car window, effectively ending the conversation.

A few minutes later, they arrived at the Coles' house, tucked into the corner of St Madoc's school grounds. In a way, Matt was relieved he had to concentrate on the matter in hand and the past had to be pushed back to where it belonged.

There was a police constable standing by the front door, and by the gate another uniformed officer was speaking to three men, one of whom carried a large camera. They walked quickly pass the pressmen, ignoring their questions, and went up the path to the Coles' front door.

It seemed to Matt that it had been no time at all since they'd been there to break the news of Amber's death to her parents. It didn't matter how many times he had to break such news to people, nothing ever made it any less of a nightmare. Earlier that day, faced with Amber's mother, a timid, mousy woman, her pale grey eyes fixed anxiously on his face, he'd wished himself anywhere but here.

"My husband says you want to talk to me about Amber," she'd said in a panicky rush, and his heart had sunk even further. Surely the man could have prepared her? Why leave it hanging like that? But Matt had thought he knew why. Telling anyone their child is dead is bad enough, telling someone you love must be unimaginably awful.

"Where is she? What's happened?" Her voice had risen, become tinged with hysteria.

Her husband had put his arm round her, pulled her rigid body against his. "Let the man speak, Cecily, do." But she'd pushed him away.

Matt had watched her carefully as he spoke. "Your daughter, Mrs Cole, has met with an accident. Her body was found this morning in the River Gwyn. I am truly sorry to have to tell you she's dead."

Her eyes had widened even further as she put a hand up to her mouth. What little colour there was in her face had drained away, leaving it sickly white. She'd opened her mouth to speak but only inarticulate sounds escaped, then her eyes had rolled up, her knees sagged, and Dilys had caught her just in time. Between them, they'd lowered her on to the sofa. Dilys had loosened her clothing and, as she'd begun to revive, held the glass of water Mr Cole had brought to Mrs Cole's lips. She'd spluttered, gasped, and slowly her eyes had focused, first on Dilys's face, then Matt, and lastly on her husband.

"Amber? Is it ... is she ..."

Her husband had taken Dilys's place. "Yes, Cecily," he said, his voice gentle as he'd put out a hand to her.

She'd hardly seemed to notice, just stared up at him, then she'd begun to speak, the broken sentences gasped out in a sibilant whisper.

"It's my fault, it's all my fault. I should have listened. Should have done as she asked. Oh God, oh God, my Amber, my poor little Amber." And she'd turned her face into the cushions and begun to weep with open-mouthed abandon. Matt needed to know what she'd meant. It hadn't been the time to press her, but he knew he'd have to follow it up soon.

* * *

Now Mr Cole opened the door before they'd even had the chance to knock. He'd obviously been watching out for them. "I'm ready," he said.

"Thank you, sir. Perhaps you would go with my colleague to the car. She'll make sure you're not bothered by anybody."

Cole looked down the path to the press men, and his mouth twisted in disgust. "What are they hanging round for?"

"I'm sorry. I'm afraid it's inevitable, sir. The best thing is to ignore them. Sergeant?"

Dilys touched Mr Cole's arm and led him down the path, and Matt turned to the constable by the door.

"Is someone with Mrs Cole?"

"Yes, sir. Her next-door neighbour, who used to be a nurse."

"Good. There'll be a team down in about half an hour to go over the girl's room. You'll have to explain what's going on to her mother, but be gentle about it, okay?"

The young constable drew himself up. "Yes, sir. It's murder, is it?"

"Yes", Matt said shortly. "Make sure you make a note of anything she may say, however trivial, understand?" The man nodded. "And keep that lot," he jerked a thumb at the press men, "under control."

He strode off down the path, neatly sidestepped the reporters, and got into the back seat next to Cole.

"This is a terrible business," Amber's step-father said as they started off. "My wife is devastated, totally distraught. She's not a strong woman at the best of times, and now this." His voice shook on the last words, he put up a hand to his mouth and paused for a moment as if trying to regain control of himself. Matt said nothing, waited. The seconds ticked by, stretched into minutes. At last Cole burst out, "I'm afraid my wife and I had differing views on Amber's upbringing, and Amber's recent excesses had made things worse. I was of the opinion that we should be firm with her, maybe cut her allowance, but my wife said it was just a phase that Amber would grow out of."

"Typical teenager perhaps," Matt suggested.

"I think it was a little more than that." His tone was brusque. "I work with the young all the time, and I can assure you, not many of my pupils present me with the kind of problems Amber did. But we have had occasional problems with drug taking at St Madoc's and I recognised the signs. I'm afraid Amber was – was dabbling in drugs of some kind, I don't know exactly what."

"Did you tackle her about it?" asked Matt.

"No. Cecily begged me not to. As I said before, she wouldn't believe me when I told her what I thought was going on. Cecily is a gentle soul, not in any way assertive, and I'm afraid she allowed Amber to run roughshod over her. Had it been entirely up to me … but, of course, it wasn't."

"It must have been very difficult for you."

"How do you mean?"

"As Miss Morgan's step-father."

"Perhaps, but we were very close when she was younger. She never really knew her own father, you see, and she used to be such a sweet little girl. But lately – well, she'd become very rebellious, staying out till all hours, sometimes she didn't even bother to come home at all, and she never bothered to let us know where she was. Her mother used to worry herself sick wondering what was happening and who she was with. I realise, at the age of eighteen, that's normal behaviour in most families, but we expected a little better of our girl."

Matt didn't comment. What could he say? He'd not been able to prevent his sister from killing herself. What did he know about this girl? Except that she, unlike Bethan, had been murdered.

"Of course, the cause of it all was that unsavoury crowd she was mixing with," Cole went on. "Quite apart from the drugs, she certainly drank too much, and as a consequence she neglected her A-levels, at least, those that would have been of any real use to her. The one thing she seemed really interested in was her art, and nothing we said seemed to make any difference." He paused and twisted his hands in his lap for a moment. "I realise I shouldn't be saying all this now with the poor girl … it's all so unbelievable. The trouble is there's no altering the fact that our beautiful girl was out of control and there was little her poor mother or I could think of to set her back on the right track."

"We will obviously be speaking to her friends," Matt said, "and we would like to have a word with Mrs Cole at some point, once she's recovered a little, of course."

"Why do you need to talk to her?"

"She may know things about her daughter's movements."

"But I really don't think my wife will be able to cope with being questioned. You saw the state she was in. I'm sure I can tell you anything you need to know."

This point always came, when you had to lay down the ground rules. "We'll be as considerate as we possibly can be, sir," Matt said firmly. "But the situation has changed. I'm afraid I have to tell you your step-daughter did not commit suicide, she was murdered."

"Oh my God," he said, and put his hand up to cover his eyes for a moment. Matt waited.

"Are you sure?"

"Yes, I'm afraid so," Matt said quietly.

"But who could do such a thing?" He answered his own question. "No doubt it was one of those louts she mixed with. I told her they were a dangerous crowd, but she wouldn't listen."

Matt didn't comment on this, just said, "We'll need to establish her movements over the last twenty-four hours. Could you tell me when you last saw her?"

"Saw her?" At first, he didn't seem to have understood the question, but a moment later he pulled himself together. "I'm sorry. I don't seem to be able to think straight."

"That's quite understandable."

"When did I – just before I went up to London, I think. I left Tuesday evening, I had to attend a conference and I didn't get back till yesterday."

"Would you mind telling me where this conference was held?"

"It was at the Commonwealth Institute and I stayed at a hotel nearby, The Beresford, together with some of the other delegates."

"And you returned home yesterday?"

"Yes. I don't remember exactly what time. Cecily was out at some church do. She spends a lot of time down there helping out with the flowers and that sort of thing."

"Perhaps your wife would remember?"

"What?"

"The time you arrived home."

The man's face tightened in annoyance. "Does it matter? I can see no reason whatever why you should need confirmation."

Matt waited, and a moment later Cole spoke again. "I'm sorry. That sounded uncooperative, and the last thing I want is to hinder your investigations. The sooner you find the bastard the better. Poor, poor Amber."

For the rest of the journey he sat with his head turned, gazing out of the window, his hands gripping his knees.

* * *

Earlier in the day, just for a moment, Matt had considered asking someone else to go with Cole to identify Amber's body, but he'd known, deep down, it wasn't an option. He was in charge of the case, being there was part of the job, and he must not let his personal feelings influence him. This had to be done, and he had to do it.

The three of them walked along the echoing corridor, its vinyl covered floor accentuating every step, the white paint and harsh lighting unforgiving in its brightness. Dilys led the way and Cole, beside Matt, held himself rigidly erect, his hands gripped into fists at his sides. Matt touched his arm as they came to a half-glazed door at the end of the corridor.

"Are you all right, sir?"

"Yes." The man took a deep, shuddering breath. "Let's get this over with."

Dilys opened the door and stood aside to let them pass. It wasn't a very large room they entered, and not unlike an operating theatre, with its strong lighting, white tiles, gleaming instruments, and the all-pervading smell of antiseptic. But there were other, more primitive smells lurking beneath this. The raw scent that rose from human flesh cut open and laid bare and, for Matt, the creeping smell of decay and death.

Pat Curtis and her assistant were there, still clothed in their blue overalls, but an effort had been made to make the scene as unobjectionable as possible. On an operating table lay a body shrouded in a sheet. Pat gave Cole a sharp but not unkind glance as Matt introduced him. She murmured some phrase of condolence, then said, more briskly, "Are you ready?"

"Yes," he said.

Gently the assistant pulled the sheet away from the top of the body revealing Amber's face and shoulders. Her face now, in the rigid repose of death, looked more like a waxwork than a human being. The jet-black hair was spread across the table and her lashes created two dark crescents above her cheeks, now slightly sunken. On the side of her face and running up into the hairline, a bruise, purple-veined, had developed. Her lips, that had been so full and red in life, held a blue tinge and seemed diminished and thinner in death.

Beside him, Matt heard Cole draw in his breath with a quiet hiss. He swayed suddenly, and Matt put out a hand and took his arm. "Are you all right, sir. Could you tell us—"

He was interrupted. "Yes. That's our girl, that's Amber. I need to go now." He turned and walked rapidly to the door and out of the room, followed by Matt and Dilys.

* * *

At eight o'clock, back at the station where an incident room had been set up, Matt had called his team together for the end of day briefing. They sat round, perched on chairs or desks, or leaning against the wall. In spite of the hour and the weather – from outside came the persistent hiss and patter of rain – they were still alert and listened intently to every word he said. He felt a wave of gratitude to them all. Thank God he had such a good team – the best in Gwent, so far as he was concerned – because he wanted this killer, badly.

"So, that's about it. Thanks, everyone, for staying on. First thing tomorrow, the diving team will start looking for that bike. If it is in the river, I can't imagine it can have travelled far. And the earring, we really want that as well, if it's somewhere in the undergrowth I want it found, okay?" There was a murmur of assent. "And also, tomorrow, you'll be delighted to know, we start on the door to doors." This time there was a groan. Matt managed a smile. "I knew you'd be pleased. Okay, folks. Get home and get some sleep."

As he drove home he thought about the last thing he'd said. Somehow, he didn't think he'd be getting much sleep himself.

Chapter 7

Pontygwyn House was on the outskirts of the town. It was a rather ugly Victorian structure, probably built by some nineteenth-century land owner to show off his wealth, but it had magnificent views over the surrounding hills, and the sweeping circular drive and well laid out grounds spoke of money and position just as much now as they had in the past. Well behaved flower beds lined the lawn with daffodils nodding in the breeze and neatly pruned rose bushes just beginning to sprout new leaf. Neville Breverton had bought it about the same time as he'd been elected to Parliament and, according to rumour, spent a small fortune on renovations and decorating. Where all the money had come from no-one was entirely sure.

In the sitting room, which looked like a room straight from the pages of Homes & Gardens with its restrained creams and corals, tastefully placed watercolours, family photos and thick carpet, the mantelpiece clock had just chimed eight o'clock and Gwen Breverton was pouring coffee for her husband and herself. She glanced across at Neville as she did so and wished, not for the first time, that he'd take more care of himself. He was an attractive man. As a young woman she'd found his rugged, full-lipped good looks extremely exciting. But at the moment, slumped as he was in his armchair, shirt unbuttoned, and a newspaper draped across his stomach, which was beginning to run to fat, he was not at his best. Perhaps she'd suggest he take advantage of the health club at the Celtic Manor resort as well as playing golf there. It might be a good move on other fronts from the point of view of meeting and greeting the right people, quite apart from any peripheral effect it would have on Neville's body.

She sighed and smoothed a hand down her skirt, part of her mind relishing the feel of the expensive fabric. She devoted a great deal of thought to her clothes, and she knew she looked as if she'd just stepped from the pages of some up-market glossy magazine. At least she looked the part even if Neville didn't, and God knows, she worked hard enough to achieve just this effect.

But she said nothing as she placed her husband's cup on a small table beside him. There'd be time later to tackle Neville about getting more exercise. Right now, she needed to go back to the subject they'd been discussing earlier.

"Neville. It's not that I don't understand he could be useful to you. It's just that his background is somewhat suspect, isn't it?"

"His background's not much different from yours, my dear," he said, with a cruel twist to his lips. "Working class boy come up in the world. And he's loaded, and influential in some circles. Paul Vaughan could be very useful on several fronts."

Gwen, slightly flushed, decided to ignore the jibe. "I realise that, darling, but you can't afford to be seen to be too friendly."

"Come on Gwen, one game of golf doesn't mean I'm about to shack up with the man."

"Neville, I'm serious about this. It's never been proved, but it's strongly rumoured some of his millions come from the drug trade."

"Load of nonsense. Those rumours are probably put about by people who're jealous of his money. You shouldn't listen to gutter gossip."

"I don't." She was angry now. "But I do keep my ear to the ground. I just think you should be careful, that's all."

For a moment their eyes met over the top of his newspaper. Gwen held his gaze, knowing he'd be the first to look away. He did.

"Okay. I'll be careful." He smiled, trying to regain lost ground, but she wasn't going to be won round that easily. Without returning the smile, she picked up a magazine and started flicking through it.

Silence reigned for a while until a sudden commotion erupted outside the room. Footsteps could be heard clattering down the stairs and, a second later, a teenage girl burst in, her eyes round with fright and her blonde hair escaping from the luminous orange clip attempting to hold it in place.

"Mum! Dad! Have you heard the news? Shit! It's awful! I just can't believe it!"

"Vanessa darling," Gwen said, her voice cool. "Do try not to be quite so loud."

"What on earth's the matter, Nessa?" her father rumbled from the depths of his chair. "Can't you see your mother and I are busy."

"Oh, that's great!" She threw herself in the armchair opposite her father. "So, you don't care that one of my best friends is dead?"

This got their attention. Her father jerked upright in his chair and the newspaper slithered to the floor. He opened his mouth to protest, but Gwen intervened.

"What are you talking about?" she asked sharply.

"Amber. She's dead, drowned. Her body was found in the Gwyn."

For a moment there was absolute silence. The shock of Vanessa's words hit Gwen as if she'd been winded and she could feel the blood draining from her face. She had time to be relieved that her makeup would probably hide it, and made an effort to compose herself as Vanessa went on.

"I just got a text from Craig. You know, the Evanses from the pub, their son. Poor old CJ, he's really cut up. He was obsessed with Amber. He said they found her body this morning, down in the bendy bit above Gwiddon Pond. Oh, Mum," she wailed, sounding very much younger than her seventeen years, "it's so awful." And with that she burst into tears.

Gwen got up and put an arm round her daughter, gave her shoulder a conventional pat and murmured comfortingly while her mind raced. Over the top of Vanessa's head her eyes met those of her husband, and what she saw in his face made her stomach contract again. Oh God, just when everything had been going so well, she thought bitterly.

A moment later she felt a cold wave of panic, she'd remembered the anonymous letter.

* * *

It had arrived early on Monday morning. Setting aside those letters addressed to Neville, she had taken her own over to her desk. Amongst them had been a large lime green envelope. It looked as if it would contain some particularly garish greeting card. The letters of the address were smudged and unclear, the printing erratic. She remembered sitting and staring at it, thinking it was probably another of those cranky begging letters that turned up from time to time.

With an exasperated sigh, she had slit the envelope open and unfolded the single sheet of lined paper. Slowly she'd read the printed words.

> I KNOW ALL ABOUT YOUR
> HUSBAND AND HIS WOMEN.
> LIKES   THEM   YOUNG

DOESN'T HE? DO THE
TABLOIDS KNOW ABOUT
THEM TOO? IF NOT I CAN
ALWAYS MAKE SURE THEY
FIND OUT, UNLESS YOU CAN
GIVE ME A GOOD REASON
NOT TO SPILL THE BEANS.

She had felt sick as she read it through again; she had
turned the paper over, but there had been nothing on the
other side. And there had been no demand for money
either. She had picked up the envelope again and tried to
decipher the postmark. It was smudged as well, but she
thought she could decipher the word 'Cardiff'. So, no real
help there. The nausea increased and, with an effort, she
had pulled herself together, tried to think clearly. Should
she tell Neville? No, not at the moment, he was too
unpredictable. In the end she had decided to hide the letter
until she could work out what to do about it.

Opening the bottom drawer of her desk, she had
lifted out a pile of old address books at the back and thrust
the letter underneath them, then closed the drawer with a
snap, but her hand remained on the handle. She'd looked
at her watch. Nine o'clock. Her sister, Betti, was expecting
her and Vanessa for lunch. There was little chance they
would be back before four or five in the afternoon. What
if someone came in and found the hidden letter? What if
Mrs Pritchard started snooping? Gwen had known it was
hardly likely, but she hadn't been able to control a shiver
of panic at the thought. Better to destroy it. She had pulled
the drawer open again and taken the letter out, walked
over to the fireplace and lifted a box of matches from the
mantelpiece, watched as the flames licked at the paper.
Then she had heard Vanessa calling.

"Mum? Hadn't we better get going?"

Panic rose. What should she do? The seconds had
ticked by as she hesitated, unable to decide. She couldn't
leave this, but Vanessa mustn't see it. She grabbed the

brush from the set of ornamental brasses that stood on the hearth, and tapped ineffectually at the burning paper. The flames died down. A moment later, with a last glance at the smouldering remains, she had left the room before Vanessa came to find her.

* * *

Fabia had watched the local news on television, but there'd been no mention of Amber's death. Matt had obviously kept the hatches well battened, but it couldn't last. Come tomorrow she was sure the media pack would be in full cry.

She found she couldn't settle to do anything. In spite of another phone call from Sheena, she hadn't even read through the manuscript, let alone started sketching out any ideas for the illustrations. There was no doubt she'd have to start soon, Sheena wouldn't let up, but Fabia just didn't feel up to concentrating on anything creative right now.

So many questions kept nagging at her. Who would want to kill Amber? Where was the second earring? Had it been torn off in a scuffle or did the murderer still have it? Why had Amber been in such a hurry? And Amber's bike, what had happened to it? A bike was large, cumbersome, not easy to get rid of.

On and on it went with no answers. She so desperately wanted to be involved in the investigation, help to answer all the questions, but knew there was little possibility of that happening. Matt had made it very clear how he felt about her involvement already. He was hardly likely to consult her. And yet she was sure she could help. She'd known the girl well, for God's sake.

A knock on the front door had her rushing to open it. But there was no lanky police officer on the doorstep. The woman who stood there was short and plump, her wildly curling hair flecked with grey and her bright red coat in stark contrast with the clerical collar around her neck.

"Fabia, my dear. I thought I'd pop round to see how you are. This is a dreadful business."

"Hallo Cath," Fabia stood aside to let her in. She liked their local vicar and was pleased to see her. At least Cath's visit would put a stop to her prowling around, wondering what Matt was up to.

"Come in, do. I really need some company."

"I'm sure you do. I gather it was you who found Amber's body. It must have been such a shock." She followed Fabia into the kitchen. "I've just come from the Coles', poor Cecily is completely distraught. Her friend who lives next door, can't remember her name, is with her. It was she who told me you were the one who found Amber's body. That poor child, she must have been desperate, or maybe it was an accident."

Fabia looked up at her, wondering if she should tell her the truth. Why not? Surely, it'd be common knowledge soon enough. Once the door to doors and the questioning started, few people in Pontygwyn would escape the effects of Amber's murder. It was only fair to warn her.

"It wasn't suicide, Cath, or an accident," she said slowly. "Amber was murdered."

"Oh my God!" Cath's hand went to her mouth, her eyes round above the lifted fingers as she subsided into a chair. "Are you sure?"

"I'm afraid so." She explained that Matt had been with her when the call came through from the pathologist. "I think we both need a drink. Whisky?"

"Please. A large one."

Nothing more was said until Fabia put a tumbler, half full of straw-coloured liquid, in front of her friend. Cath picked it up and gulped at the contents, spluttered a little, then recovered herself. "Who would do such a dreadful thing?"

Fabia shook her head, knowing there was no answer to that question yet. "Matt Lambert's very good. I used to work with him. He'll be particularly determined on this one."

"What do you mean?"

Fabia took a deep breath, again unsure for a minute how much she should say, but this was Cath, she had keep it to herself. "His sister, Bethan, was drowned when she was seventeen. It wasn't murder or an accident, she committed suicide, but there are similarities with this business. Bethan jumped off a bridge into the Usk when it was running very fast. There had been a hell of a lot of rain on the Beacons, and you know the effect that has. Her body became entangled in some fallen branches and that's how they recovered it from the water, just like Amber. Matt had to identify her. He was working with me in Newport at the time. I thought he was going to crack up completely. He and Bethan had been very close and he blamed himself for her death."

"Why did she do it?"

"It's a long story. She was always fragile, mentally, almost as if she was born with an outer layer of skin missing. Do you know what I mean? I think she'd have been diagnosed as a manic depressive if her parents had ever thought to consult a specialist. The trouble was neither of them was aware enough really, and they had too many problems of their own. Matt's father was an unworldly theologian who was never that close to his children – should have been a monk really."

"His father was a parson, was he?"

"Oh yes, so's Matt's brother Pierre. His mother, well, she was simply over-worked, she had a full-time job, as a primary school teacher, quite apart from being an unpaid curate as all parson's wives used to be. She was half Norman French, half Guernsey, both – according to Matt – people who don't show their emotions easily, just have a 'get on with it' attitude to life. He says neither of them ever understood Bethan. Matt was more of a father to Bethan

than their dad ever was. She was ten years younger than him and he adored her."

Fabia sat silent for a moment, sipping at her whisky and thinking back to that dreadful time just after Bethan died. Matt had blamed himself, saying time and time again that he should have known, should have got help for her. At first, she'd protested, assured him it wasn't his fault, insisted he couldn't have known what Bethan intended, let alone prevented her suicide, but whatever she'd said had made no difference. In the end, she'd resorted to listening in silence and making sure he was kept so busy he had no time for brooding. Gradually, he'd stopped talking about Bethan, but she knew very well thoughts of her were never far from his mind, and now this had probably brought it all flooding back to him, and what grieved her most is that she wasn't able to help.

Cath's sympathetic voice brought her back to the present. "How awful, and now he has to deal with this. Can't someone else take charge?"

"I don't think he'd let them. If I know anything about Matt, he'll stick to it like a leech. He's not going to let go until he finds out exactly what happened to Amber and he has her killer, or killers, behind bars."

Cath sighed. "I can't get my mind round the idea of Amber dead. She was so full of life."

"Overflowing with it. I was talking to Matt earlier on about how talented she was, and she'd got such plans for the future. Did you know she had a final interview at Cardiff the day before yesterday and one coming up at St Martin's? She was almost certain to have been offered a place."

"Poor Cecily, how is she going to cope?"

"God knows. Amber might have been a bit wild, but she was devoted to her mother in her own way, very protective of her. She told me her father, Cecily's first husband, was an artist, and her mother was particularly delighted his talent had been passed on to Amber." She thumped the table with her fist. "What a waste! Christ, I'd like to get my hands on whoever's responsible!"

"It feels as if whoever killed her has attacked us all in a way. Maybe it was some lunatic, someone passing through."

"Part of me hopes so. But, whoever it was, like a pebble in a pool, the repercussions will reach out through the whole community. Youngsters will find their parents wanting to know exactly where they are all the time, and women will be warier of going out alone, and if it does turn out to be someone we all know, that'll make it even more difficult for the community to recover. It's awful, Cath, just awful."

Cath was looking at her, horror in her eyes. "You're right. I hate thinking about it but can't avoid doing so."

Cath didn't say anything for a moment, just sat frowning down at the kitchen table, tracing a finger slowly up and down on the surface. Fabia watched her hand, not really seeing it until it nearly touched a bright green envelope.

"Oh Lord!" Fabia said aloud, putting a hand up to her forehead.

"What's the matter?"

"I've just remembered something."

"About Amber?"

"No, Rhona. Look, you might be able to advise me," she said, feeling relieved at having someone to share the problem with. "I'm not at all sure what I should do about it." She picked up the envelope, and quickly told Cath how it came to be on her kitchen table. "What with everything that's happened, it'd gone right out of my mind – until now."

"What does it say?" asked Cath.

Reluctantly Fabia took the piece of paper from the envelope and, with a grimace at Cath, began to read. "*I saw you slobbering over him. Told you to bugger off, didn't he?*

Whatever made you think he'd want to screw a shrivelled old heap like you? Better watch out or I'll tell what I saw.' Awful isn't it?"

"Oh Lord," said Cath, "that's pretty nasty."

"I know, and what the hell am I going to do about it?"

Cath didn't answer immediately. Her eyes moved from Fabia's face to the envelope and back again, and a spurt of slightly hysterical laughter bubbled up in her throat but was quickly suppressed.

"God, Cath," Fabia said, "it's not funny." But she couldn't prevent a grin twitching at her lips.

"No, it certainly isn't. Sorry. I suppose you could just bung it through the letterbox," Cath said doubtfully.

"Oh, I don't think so. She'll need help dealing with it. I think I'll have to give it to her."

"Yes, you're right. You can offer to ring the police on her behalf or take it to them."

"Yes. That's what I'll do. But it's too late now. I'll take it round tomorrow morning."

"That's best, I think," said Cath.

Chapter 8

Fabia did not sleep well, but she hadn't expected to. The events of the day crowded into her head the moment she closed her eyes and, as she floated in that half-world between waking and sleeping, the image of Amber's dead body thrust itself back in. Instantly she was wide awake again and her thoughts started their repetitive round once more.

However hard she tried, she couldn't keep Matt out of her mind either. That last horrific row they'd had. She hadn't thought about it for months, hadn't let herself. Now the memories wouldn't be denied.

"What the hell do you mean, extended sick leave?" He'd been so angry, but there'd been more to it than that, she'd sensed deep disappointment as well. "You're never sick."

"Well, this time I am. Anyway, that's what they want me to call it for now. Sorry, Matt, but I've had enough. In a couple of years, they'll accept my resignation, quietly, and I may keep some of my pension."

"But that's tantamount to admitting you were involved."

"What the hell's the difference? Nobody believes my side of the story anyway. All that whispering in the canteen, picking away like a bunch of vultures. They've done too good a job." She'd seen straight through the facade he'd tried to hide behind. "Come on, Matt, admit it, you've got your doubts."

Desperate for him to deny it, she'd held her breath as she'd waited for his response. He'd said nothing.

"Oh, for Christ's sake!" she'd cried despairingly. "You could at least do me the courtesy of being honest with me, you of all people."

He'd stood there, looking sick and resentful, and she knew she'd put into words what he'd hardly admitted to himself.

"I've been given to understand that this way," she went on bitterly, "if I go quietly, I suppose you'd call it, I won't lose all my pension, and they'll keep me on full pay for now. What really happened, the truth," she spat the word out, "has no currency in these circumstances. And when friends like you have doubts—" Ignoring his protests, she'd ploughed on, "Oh, shut up, Matt. Even you have this sneaking feeling I just might have been involved. In these circumstances, I don't think I want to stick around anymore."

"I'd never put you down as a coward before."

She could hardly believe what he'd said. The blaze of anger that swept over her was like a physical blow. For a second, she thought she might lash out at him.

He'd reached a hand out to her, said, "Fabia, I'm sorry—" but she'd shaken him off, and the worst thing had been the tears crowding up in her throat and threatening to overflow. She never cried.

"Well, now you know." She'd said on a long, shuddering breath, making a supreme effort to pull herself together. "Enough's enough," she'd said. "I'm going." And that was the last time she'd seen him until two days ago.

Misery swept over her. What a bloody awful mess. But nothing to do about it. She turned her pillow over yet again, straightened the duvet and, in an effort to distract herself from the painful memories, went through what she knew so far about Amber's death, going over and over the sequence of events as she knew them, and desperately trying to delve into the mind of the unknown killer.

In the grey early hours, she finally fell into an exhausted sleep, only to be woken, she was sure mere minutes later, by the ringing of her mobile. She scrabbled around on her bedside table, picked it up and, as she did so, looked at the clock. It was just after nine.

"Hallo?" she muttered.

"It's me, Matt."

Her heart gave a lurch at the sound of his voice and immediately she was wide awake. Throwing back the duvet, she swung her legs out of bed, searched for her slippers. "Good morning," she said, her voice as neutral as she could get it. "What can I do for you?"

"Look – um – we've got a bit of a problem and Dilys suggested you might be able to help."

"Did she, now?" And why didn't you think of that? Fabia thought. She could imagine how much this was costing him, but she dug her heels in, determined not to make it any easier for him, not yet.

"Yes, well, it's Amber's diary, the one you mentioned yesterday. One of my chaps found it when he was going over her bedroom. Our problem is, she's used some kind of code for people's names and, well, we can't work them out. We were wondering if you'd be able to help us decipher it."

"You haven't spoken to her parents about it?"

"No, not yet." His voice was clipped. "Obviously I will be doing so, but I'd rather get a handle on it first, so that I've got a better idea of what to look for when I talk to them. And anyway, Mrs Cole had been sedated by her doctor and wasn't fit to be interviewed last night, still isn't this morning, and by the time we got her husband back from the mortuary last night, he'd had about as much as he could take."

"He did the ID?"

"Yes."

"Poor man," Fabia said, then added, "Where are you now?"

"In my office. I can be with you in, say, forty minutes."

"Okay, I'll see you then," Fabia said and put the phone down, unable to suppress a grin of satisfaction as she did so. A moment later the phone rang again.

"It's Cath. I thought I'd better let you know we're going ahead Saturday morning in spite of everything."

"What with?"

"Sorting the nearly new stuff for the women's refuge fundraiser. You said you'd be able to give us a hand. Had you forgotten?"

Fabia sighed. "Oh Lord, yes. It'd gone right out of my mind. What time did we say?"

"Half past ten in the church hall. It shouldn't take too long. I hate to nag, but we're a bit down on helpers, what with Cecily ... well, you can see what I mean."

"Of course. Don't worry. I'll be there."

She showered and dressed quickly and went down to the kitchen, in desperate need of some strong coffee, but as she walked in she saw the green envelope on the table. There was no getting away from it. Best to get this over with now, not knowing when she'd get another opportunity. She picked up the envelope and, with a sinking feeling in the pit of her stomach, made her way next door.

Rhona opened the door to her knock. "Oh, it's you," she said, her pointed face unsmiling. It was obvious she'd not forgiven Fabia for her teasing the day before. Oh Lord, Fabia thought, and the bloody letter is going to make things so much worse. She conjured up what she hoped was a friendly smile and plunged in.

"Hallo Rhona. I'm sorry about this, but I've been trying to catch up with you since yesterday. This was delivered to me by mistake yesterday and I opened it without thinking. I really am sorry, I–"

The small eyes glanced quickly down at the envelope Fabia was holding out. Before she could say another word, Rhona snatched it from her hand, snapped, "Thank you," and closed the door in her face.

"For goodness sake!" Fabia said aloud, almost laughing, but also perturbed by the whole business. She lifted her hand to knock again, then stopped. There was no doubt she'd have to talk to Rhona about the letter some time, having read it she could hardly just leave it, but now wasn't the time. Matt would be here soon, and that had to take priority. With a shrug of resignation, she went back inside to wait for him to arrive.

* * *

Fabia was shocked at how exhausted Matt looked when she saw him – sunken cheeks, inky shadows under his eyes and his dark hair in a tangled mess. It was obvious, just as she'd feared, that this case was getting to him. She wanted to ask him if he'd slept or give him an opportunity to talk about Bethan. In the past, it would have been the most natural thing to do, but not now. But she was a good deal gentler with him as a consequence, insisting he have a cup of coffee and putting a plate of biscuits on the table.

Better get the worst over first. He had every right to be angry she'd not told him about Amber and Rhona's quarrel yet. As he gulped at the steaming mug and helped himself, absent-mindedly, to the biscuits, she plunged in.

"There's something I really should have told you yesterday," Fabia began. Matt's eyebrows rose but she didn't give him the chance to respond. Quickly she told him all about the encounter on the bridge. He frowned as she spoke, but the expected explosion didn't come.

"That could be useful," his voice was cool but not angry.

"I know. I'm sorry I forgot about it yesterday."

He gave her a slightly twisted smile. "Even you slip up sometimes, Fabia." Then, obviously realising this wasn't the most tactful thing to say, he went on quickly. "Amber seems to have been a bright kid. She'd got the hang of hiding things so that they're seen but not recognised. Pryce finally found the diary in a bookcase they'd already been through. She'd wrapped it very neatly in the dust cover from an old children's picture book of exactly the same size."

"She was bright." Yet again Fabia felt the deep-down regret at the waste of so much potential. "Anyway," she said, deciding the best way was to keep things as businesslike as possible, "let's have a look at this diary."

He handed her a sheaf of photocopy paper. Someone had flattened the diary out on the machine and copied two pages at a time. The actual size of the book must be A5, Fabia thought, with faint lines and a margin. An ordinary notebook. On the left, in a flowing hand, was the name Amber Jane Morgan, with the word PRIVATE beneath it. Around her name and the word, she'd drawn an intricate border of twisted, thorn filled vines. On the right, the much more closely written script began. 29th October was the first date.

Silence reigned as Fabia sat reading, turning a page occasionally. There weren't that many. Amber hadn't written in her diary every day. There were gaps here and there of several days at a time. Fabia flipped through to see what the last date was. It was the day before she died.

"I can guess at the identity of some of the people she mentions. CJ, for instance, is probably the Evans boy from The Oaks. His second name's John – can't remember why I know that – he and Amber were close. But Viz, no, don't know that one, but wait a minute–" Fabia pressed a hand to her forehead, closed her eyes in concentration. "Viz, could be Vanessa Breverton, she was a friend of Amber's too. The three of them went around a lot together, much to Gwen Breverton's disgust. I don't think she approved of Amber one little bit. They do seem to pop up quite a few times in here as a threesome, see this here, and on the next page." Matt leant forward to look at the pages, then leant back to continue taking notes as he'd been doing since she started.

Fabia pointed to another passage. "And this bit here, *'Mouse gave me a pile of dosh for my birthday, just between the two of us she said'* – Amber told me her mother had given her money for her birthday, much more than usual which is probably why she mentioned it, so maybe Mouse is Cecily." She looked up at Matt. "It would fit perfectly. Cecily is a very timid person, quite apart from having mousey brown hair. Colours mattered to Amber."

Matt nodded. "Go on."

"As to Lecter, I've no idea. Presumably a man, and certainly someone she didn't like if she gave him a nickname like that." She paused then said triumphantly, "Yes, I definitely think Viz is Vanessa, because she mentions a big party at her house on the 2nd of December, and there was one up at the Breverton's house that day, a couple of hundred people according to Cath – our vicar, Cath Temple, she was invited, and I went with her to buy something to wear. And this bit here, about Drummer, I think that might be Paul Vaughan up at Bryn-y-Mor Lodge. In his early days in the music business he was a drummer in a group, what was it called? Coffee House? No, Coffee Club."

She glanced across the table at Matt and noticed the ghost of a smile on his face. "Your memory always did amaze me," he said.

Fabia didn't want to risk commenting. Any kind of reminiscing would entail trying to cross the yawning chasm of misunderstanding and pain that stretched between them. Not a good idea. Not now. Quickly she went back to the diary. "I know Paul Vaughan owns a studio and I think he's also a music promoter of some kind, so that's probably how he got her tickets for the Death's Head gig." She turned the paper towards Matt, indicating a point halfway down the page. "I wonder what she means by this bit here. *Just as well he'* – that's CJ she's talking about – *'doesn't know why Drummer got them for me!'*, and here she says, *'Wonder what his tart would think if she knew'*. If Drummer is Paul, I suppose she'd be referring to Mel Franklin, Paul's partner. Then a little later she says, *'Naomi found out about Drummer and me. I certainly know now where his priorities lie, the bastard'*. Now Mel is a fashion model so Naomi, as in Naomi Campbell, could be a predictable nickname for her. Looks to me as if Amber and Paul knew each other rather well."

"In the biblical sense," Matt said sardonically.

"How delicately you put it. This bit's about the Breverton's party." She read on for a while then suddenly exclaimed, "Shit! The poor child."

Matt leant forward to check how far Fabia had got. "Oh yes," he said, his voice expressionless. "It seems she was on the game, more or less, well, sex for favours as much as for money. Trouble is, with the number of people at that party, this Bulldog person she says she *'gave it to'* could be any one of dozens of …"

"But in the next entry," Fabia interrupted, "she mentions meeting him in the High Street. Surely that means he must be local?"

"Could be, but not necessarily. Maybe just visiting. Anyway, does the word 'Bulldog' mean anything to you?"

"Not immediately. Perhaps his name is actually Churchill, although I can't think of anyone of that name round here, not offhand. And I wouldn't have thought that'd be a connection a seventeen-year-old would come up with, although that advert on television might have prompted her to use it."

"Possibly."

"And who's this Ferret person?" went on Fabia. "She mentioned her – it seems to be a her – earlier on, said she found out about Drummer, alias Paul, and told Mouse, alias Cecily. God this is complicated. It's hard to keep up." She frowned. "I can't work out who Lecter is yet. Here she seems to have overheard something between him and this Ferret person. *'Overheard her coming on to him – gross!'* But that could be just Amber's imagination, she certainly had a lively one, not to say lurid at times. It could have been a completely innocent encounter. She finishes that entry, *'That'll teach her to blab about me and Drummer'*. You know what, I think The Ferret might be Rhona Griffiths, my next-door neighbour."

"Why?"

"Well, she is awfully nosey, always spying on people, and she does look a bit like a ferret. But no, perhaps it's just that she's on my mind at the moment."

Fabia was nearing the end. Just one more page to go. She went on and finished without further comment, then exclaimed suddenly. "Stupid woman, I missed this earlier on."

"What?"

"This bit about posting the letters."

"Oh yes. It wasn't just the diary we found," Matt said. "There was some other rather interesting stuff well hidden in some CD box sets beside the girl's TV."

"What was it?" asked Fabia.

"There was one of those old-fashioned John Bull printing sets, do you remember them? You know, little rubber letters, tweezers to pick them up with and an ink pad. All the kit was there, and some pieces of paper which she appears to have been practising on, together with some notes in her own writing. It all looked like drafts of a poison pen letter, or perhaps more than one."

Fabia's eyes widened but she didn't interrupt.

"There're several versions, some just the odd phrase. But it's pretty obvious what they were intended for, although there are no names and no indication of whom they were sent to. From that entry in the diary, it seems she actually sent them off."

"She did. At least, she sent one off." Quickly she told him about the letter to Rhona and her efforts to return it, and Rhona's reaction that morning when she'd finally succeeded in doing so. Matt's eyes widened. She could see he was angry, but she forestalled any outburst. "Don't start on me for not mentioning this earlier. I had absolutely no reason to until I read this."

"Okay. But it certainly puts a different complexion on things. I'll have to have a word with Miss Griffiths as soon as possible."

"But I'd speak to young Craig Evans first if I were you," she said without thinking.

"Obviously we'll be talking to everyone involved." His tone was chilly.

"Yes, of course," she said stiffly, feeling snubbed. She went back to the diary. "That last entry, when was it? Damn, it's not dated. Had you noticed the language is different? Less theatrical, much more serious? What was it she found out? And she talks about needing to talk to CJ. I wonder if she had the chance to do so. I'm sure whatever it was shocked her, but it also made her very angry."

Matt glanced down the last page again. "I see what you mean. At this stage we've no way of knowing what it was, we'll just have to keep delving, speculation's going to get us nowhere."

"Maybe not, but an educated guess or two might help."

"I'm not going to start guessing, Fabia." The frosty tone resumed. "You should know me better than that."

She made no comment. What would be the point?

"Well, thank you very much," Matt said, formal now. "You've been very helpful."

"That's okay," she said awkwardly. "Would you mind if I kept these copies? I'd like to look through it all again, get a better feel for it. I'll let you know if I think of anything else."

He hesitated for a moment but, after a sideways glance at her said, "Fine, so long as you keep them strictly to yourself."

"Of course," she said coldly. "What else would I do?"

He ignored this. "I'd better be going then. Thanks for the coffee. I'll... um... I'll keep you posted."

For a long while after he'd gone, Fabia sat on at the kitchen table, wishing things were as they used to be between them, but knowing they never would be. To distract herself, she pulled the photocopied sheets towards her, began to read them again. What on earth had possessed Amber to send that letter to Rhona? For Fabia was sure now that she had. She thought back, trying to remember what the letter had said, and wishing now she'd taken a copy. That last line, something about watching out or she'd tell what she'd seen. Had Amber told what she'd seen? Was that why she'd been killed? But Rhona hadn't seen the letter until after Amber died. Still, that might not make any difference, if she'd felt threatened by Amber in some other way, perhaps she'd lashed out. No, thought Fabia, I just can't see Rhona as a murderer, but still, as a policewoman she knew only too well there was no particular type who committed this kind of crime. There was no such thing as a typical murderer.

Chapter 9

Matt felt misery close in on him as he drove away from Fabia's. It was bad enough that this case brought his sister so strongly back into his mind, but Fabia's involvement made things even worse. He felt angry with her for being involved and, however much he told himself that was unreasonable, it made no difference, the anger still simmered. And yet part of him was elated at meeting up with her again. She hadn't changed, not one bit, still as assertive as ever, and as attractive.

He couldn't stop himself wondering how different things would be now if she'd given in that weekend when he'd helped her decorate the kitchen. Standing there in the middle of the room, brush in hand, his clothes flecked with paint, he'd stared at her. "Don't be obtuse, Fabia. Surely by now you know what I want."

"Yes, but it's just not on, Matt, it really isn't." Her gentle tone belied the words. She'd turned and begun to rinse out some brushes in the sink.

"We work too closely together," she'd told him. "You know how difficult it is to keep a relationship going with our job, and when it's with someone else in the force, that just adds to the problems. Believe me, I know what I'm talking about here."

"How come?"

"It's a long story. I'll tell you one day. You're such a good friend to me, I don't want to lose that."

"I wouldn't stop being your friend, I'd just be your–" he'd paused, come closer, turned her to face him, put out a hand and gently run a finger down her cheek and neck. Before he got any further down, she'd stopped his hand with her own.

"No, Matt. Please don't."

"Why not? Is it to do with the fact you out-rank me? I grant you that could be a problem, but surely not one we can't overcome. I could ask for a transfer to Cardiff or somewhere."

"No, it's not that."

"Well, what then? The age difference?"

She'd smiled ruefully. "Don't be silly, what does five years matter? If it was you that was older than me, no-one would even think about it. No, it's – it's just that I don't want to lose you…" He'd felt a stirring of hope, but she'd hurried on before he could say anything. "I don't want to lose what we have already. You're, sort of, the closest I've ever had to a brother."

"Oh, for God's sake Fabia, that's positively incestuous."

Her eyes had slid away from his. "Matt, I love you, very much, but as a friend, nothing else. Can't we leave it like that?"

He'd stood there, utterly still, looking down at her and studying her face minutely, then he'd sighed. He didn't believe her, but couldn't say so. "Okay. For now. But I'm not going to give up."

Of course, in the end he had, and now it was pointless to speculate how different life would have been if she'd given in that day. And now he'd met up with her again and discovered his feelings for her were as strong as ever. He still longed to run his fingers through that mass of untidy curls – he stopped this thought in its tracks. Don't go there, he told himself firmly. It'll only make things worse. Concentrate on the job.

Half an hour later, he picked Dilys up from the station where she'd been checking through a mountain of paperwork. Matt wanted her with him for their next two calls. Dilys had arranged a visit to Rhona Griffiths later in the day, but their first call was at The Oaks pub to have a word with Amber's friend, Craig Evans.

The Oaks was an old building, parts of it probably dated back to the seventeenth century. It had been a coaching inn and, where the stables and coach house had been, there was now a car park and a beer garden. In the summer, Matt thought, it would be pleasant to sit out here – the place bright with geraniums, petunias and busy lizzies – and relax with a pint. Now, though, he and Dilys parked in the empty car park – it was still a little early for the lunchtime trade – and entered through a door at the back. Matt had to duck to avoid first the lintel and then a dark wood beam, obviously an original, halfway along the passageway. At the end, they found a door that opened into a bar full of the same dark wood. Horse brasses decorated the walls, along with some willow patterned plates and a few rather attractive hunting prints. Matt liked the traditional decor. It wasn't particularly imaginative, but it was comfortable and welcoming.

The same could not be said of the publican who stood behind the bar. George Evans looked up from wiping glasses as they walked in. He frowned at the sight of them; obviously he knew full well they weren't customers, and he wasn't in the slightest bit pleased to see them. A second later, his eyes were veiled, revealing no more.

"Don't think he likes the look of us," muttered Dilys. Matt didn't comment, after all, it was a reaction every member of the police force was used to.

"Good morning, Mr Evans. DCI Lambert and Sergeant Bevan." Matt showed his warrant card. "We're investigating the death of Amber Morgan."

"Ah." George's face fell automatically into an expression of concern. "Poor dab, that's sad. A terrible thing to happen. Terrible thing…" he rumbled.

"Yes, it is," Matt interrupted, following this up with a brisk request to see George's son, Craig. "He was a close friend of Miss Morgan, wasn't he?"

"They was pals, yes." The publican sounded more cautious now. "Used to knock around together, see. They weren't that close."

"We understood they were very close."

George shrugged his massive shoulders. "You know how it is with these kids."

"Could we have a word with him?"

"I'm not sure."

Once more Matt interrupted, "It's important. Obviously, you would want to help us find out who's responsible, given that Amber was a friend?"

"Yea, well – rightio then. Hang on a moment, I'll just check out the back, see if he's there."

George disappeared through a door behind the bar and Matt looked around the empty room. It smelt of stale beer with an overlay of furniture polish.

"Sounds as if he comes from Swansea way, Mr Evans," he said while they waited.

"Sounds like it. He's definitely not local."

"What about his wife?"

"I'm told she's from round here. Born in Newport, apparently."

When he returned, George took them through to the family's private kitchen, a large, untidy room at the back of the building that obviously doubled as an office. There was a desk in the corner, piled high with papers of all kinds, a computer to one side half buried in the mess.

Standing by a round table in the middle of the room, chewing at a thumbnail, shoulders hunched, was a gangly lad of about eighteen, his hair carefully shaved on either side of his head, what was left arranged in untidy spikes.

"This is my boy Craig." George said, looking from Matt to Dilys. After a moment's hesitation and a nervous glance at his son, he went on. "Well, I'll leave you to it. I'll be in the bar if you need me," he said pointedly to his son, and left the room.

It was obvious Craig had been crying. His blue eyes were red-rimmed and his cheeks blotchy. But he had himself well in hand as he sat down at the table. Matt and Dilys took seats opposite him.

"You gonna find out what happened to Amber then?" was the first thing he said, his tone aggressive.

"We intend to do so, yes, with help from people like you," said Matt.

"Why me?"

"I would have thought that was obvious. You were her friend. You might well have information that would be helpful in our enquiries."

Craig made a pathetic attempt to sneer. "Helping the police with their enquiries, think I don't know what that means?"

"It means just that. We're making enquiries, you're helping us. What's wrong with that?"

Craig made a derisive sound. "I knows what I knows," he said cryptically, and slouched back in his chair, folding his arms across his chest. He looked Matt defiantly in the eye. "So? What do you want to know?"

Matt sighed and ploughed on. "I'm sure you're as anxious as we are to find out who killed your girlfriend. Amber was your girlfriend, wasn't she?"

"No. Not so's you'd notice. Just a friend."

"But you cared about her?"

"S'pose."

"Well then, cooperating with us is your best chance of seeing whoever did it brought to justice." God, I sound pompous, Matt thought, as he went on. "So, shall we start again without all the macho crap?"

It was obvious Craig was struggling with his desire to keep up his defiant stance. But it was a losing battle. A look of pain flitted across his face, then he swallowed hard, sat up straighter and muttered, "Okay. S'pose you're only doing your job."

They took him through his last encounter with Amber. That had been on Wednesday afternoon, he said, on the bridge. "She was going on about this interview she'd had at some fancy college. She'd just got back, texted me to meet her, full of it, she was. She was good, Amber, at painting and that. We was having a laugh, see, and I was showing her my new bike." For a moment, there was animation in his face, "It's a Yamaha TTR 750 cc. Lovely machine, goes sweet as a nut." But it didn't last long. Soon his eyes darkened again. "Then that old crone come past, stupid cow."

"Which old crone is that?"

"Miss bloody high and mighty Rhona Griffiths. Thinks she's so fuckin' important, she does." His voice was loaded with scorn. "Told me to get my bike off the pavement. Amber dealt with her all right. Sent her off with a flea in her ear. She was good at that sort of thing, Amb."

"What did she say?"

"Told her what she needed was a good screw," he said defiantly. "Said something 'bout she should wait till tomorrow, then she'd know all about it."

"Did she?" Matt glanced at Dilys, wondering if she'd picked up on this.

"What did she mean by that?"

"Dunno."

"Are you sure?"

Craig met this question with sullen silence, so Matt changed tack. "And what was Miss Griffiths' reaction to what Amber said?"

"Usual sort of stuff for her, popping eyes, spluttering, and then she stomped off. She told Amb she was going to talk to her Mam. Amber didn't like that, she hates," a spasm of pain crossed his face, then he corrected himself, "hated it when people said things about her Mam. She didn't like her upset, see?"

This was a new slant on Amber, and Matt added it to the picture he was building up of the murdered girl. "Did you notice anything unusual about her that afternoon? Anything out of the ordinary?"

Craig frowned and chewed at his bottom lip, obviously thinking hard about these questions. After a while he said, "I don't know as there was anything unusual exactly. She was a bit uptight, sort of excited, but inside, you know. I thought it was because of that art school. She wanted me to take her for a spin on my bike, but I couldn't. That annoyed her."

"But she was normal otherwise?"

"Yea, maybe. She was always moody, like, up and down."

"Was it enough for you to notice a difference that particular evening?"

"I s'pose, but only when I thought about it after – you know – when I heard." He paused, frowning, and pressed a thumb and forefinger to the corners of his eyes. "It was only when I went past her, as I was riding home, she waved, and I thought at the time it was just ordinary waving like, but now I think maybe she was trying to get me to stop. I don't know. Maybe not."

"So, she hadn't mentioned anything that was worrying her?"

Craig leant forward aggressively. "Haven't I just said? Nothing out of the ordinary happened, other than that old crow and her yakking. Don't you think that was enough to make anybody angry? I s'pose you think Amb should have done the yes miss, no miss shit with the stupid old bag?" He slouched back again and began to chew at a fingernail.

With a glance at Matt, Dilys took over. "How soon after the encounter with Miss Griffiths did the two of you go home?"

"Not long," Craig said, calmer now. "Amb walked up the High Street and along up St Madoc's Road."

"How long would that have taken her?"

"Fifteen minutes, no more." Craig shrugged. "She probably got back to her place about half five."

"And did you make any arrangements to meet later that evening?" Matt asked.

"Sort of, we met up most nights." There was a second of absolute stillness, then he realised what he'd said. The colour drained from his face and his hands clenched convulsively where they lay clasped before him on the table. "But I didn't see her, not Wednesday evening. You trying to trick me or something? I've got an alibi, I have. You ask Viz—"

Dilys's eyes widened but Matt forestalled her, "Who's Viz?"

"Vanessa Breverton, she's a mate too, not bad considering her mam and da are such nobs," Craig remarked with an incongruous diversion into mundanity. "The three of us were going to go into Newport, have a few drinks, go to a club, but Amb never showed. We... we didn't think that much of it. Sometimes her folks got stupid, told her she couldn't go out and that, and we thought maybe that was it, you know?"

"And where had you arranged to meet her?"

"Back there on..." His voice petered out and he made a little choking noise, put his hand up and pressed his thumb and fingertips to his eyes.

Matt glanced at Dilys, eyebrows raised. They waited a moment, then he asked, his voice firm but not unsympathetic. "Craig, I know this is difficult, but we really do need to know everyone's movements. Where did you arrange to meet Amber?"

Taking a shuddering breath and rubbing at his eyes with the heel of his hand he said, almost inaudibly, "Down by the street lamp, on the bridge."

"What time?"

"Nine."

"And did you go down at that time?"

"Yes, but she never showed." His voice was anguished, then it changed, and he said dully, "In the end me and Viz just went back to the pub."

"You arrived at the bridge at the same time, you and Vanessa?"

"Yea. We met up in the High Street. She's got a car and she picked me up."

"And there was no sign of Amber?"

"No." A look of horror gradually growing in his eyes, he asked, "Was she – was she dead then?"

"We don't know yet when she died, but we're pretty sure she fell from the bridge itself." A small part of Matt regretted the shock tactics, but it was sometimes useful.

"Fuck, fuck, fuck," Craig said with soft violence, banging on the table with clenched fists. A moment later he put his hands up to his face once more and quietly began to sob.

It was precisely at this moment that the door was thrust open and a woman burst into the room. She reminded Matt of a Russian singer he'd seen at the Welsh National Opera, a Rubenesque figure, taller than average, with improbably black hair curling down her shoulders. She glanced at her son and then turned on them, obviously very angry.

"What d'you think you're doing to my boy? Hasn't he had enough to put up with, what with his girlfriend dead in the river? All the same, you bloody police. Bloody bullies, that's what." She put an arm round Craig's shoulders and glared across at them as she stroked his hair with her other hand. "You leave him alone. Can't you see he's that upset he hardly knows what he's saying?"

"I'm sorry, Mrs Evans," Matt said calmly, "but this has to be done. Murder is very hard on everyone involved, family, friends, everyone. If we're to find Amber's killer, I'm afraid questions have to be asked."

Craig shrugged off his mother's arm, rubbed at his face with a tissue he'd rummaged from his pocket, and muttered, "It's okay Mam. I want to help find the fucking bastard."

"Language," his mother said, but it was only a reflex action. She continued to glare at them as she settled back in a chair next to her son. "Okay, but I'm staying, understand?"

"By all means, Mrs Evans," Matt said smoothly.

Her description of Amber as Craig's girlfriend was not lost on Matt. He wondered who was closest to the truth, Craig or his mother. But then, if the boy had found out about Amber's activities with the two men mentioned in her diary, and there could have been others, maybe there'd been a falling out between them. Enough for Craig to lose his temper and lash out at Amber in a jealous rage? That remained to be seen. At the moment, he looked anxious to find her killer and his grieving seemed sincere. Of course, his distress could just as easily be caused by the knowledge of his own guilt.

Matt leant forward and rested his arms on the table. "So, Craig, you last saw Amber on Wednesday afternoon?"

"Yes."

"And he was working Wednesday evening behind the bar," Craig's mother said in a challenging voice.

"Until he went out a bit later," Matt said firmly, then decided on another tack. "As I said before, we'd like you to help us, and by that I mean help find the person who killed your girlfriend. Can you think of anyone who might have had reason to harm her?"

Craig simply shook his head and the silence stretched out, each of them waiting for the other to break it. Matt glanced at his sergeant and Dilys leant forward.

"You do understand, don't you?" she said, "how important it is that we get some idea of Amber's movements in the last few hours before she died?"

"But I told you I didn't see her again that day. Don't you think I wish I had?"

"Do you think she was with somebody else on Wednesday evening?"

"What d'you mean?"

"Well, she was an attractive girl," Dilys said. "We've heard she had plenty of boyfriends. Did she mention anyone to you?"

Craig stared straight ahead, sullenly uncooperative, but Matt noticed that he wasn't willing to look Dilys in the eye.

"Who do you think she might have been with?" he demanded. "Come on. This could be really important, Craig. You said you wanted her killer caught, so help us do so."

"I don't know, do I? I wasn't her keeper." But he was weakening. "Okay, so she may have been with Paul. She'd been out with him a few times."

"Paul who?" Matt asked.

"Paul Vaughan from Bryn-y-Mor Lodge. He's okay, Paul. Has his own studio and everything. Got us tickets for some gigs. Amber talked about him a bit, said he gave her–"

"Gave her what?"

"A good time; said he was a good bloke."

But Matt was sure that wasn't what he'd intended to say.

Chapter 10

As they left the pub Dilys asked, "Do you think he had anything to do with it, sir?"

"Hard to tell at the moment. I think he was genuinely fond of the girl. Maybe she made him so jealous, carrying on with other men, that he hit out at her. It's a possibility."

"He's not very fond of us."

"That's par for the course, particularly if he's in with that group from the Golden Monkey. He could be afraid we'll turn something up on him almost by default."

"I'd certainly like to know how he came by enough money to buy that Yamaha. That's some bike." Dilys sounded as if she knew what she was talking about.

"Into bikes, are you?"

"Not really, but my brother'd give his eyeteeth for one like that. They cost a small fortune, particularly for a lad that age."

"Get Pryce to check out where he got it from, and what money he's got coming in, part-time jobs, that sort of thing. And it's worth doing a double check on him when it comes to the drugs business. See to it, would you?"

"Will do."

Matt frowned through the windscreen as he started up the car. "And I don't think he was being entirely honest right at the end there. Said Paul Vaughan gave her a good time, no, I don't buy that. I think he was just about to say he gave her drugs or something like that."

"I think you might be right there. So, where now?"

"A visit to Mr Vaughan would be a good idea, I think, but let's do some checks on him first. Right now, since we've got a few minutes, I want to pop in and have a word with Amber's stepfather."

They drove through Pontygwyn and on up St Madoc's Road to the Coles' house. Murray Cole opened the door, looking haggard. His skin had a grey tinge to it and there were deep grooves either side of his mouth which had added years to him since the day before. But he was as polite as ever as he invited them into the house.

"I've got the results of the post-mortem," Matt told him. "I thought you'd want to know what was found."

"Yes, yes," Cole said, but the ghost of a shudder ran through him as he spoke.

They stood in an awkward little group in the middle of the incredibly neat sitting room as Matt outlined Dr Curtis's findings.

"So," he finished, "I'm afraid there's very little doubt your stepdaughter was murdered, Mr Cole."

"Oh God. You're absolutely sure, are you?"

"I'm afraid we are, yes," Matt said gently. "Would you like us to speak to Mrs Cole ourselves? We will have to interview her at some point."

"No, I'll tell her," he said quickly. "She's sleeping at the moment. Dr Page still has her sedated."

"I see. Well, perhaps you could help us on one other point, sir."

"Of course."

"We believe your step-daughter was sending poison pen letters." Matt watched the man's face carefully as he said this, ready to pick up on the slightest reaction. There was none at first. His expression barely changed at all, nor did he make any comment, but the muscles in his cheeks tightened until the skin went white. Matt went on. "We're hoping that your wife, in particular, might be able to help us work out who she sent the letters to."

"Why would my wife know?" he said sharply, as if they'd accused his wife of sending the letters herself.

"As Amber's mother she might well–"

"I see no reason at all why she should know anything about it." He was sounding angrily protective now. "Are you certain she was writing them?"

"We know of at least one she'd sent, we're hoping to interview the person who received it later today."

"I'd like to see this evidence."

"That won't be possible at the moment, sir."

"Why?"

"It's with our forensics team."

"But you're willing to show it to my wife." He was beginning to pace up and down the room in agitation.

"In due course, yes. But then, she is Amber's mother."

Cole swung round and glared at Matt. "And I have been her father since she was six years old. You think I don't know her? Don't care about her?"

"That's not what I said, sir."

Cole took a deep breath, obviously trying to calm down. "I'm sorry. Of course, I know you'll have to speak to Cecily soon. It's just that I don't want her upset any more than she is already."

"I understand, sir, but as I said before, we will have to talk to her," Matt said firmly. "Can you tell us when that would be possible?"

"Tomorrow, maybe." It was obvious his mind was no longer on them. He continued to pace up and down, muttering almost to himself. "We loved Amber very much, both of us, but there's no denying she was a difficult child, and always has... had been. And now still it goes on."

Dilys caught Matt's eye, opened her mouth to say something, then seemed to change her mind. Matt was glad she had. Better not to interrupt him.

His pacing had brought him round to face them and he seemed to come to realise they were still there. "I'm sorry, Chief Inspector. This tragic business is getting to all of us. It was only a few days ago Cecily had Rhona Griffiths complaining about Amber's behaviour in extremely strong terms. My poor wife was very upset."

"What exactly did Miss Griffiths say?"

"I'm not sure exactly. She objected to Amber's clothes, and her behaviour – said Amber was always being rude to her. The Griffiths woman was most upset, in fact Cecily described it as 'beside herself'. She ranted and raved, said if we didn't deal with Amber she'd have to do so herself."

Matt hoped his face remained impassive. "And what do you think she meant by that?"

"The Lord knows." Cole seemed completely unaware of the implications of what he'd said. "She's completely round the bend, probably got hormonal troubles, not responsible for her actions, you know what I mean. I'm afraid Amber would have enjoyed winding her up." He gave Matt a sharp look from under his brows. "Is that who she was sending the letters to?"

"As yet we're not sure exactly who they were sent to," Matt said. There was no way he was going to be more specific at the moment.

"Might be worth checking. She's the sort of person Amber might have targeted."

"We'll bear it in mind, sir."

Matt could see that he was making an effort to pull himself together. "As to my wife, would it be convenient if I let you know you when she's fit to see you?"

"Yes, thank you. I'm sure you realise how urgent it is, Mr Cole. It will have to be within the next few days." Matt waited for the protest, but it didn't come. "We'll get out of your way now then, sir. And if you do think of anyone else Amber might have written letters to, here's my card."

Cole took it without looking at it. "Of course. Anything I can do to help, anything. I'll not rest until the monster who's done this dreadful thing is behind bars." He edged towards the door and held it open, obviously relieved at the prospect of their departure. "I'll see you out."

* * *

Matt had hopes of the interview with Rhona Griffiths. Apart from her involvement with Amber and the letter, he remembered what Fabia had said – Rhona was a nosy woman who always knew everyone else's business. People like that could be very useful. He hoped to be able to glean a good deal of background from her, quite apart from any specific information. And there was what Cole had said about her state of mind and her reaction to Amber, that mustn't be forgotten either. But would someone really kill out of a warped mixture of jealousy and outrage? God only knew. In Matt's experience, murder had been committed for much less.

They parked directly outside the house and Matt couldn't resist a glance next door to see if there was any sign of life at Fabia's. There wasn't. Friday afternoon she could be doing the church flowers or something. That was something she'd done in the past, and it'd always surprised him. He remembered the arguments they used to have about her church going.

"Don't know why you bother," he used to tease. "Load of superstitious nonsense. How can you believe in all that with the job you've got?" And she'd usually responded with a grin and a remark about his family. "Shame on you, a parson's son, and your brother a parson too. You should know better."

He pushed these thoughts out of his mind and followed Dilys up the path to Rhona Griffiths' front door.

As he did so, he noticed the lace curtain in a downstairs window dropping back into place. Barely a second after they'd knocked, the door opened. Matt thought he saw a flash of disappointment in the woman's eyes when she saw Dilys standing there, then she caught sight of him and her eyes lit up. Oh Lord, he thought, here we go.

"Chief Inspector Lambert," Matt said, holding out his warrant card. "This is Sergeant Dilys Bevan and we'd like to talk to you about Amber Morgan."

"Oh yes, yes," she said, her voice high and sibilant. "Do please come in. Such a tragedy, but one waiting to happen, I'm afraid."

They followed her into an impossibly cluttered lounge. On the walls were dark oil paintings, one a sentimental study of a father and child, two others rather dour landscapes, their jutting gold frames heavy around them, and here and there hung family photographs, all rather rigidly posed. The furniture was predominantly Victorian, over-ornamented mahogany, and even the armchairs and settee looked rigid and uncompromising. Every surface contained brass, china or glass ornaments, and every cushion had its brightly coloured embroidered or crocheted cover. Matt found the crowded, oppressive feel of the place depressing and longed to escape.

"What makes you say that?" he asked.

Her beady little eyes gazed at him, but she didn't answer, obviously put out by his direct question. After goggling at him for a moment without answering, she invited them to sit down. She twittered around offering them tea, which they refused. Anything else? Again, they refused. Finally, she came to rest, perched on an upright chair with her hands clasped tightly in her lap, staring relentlessly at Matt while totally ignoring Dilys.

Matt asked again, "What made you think this tragedy was waiting to happen?" He watched as the colour in her cheeks deepened a little.

"Perhaps I shouldn't have said that. *De mortuis nil nisi bonum*, as my dear father would have said."

"But sometimes in a murder investigation, unfortunate though it may be," Matt said earnestly, thanking his lucky stars he was well up on Latin tags, "it becomes necessary to speak ill of the dead in the interests of justice."

Rhona looked deeply impressed by this. "Oh, do you really think so, Chief Inspector? Of course, you would know best, wouldn't you?" She gave a strange little snigger, then looked embarrassed and added hastily, "I mean, in your job."

"Yes indeed," Matt said, relieved that he seemed to have hit the right note. "We'd be most grateful if you could give us your honest opinion of Amber Morgan. It would certainly help us enormously." He gave her one of his most deprecating smiles and watched with mounting distaste as her colour deepened even more and she put up a hand to pat at her hair. The silence lengthened while an ugly porcelain clock on the mantelpiece ticked away the seconds, and Rhona Griffiths' unblinking little eyes gazed at him intently over the fingers now pressed to her lips.

Slowly she lowered the hand and said, "You say this is a murder investigation, but surely, she could have committed suicide." She whispered the last two words as if she could hardly bring herself to voice them. "In my opinion it would not be surprising if a girl such as Amber was driven to such lengths, mortal sin though it is. The final sin of Judas, as we well know. She, of course, was not a believer, in fact she mocked most disgracefully at those of us who are of the faith." Suddenly, her precise, old-fashioned style of speech slipped and she spat out. "And look where it's got her."

Good God, Matt thought, this woman's like some caricature of an old maid from decades back. He glanced at Dilys, surprised to see a look of deep disgust in her eyes, he looked quickly away. Obviously, he wasn't the only one who was finding Rhona Griffiths distasteful. Give me a straightforward villain into burglary or a spot of fraud any day, rather than this ghastly female, he thought. But needs must.

"We have considered that it might be suicide," he said, keeping his voice blandly expressionless, "but the evidence points in a different direction."

"Be that as it may, I don't think you should discard that route of investigation," she said earnestly, returning to her usual style. "Amber was a very wild girl, a very bad girl. I really wouldn't put it past her, if only for the sake of the effect it might have on her nearest and dearest. She was a terrible attention seeker. But," she said, piously folding her hands in her lap again, "she has her punishment. In Revelations it is said of such as her, I will cast her on a bed of suffering. How true. How true."

Matt could find no appropriate response to this, so he waited for the awful little woman to continue.

"Her poor stepfather had a great deal of trouble with her," she said, shaking her head slowly from side to side. "Her mother, I'm afraid, indulged her dreadfully. My dearest Da always said discipline was at the cornerstone of a good relationship between parent and child. I do so agree with him, don't you?"

Matt by-passed this question with a stiff smile and asked. "What kind of trouble did her parents have with her?"

"Oh, I don't really like to go into details—"

"—but it would help us a great deal if you would, Miss Griffiths."

Rhona licked at her top lip, her pink tongue flashing from side to side with great speed, then she went on, with obvious relish. "She had a lot of men friends." Her voice dropped to a breathy whisper. "Not just boys, you know. Older men too."

"Do you know who exactly?"

"Oh, no, no, no. Her mother told me about it." She took a sharp little breath. "At least, she hinted at it, but she didn't say exactly who."

Matt found this hard to believe. He doubted very much that Amber's mother would confide such things to this vicious little gossip. He tried to probe, framing and reframing more or less the same questions in an effort to find out which of Amber's men friends Rhona had in mind, and how she'd found out about them – if, of course, she had. But it was no good. He could get nothing more out of her on that front. In the end, he changed tack.

"I gather you were on Pontygwyn Bridge late on Wednesday afternoon and that you had a difference of opinion with Amber Morgan. Could you tell us exactly what happened?"

Chapter 11

Rhona's sharply drawn eyebrows rose and her lips tightened into a straight line. Matt expected her to ask how he knew, but she didn't. Unexpectedly she smiled, but it didn't reach her eyes.

"Yes, I was. I'd been to visit a friend of mine who has a bungalow in that rather exclusive little estate on the other side of Cobett's Field. She's a member of the Mansel-Pryce family, they're a very old and respected family in Gwent and she's a distant connection of mine. As my father used to say, there's no substitute for true class. Her mother was an Honourable, you know."

Her sharp eyes waited for him to respond to this. She obviously expected him to be impressed and to comment accordingly, but Matt said nothing. He wasn't going to be distracted.

"Can you tell me exactly what happened on the bridge?"

At first, she just stared at him, said nothing, then she gave an almost imperceptible sniff and went on.

"As I say, I was returning from my friend's house when I happened to encounter Amber." Suddenly she went off on a different tack, hitching herself forward in her chair in a conspiratorial fashion and dropping her voice to a sibilant whisper. "Do you know she even corrupted some of the other young girls in the neighbourhood? Our new member of parliament, Neville Breverton, such a dear man, just as he should be, they're regular churchgoers, he and his wife, always attends Sunday service when he's at home. So charismatic, so attentive. I think he'll become a particular friend. He has a delightful young daughter, very well spoken, been to the best schools. Well, would you believe I saw her the other day with Amber and that young Evans boy? I do hope her parents realise what's going on. Obviously, I shall have to speak to them. It's my duty to do so, I'm sure you'll agree."

Matt would have liked to be able to tell her precisely what he thought. Instead he murmured that it was up to her, but she wasn't really listening.

"It was a disgrace the way that girl behaved. So disrespectful, so... so vulgar. Her language was disgusting; disgusting, from the gutter..." Her voice had risen to a slightly hysterical squeak before she pulled herself up short and fell silent, her lips working and her fingers plucking incessantly at the neck of her blouse.

"What happened when you encountered Amber?" Matt asked, trying to steer her back on course.

"She was on the bridge, sitting there banging those beautiful ancient stones with her horrible boots. Of course, I had to remonstrate with her, it was my duty," she said again. "I'm sure anyone who knows me will tell you that I never shirk my duty."

Okay, okay, thought Matt, in your book all this is down to duty, in my book it's being an interfering old bag. But you could be useful to us, so keep going. He didn't dare look at Dilys in case his thoughts were echoed in her face.

"Heaven be praised," Rhona went on, "when I telephoned the Coles' to speak to Cecily, she was out and I was able to talk to Amber's stepfather. A good man, very caring, but firm. He always knows just what's needed, whereas Cecily, I have to say, was far too indulgent with her daughter. She's always spoilt her most disgracefully, hence her behaviour. A weak mother breeds a wild child, as my dearest father used to say."

A second later, her expression changed. A strange little smile appeared round the edge of her mouth. Matt noticed her hands clasped together so hard in her lap that the skin shone tight over the knuckles. He wondered what on earth was coming next.

"Amber's stepfather is a very different matter. A most capable man, and devoted to Amber, in spite of her behaviour. I saw him later that evening. He drove past and gave me such a friendly wave. I thought at the time he must be returning from singing practice. He has a beautiful tenor voice, you know, you might almost think him a Welsh man born and bred. Such a busy man, and so very conscientious. A great asset to St Madoc's. He's their deputy head, you know." Her cheeks were pink. "He always waves to me as he passes, and smiles, very friendly."

"Where was this?" Matt asked.

"In the High Street. I was coming back from checking that the church silver had been cleaned. I'm in charge of the team who do the cleaning at St Mary's. One must do one's bit after all." She gave a deprecating little smile, then sniffed. "Some people aren't as particular as they should be, so I just popped in to make sure the job had been done properly. One can't be too careful, particularly now we have to suffer this modern phenomenon, a female vicar, with no vicar's wife to oversee the smooth running of things. Not as it should be, as I'm sure you agree. Such a pity, but there you are." She gave a little shudder. "Ladies of the cloth, it just doesn't sound right, does it?"

She might as well have said ladies of the night, Matt thought. He ignored this digression and asked, "Do you remember the time?"

"Yes I do, as a matter of fact. It was exactly half-past seven. I know that because I remember hearing the church clock chime the half hour. And when I got home, I telephoned to speak to Cecily again, and would you believe she was still out?" she said in shocked tones. "I would have thought she'd be at home to welcome her husband on his return. But no. I don't think she gives him nearly as much support as she should, particularly not when it comes to Amber's more outrageous behaviour. Once, when I remonstrated with her about it, she was quite sharp with me – but the least said about that the better perhaps."

Matt glanced at Dilys and she raised her eyebrows slightly but didn't intervene. Time was pressing. They had to get to the poison pen letters, and he'd been hoping to lead Rhona gently towards the subject, or even better, that she'd mention it herself, but he now had a pretty shrewd idea she wouldn't do so. He'd have to plunge in regardless.

"One thing I would like to ask you, Miss Griffiths. Can you tell us about the letter, addressed to you, that was delivered to Miss Havard next door by mistake?"

He watched as her already protuberant eyes widened, and the colour drained slowly from her cheeks. At first her lips moved and no sound came out, but then she said in a sibilant whisper, "What... what letter is that?"

"The one in a bright green envelope. Miss Havard tells us she opened it thinking it was for her. She was disturbed at what she read and, on looking at the envelope again, realised it was addressed to you. I think she managed to catch up with you this morning to hand it over, hoping to be able to offer her help in dealing with it. Would you let us have a look at it?"

"I don't know what you're talking about."

"But surely you remember?"

She gave a high-pitched little giggle. "Remember? Remember what?"

"That Miss Havard," Matt said, slowly and patiently, "came round early this morning and gave you a letter, which was addressed to you, but had been delivered to her by mistake. She thought it looked like a poison pen letter. They're very nasty and really ought to be reported to the police so that we can deal with the perpetrator."

"This is all such nonsense. I don't know what Fabia Havard may have chosen to tell you, but it's lies, all lies. I can't imagine what's got into her."

"I beg your pardon, Miss Griffiths, but I don't think she had any reason to lie."

"Why not, may I ask? She's a dreadful troublemaker that woman. And so... so coarse." A glint of pure malice came into her small eyes. "I suppose it was from her that you heard about Amber being so rude to me. She came upon us on the bridge but did nothing to help me in my predicament. Of course, she was always far too friendly with that girl."

"What was in this letter?" Matt asked, trying to drag her back to the matter in hand. But it was no good.

"Of course, you stick together, you people. That's it, isn't it? You'll even stand by someone who's been thrown out of the police force, for the Lord knows what kind of disgusting misconduct. Oh, I know they call it sick leave, but we all know what that means. I've read about it in the papers. No doubt she had affairs. These artists..." Spittle sprayed from her mouth with the force of the words as she stared at him malevolently, "they're never to be trusted, particularly not with men. Do you know why she was sacked? Because that's what it amounts to, isn't it? Do you know what she got up to?"

Matt felt a wave of anger rise up inside him and a desperate urge to get away from this poisonous little woman. He glanced at Dilys. There was a look of disgust on her face, though tinged with pity. But he couldn't find it in himself to pity Rhona Griffiths, not at the moment.

"Miss Griffiths," he said as calmly as he could manage, "we do need to see that letter. Please would you allow us to do so?"

"No! No! There was no letter. It's gone. I... I burnt–" A hand flew up to her mouth as she realised that she'd given herself away.

"That is a great pity," Matt said. He got to his feet, looked down at the spluttering woman before him, and said, "I'm sorry you don't wish to co-operate with us. I realise it must be very difficult–"

"Enough! I will not be subjected to any more of this... this–" She jumped up from her chair. "I would like you to leave now. You're... you're harassing me." She looked as if any minute she'd burst into tears.

"Very well, but if you change your mind I would like you to phone me on this number." He held out a card with his name and phone number on it. She snatched it from his hand but didn't look at it. "And do remember, Miss Griffiths, this is a murder enquiry and we have the power to subpoena evidence if we feel it is necessary."

As they walked rapidly down the path to the gate, with the echo of the slammed door ringing in their ears, Dilys muttered, "Shouldn't we have insisted, sir, on seeing the letter or, well, the remains of it?"

"Probably, but the likelihood is she flushed the remains down the loo or something. We'll leave her to stew a bit, try again when she's had time to think back on how revealing some of what she said actually was." But in the back of his mind Matt felt he'd handled things badly. He'd wanted to get away from Rhona Griffiths as fast as possible, away from the stream of poison that had clouded his judgement. He should have pressed her, insisted she tell them what she'd done with the letter, or at least told them what it had said. Too late now.

"God Almighty." This was strong language for Dilys. Unconsciously she echoed his thoughts. "What a poisonous woman. And she's certainly one for the men, isn't she?"

"What do you mean?"

"First her eyes light up like beacons at the sight of you, then it's the MP, Neville Breverton, and how charismatic he is, then it's Mr Cole and what a marvellous teacher and father he is, and how his wife neglects him! I wouldn't mind betting she was jealous as hell of Amber and all those boyfriends."

"You might be right. Remember what Fabia said about how attractive Amber was, loads of sexual chemistry. Who knows what contact with such a person does to a warped little woman like that? And Amber seemed to have delighted in winding her up, using language she knew would get her going, like suggesting she needed a good screw for a start." Matt gave Dilys a twisted grin.

"Ugh!" she said.

Once again Matt glanced at Fabia's door as they went down the path, but there was still no sign of life. He couldn't help wondering if she was at home and what she was doing. Thinking about it, he decided she was probably as preoccupied with Amber's murder as he was. He felt a wave of frustration at not being able to go over the case with her – how he would have loved to do so! In the past they'd spent many an evening sitting in his flat or her house, discussing their current case, takeaway cartons spread around, wine glasses gradually emptying. The way each of them worked had complemented the other, Matt thought, he with his analytical, precise dissecting of evidence, Fabia with her flair for going straight to the heart of a problem, and her famous hunches. They'd had many an argument about method, but had always been as one in their determination to get a result. And now, with this gulf of misunderstanding and anger between them, there was no way he could phone her when he came up against a problem, pick her brains and have her flair and intuition help him towards a solution.

He asked Dilys to drive. He wanted time to think. Settling himself in the passenger seat, he put his head back against the rest and closed his eyes. Now he and Fabia had been thrown together again, surely they could sort out their differences – couldn't they? But the yawning gulf between them couldn't be crossed easily; it's my fault we fell out, he thought, admitting that to himself for the first time since that last awful row. If this was going to be sorted, it had to come from him, he decided, but how? That was the problem. How on earth was he going to do it?

Chapter 12

Cath was struggling valiantly with a clothes rail when Fabia arrived at the church hall. "Bloody thing. This notch is meant to slip into there, but it just won't."

"Nobody else here yet?" Fabia asked as she helped to put the rail together.

"No. Gwen Breverton said she'd come, and Rhona too."

"Oh Lord."

"I know," said Cath, smiling ruefully, "but she is very good at offering to help, not that she doesn't always give herself a pat on the back for doing so. What did you do about that letter in the end?"

"I knocked and handed it over, offered to help but she wouldn't have it, just slammed the door in my face."

"Ah well. It's up to her I suppose."

"Who else do you think will turn up?" Fabia asked.

"Mary Page, you know, Dr Page's wife, and some of the girls from the choir. I do hope they come. It'll take us ages otherwise, and I've still got a sermon to write." Cath ran a hand through her curls. "What can I say, Fabia? I've been going over and over it, trying to think of an appropriate text, I even looked up the words murder and suicide in my Complete Concordance, but that wasn't really any help. I suppose I could use 'let he who is without sin cast the first stone', or should I make it more practical? 'Don't let your kids do drugs' and stuff, that's assuming Amber was. But when it comes down to it, I'm going to be standing in that pulpit not knowing if Amber's murderer is one of the faces looking up at me. It's a nightmare."

"It is, indeed," Fabia said, and put an arm round Cath's shoulders. "But I'm sure you'll come up with something. You always do. You've an instinct for saying the right thing at the right time."

"Do you really think so?"

"I do," Fabia said firmly.

"Thank you. Ah well, we'd better get on with this. We've got to go through all the clothes and hang up the ones that are suitable. They're in the black sacks over there. Those that aren't good enough can go back into the sacks for the next jumble sale. Let's get going."

"Might as well."

But still Cath didn't move. "Awful to think that when I was collecting the bags from Cecily on Friday morning, Amber was already dead. It seems like aeons ago now."

"That's the way of these things," Fabia sympathised. "One minute, life's pottering along just as normal, the next, everything's turned upside down."

"All I can think about is that poor child and her parents. I called on Cecily, but Murray said she'd been sedated by the doctor, which is just as well, I suppose, but it won't bring Amber back, will it? I'll try again tomorrow, she'll need an awful lot of support."

"She will indeed," Fabia said bleakly.

"Do you know anything more about what happened?"

"Not much. It definitely wasn't suicide. If it's any comfort she was probably unconscious when she went into the water, so she wouldn't have known much about it."

"She drowned then?"

"It's not been confirmed yet."

"Oh God! It's awful. Only eighteen. She had so much to live for." Her round, normally smiling face was drawn down and sombre. "Heaven knows when the body will be released for burial. And then there'll be the funeral. I don't think I've ever held one for a murder victim before."

Fabia could think of no response to this and was relieved when there was a rattle at the main door of the hall and it was pushed open.

"Coo-ee," Rhona said as she peered round the door, and her feeling of relief died. She bustled into the room, glanced at Fabia then cut her dead. Obviously, she still hadn't been forgiven. What with the letter and all, it was hardly surprising.

Rhona was talking to Cath, sounding friendlier towards her than Fabia had ever heard before. "So sorry I'm late. I've been so busy. Forgot the time, silly me." She was followed by three teenage girls, all of whom Fabia recognised as members of Cath's church choir, and a moment later by Gwen Breverton and Mary Page.

Cath explained what had to be done. The three girls took two black bags and started to sort through them, talking in rapid but inaudible whispers as they did so. The doctor's wife and Rhona took two more.

"Damn," Cath said, after doing a rapid count. "I've left a couple of bags at the vicarage. I'll just go and fetch them. Won't be long."

With a sinking heart Fabia realised this meant she was lumbered with Gwen. There was really no way she could avoid it, much as she'd dearly love to do so.

For Fabia one of the enduring memories of her school life had been the unfulfilled desire to be popular. She'd always been streets ahead of her peers academically, but popular she was not. And when it came to boys it was even worse. Too sharp, too defensive and, she'd comforted herself, too damned intelligent. But Gwen, née

Jenkins, now Breverton, had been an altogether different kettle of fish.

At school she'd been in the year above Fabia. She'd always pushed the uniform to its limits, her skirts shorter and her blouses more revealing than anyone else's. Her rather hard, strongly accented voice would rise above any other noise in the school grounds. And after school she was invariably the centre of a coterie of boys.

Fabia had envied Gwen, but despised herself for doing so. She remembered that time all too clearly and, even though none of it really mattered any more, she could still conjure up the feelings, the heartache and insecurity.

Looking at Gwen now she wondered how much effort she'd put into acquiring the deeper, softer voice and getting rid of the accent; how much work had gone into developing her present poise, and how much money was spent on her oh-so-different clothes. She also wondered who was the brains behind the Breverton success story. Neville was clever, and totally unscrupulous, as she'd good reason to know, but she couldn't help thinking that the better brain was Gwen's.

Fabia gave herself a little shake. What stupid brooding at a time like this. Anyway, there was a job to do. Might as well get on with it and get it over. Dragging a bag forward she asked coolly, "Shall we start on these? I'll unload, you hang up, okay?"

"Fine." Gwen's tone was clipped. She'd obviously no liking for the situation either, which made Fabia feel a little better. Being a thorn in Gwen's flesh was not altogether unpleasing.

For a while they worked in polite, frosty silence, but it wasn't long before Fabia rebelled. Sod this, she thought, why shouldn't I do a bit of probing while I'm here. It's nothing to do with the past. This is now and there's one subject on all our minds, no point in pretending it's not.

"Your Vanessa was a friend of Amber Morgan's, wasn't she?" she said. Might as well come straight to the point.

"Yes, she was." Gwen's voice was flat and noncommittal.

"Such a dreadful thing to happen. I hope she's coping okay." She glanced at the other woman's face as she spoke, but it gave nothing away.

"She's upset. Who wouldn't be?"

"Absolutely. Has she any theories as to what's behind this tragic business?"

"No." The word was snapped out. "No. Of course not."

"But you must have talked about it."

"No... yes... well, a bit." Now she was beginning to sound rattled. Fabia's curiosity was aroused and she probed further.

"Has she been interviewed by the police yet?"

"No. Why should she be?"

"Routine mainly. They'll want to speak to all of Amber's friends. Vanessa could be very useful to them. She might know things she doesn't even realise are relevant. It's often the case with friends of the victim. For instance, any man Amber was involved with would almost certainly be known to her girlfriends."

"What makes you say that?" Gwen stood gazing at Fabia across the pile of clothes, a look of horror in her eyes.

What on earth's going on here? Fabia wondered and said, "Experience, really. Interview a teenager's parents and you'll usually find they know very little about their own child's activities, but interview that teenager's friends and you'll get the information you need."

"But that's ridiculous. Vanessa would have no idea..." There was a note of panic in Gwen's voice. She took a deep breath. "Chief Inspector Lambert is coming to consult Neville tomorrow morning, but he mentioned nothing about interviewing Vanessa. Perhaps he realises it's not necessary." She was gradually recovering her poise.

Consult, no less, thought Fabia. Let's hope Matt realises that's what's expected of him.

"Anyway," Gwen went on. "I'd rather not talk about it. It feels so ghoulish to be dwelling on the poor girl's death." Now she had herself well in hand. "I don't suppose this kind of thing affects you much, what with your having no children. I seem to remember you always were rather thick skinned. Police work must have suited you. Although I gather you've been on what's euphemistically called sick leave. How long is it now? Two years? A long time."

Fabia looked straight at her, wondering how much she knew, and surprised such a look of loathing in Gwen's eyes that, for a moment, she was taken aback. But a second later it was gone, the shutters had come down. What could cause such a reaction? Had she imagined it? After all, if damage had been done, it had been by Neville Breverton, and she'd been the victim, not the other way round. She pulled a coat out of the sack, but her mind wasn't on what she was doing. She hung it on a hanger, not really noticing the tear under the arm and a grubby mark down one side, then pulled out a tartan skirt that had definitely seen better days and hung that up too.

Nothing more was said and when Cath returned, Fabia moved over to help her. Unfortunately, this brought her nearer to Rhona who looked round and saw her. Her eyes widened, and she licked at her top lip with the tip of the tongue, back and forth, back and forth, a mannerism Fabia had noticed before when Rhona was agitated. She decided she really ought to mention the letter. There was no point in pretending it didn't exist, and since there was no-one else within earshot she said, "I'm sorry about that letter business, Rhona. Can I help at all? Horrid things. You'd best show it to the police."

"Be quiet," Rhona said in a sibilant whisper, then added, "I don't know what you're talking about."

Exasperated, Fabia tried again. "I did see what that letter was, and I know it must have upset you. Would you like me to tell them what was in it? I really would advise you to tell Chief Inspector Lambert about it. You wouldn't want him to think you were withholding evidence, would you?"

Rhona's protuberant eyes seemed to be in danger of popping out of her head. "I don't know what you're talking about. What do you mean, evidence?"

But Fabia knew she couldn't tell Rhona about the diary. Annoyed with herself for saying too much already, she didn't respond immediately to Rhona's question. She stood there wondering what to say next, but Rhona saved her the trouble.

"I know my duty. I told him everything I should. He was definitely most grateful, a very nice young man, I have to say. But I certainly won't be telling you what I told him. You seem to forget, my dear Fabia," she said with a spiteful little titter, "that you're no longer an active member of the police force. Although it does seem rather strange, your situation. It does make one wonder what the full story is."

Fabia stood staring after her as she flounced off. Bloody woman. Gwen first, and then Rhona, was more than she'd bargained for. Definitely time to get out of here. If she didn't escape soon she'd probably throttle somebody.

"Cath, sorry love, but I must get going. If you want any more help I can give you some time early tomorrow."

"Don't worry. We've nearly finished. Thanks for coming."

"Oh shit! Oh shit!" They both turned, startled, to see who'd spoken. It was one of the girls from the choir. She was standing holding up a pair of dark purple satin flares, gazing at them with a stricken look on her face. A moment later she let them drop, covered her face with her hands and burst into tears. Cath and Fabia hurried over.

"What is it, Dionne?" Cath asked, putting an arm round her shaking shoulders. But the distraught girl shook her head, unable to speak. White in the face, her friend answered for her.

"They were Amber's. We both remember her wearing them. It just brings it home to you like. It got to Dionne a bit."

"Oh dear," Cath said, her arm still round the girl's shoulders. "That's one of the bags I collected from Cecily. Let me do the rest. You two get off. You've done enough."

"Are you sure you can manage?" Fabia asked.

"Yes, of course. There's only half a bag to do."

Neither of them had noticed Rhona sidling up. "I'm afraid I really don't think I could help, Catherine. I don't think I could bring myself to touch that child's clothing. I'd find it far too distressing. My dear Da always said I had such delicate sensibilities."

Before Cath could say anything, Fabia intervened. "Did he now, Rhona? Funny, it's not something I'd ever have said of you. In fact, I'd say, deep down, you're as tough as old boots. Strange how we all have different views of people."

She turned her back on a gaping Rhona and looked directly at Cath, surprised a wicked gleam of amusement in the vicar's eyes, and said her goodbyes quickly. Best escape before she said any more.

Shoulders hunched and walking as fast as she could, Fabia headed for home. Why did she let these blasted women get under her skin? Gwen with her venom and Rhona with her nosiness and malicious hinting. Poisonous pair. Thank God for people like Cath.

But still she had to admit it hadn't been an entirely unproductive hour. Maybe when she got home she'd give Matt a ring, find out how things were going. What reason could she give? Surely, he'd be interested in Gwen and Rhona's behaviour this morning. But she knew she was grasping at straws.

It wasn't until she was nearly home that she realised something was niggling at the back of her mind, just out of reach. Something that slipped up from her subconscious for a second and disappeared again. Damn! What was it? But there was no point in worrying away at it. From experience, she knew she'd just have to wait for it to come to the surface again.

Chapter 13

Fabia was nearly home, head down and still walking fast, when she almost walked straight into someone coming the other way. Looking up, she saw it was Mrs Pritchard, a cleaner who worked for several people in the village, including Fabia occasionally.

"I'm so sorry, Mrs Pritchard. I was miles away."

"Oh Miss Havard, oh dear, oh dear," Mrs Pritchard said, a hand to her chest. "I'm so glad I bumped into you. I just don't know what to do for the best."

Fabia put a hand on the woman's arm. "What's wrong?"

"It's just... well... after this awful business with Amber. I hardly know what to do. I wonder if, seeing as how you was in the police force, perhaps you'd advise me."

At mention of Amber, Fabia's interest sharpened. "Of course, I'll do my best. What's the problem?" They were standing just by Fabia's front gate. "Look, come in. You're obviously upset. I'll make a cup of tea and you can tell me all about it."

* * *

Matt got back to Newport mid-morning. The divers had found Amber's bike in the river, not far from the bridge and stuck fast in the mud, and he'd been out to have a word with them. Forensics would now go over it with a fine-tooth comb, but he doubted they'd find anything useful. As he got out of the car, he was hailed by a thickset man in uniform and recognised Inspector Alun Richards from Traffic.

"You on this case up to Pontygwyn?" Richards asked.

"Yes. Why do you ask?"

"Bit of a coincidence. I saw Fabia Havard Wednesday evening, she lives in Pontygwyn. A few of us get together occasionally for old times' sake, this time it was at hers. We were celebrating her resignation, if that's what you call it. Nothing to celebrate in my opinion. Anyway, asking after you, she was." There was more than a glint of mischief in the man's eyes.

"Was she?" Matt said shortly.

"Didn't know about your promotion, which surprised me, since you two used to be so close." There was a lot more than mischief there now. Matt clenched his teeth, willing himself not to react as Alun went on, "Anyway, should be useful to you, having Fabia on the spot. One of the best officers ever, that woman. Tragedy what's happened to her. Still, you'll be able to pick her brains about the local scene, should be a help."

"You could call it that," Matt said coolly. Alun fell into step beside him. Matt couldn't resist asking, "So, you see a lot of Fabia, do you?"

"Not that much, but we always enjoy it when we do. Got to make sure she realises some of us don't believe the crap that's been put about concerning her."

"What crap's that?" Matt was determined not to rise to the bait.

"Come on, butt, you can't tell me you don't know all about it. It must be difficult for her to have that bastard, Neville Breverton, living so close."

"What do you mean by that?"

Alun stopped by the door of the station and glanced up at him, a curious look in his eyes. He frowned. "You telling me you really don't know what went on?"

"I try not to take much notice of gossip," Matt said, and immediately wished he hadn't. It sounded like a snub, and he really wanted to hear more. "And, of course, I was away when she was put on sick leave."

"But you must have asked her, or at least asked around?" Alun's tone was a mixture of incredulity and accusation.

Matt knew he should be getting on, there was so much to do, and yet he desperately wanted to know what Richards had to say. "Look," he said quickly, "could we have a drink at some point? I'd like to pick your brains. Pontygwyn's part of your manor, isn't it?"

"Okay, if you think it'll help," Alun said, then with a hard look, he added. "And as for Fabia, I know she doesn't like it talked about, but I wouldn't like to think you'd got the wrong idea about her, see. She was a bloody good officer, one of the best, and she was shafted good and proper."

"Well, let me buy you a drink, this evening maybe, and you can put me in the picture."

"Okay. Make it the Cledwyn Arms, in Derwen Road, it's my local. I should be there round nine."

"Good, I'll be there."

Matt took the steps two at a time, pleased that he'd made what he thought of as the first move towards sorting out the Fabia situation. He threw his coat over a chair and sat down at his desk. He was just about to start on a mountain of messages, but barely had time to look at the first one when he was summoned to his chief's office.

* * *

Chief Superintendent Rees-Jones glared up at him as he walked in, his bushy eyebrows almost meeting above his flat boxer's nose. He was a big man, running a little to fat now with a somewhat unhealthy flush to his skin. Ripe for a heart attack, Matt thought, if he doesn't get more exercise and cut down on the rich food and booze. Rees-Jones's love of the table was legendary within the force, although some of the stories about his capacity were almost certainly exaggerated. He sat back in his chair and Matt could hear it protest as he took a seat opposite.

"I've had a call from Neville Breverton," Rees-Jones said. "He's doesn't want this drowning case dragging on and the tabloids getting hold of it. He lives in Pontygwyn."

As if I didn't know that, Matt thought, irritated. It's only a week since you sent me to waste my time talking about his bloody security system, remember? And as to the tabloids, best of luck to them when it comes to the Neville Brevertons of this world. But all he said was, "I know, sir."

"Well, unpleasant for him, all this happening on his doorstep. What's worse is his daughter was a friend of the dead girl."

"It's pretty unpleasant for everybody I think," Matt said, "particularly the victim's family."

The scowl on Rees-Jones ruddy, humourless face became more pronounced. "No need to use that tone with me, Chief Inspector."

"No, sir." But Matt didn't apologise.

"Have you made any progress at all?" he snapped.

"It's early days yet. I've got the incident room set up and my team's hard at work. Dr Curtis fast-tracked the PM for us and it's confirmed now that we've a murder investigation on our hands."

"Sure of that?"

"As I said, it's confirmed. I've spoken to the step-father, but I've yet to have a word with the girl's mother. At the moment her doctor's got her heavily sedated. I've also spoken to Fabia Havard, who found the body." Matt tensed, waiting for a reaction to Fabia's name. His boss's head jerked up and he stared at Matt, eyes cold, the line of his jaw tensing as if he'd clenched his teeth, but he didn't actually say a word. Matt would have expected him to make some kind of comment, probably derogatory, but he didn't. Strange. After a moment Rees-Jones looked down at his desk, straightened a file, adjusted the position of two pens, then said shortly, "Go on."

Matt went on to tell him about the search for and discovery of the bicycle, about the diary, missing out the help he'd received from Fabia, and then touched on his interviews with Craig and Rhona Griffiths, ending up with his plans for the rest of the day.

When he'd finished, the Chief Superintendent glared across the desk at him. Matt got the distinct impression he was trying to pick on some area with which he could find fault. He was obviously unsuccessful. "Just put your back into it and make sure you show Breverton the respect due to his position," he said, and followed that up by growling, "I want a quick result on this one, Lambert. Understand?"

Matt said nothing.

"Do you need any more men?"

"I could always do with more help, particularly with the house to house," Matt said, finding it hard to believe his luck. Maybe having an MP involved wasn't so bad after all.

"Well, you've got my say so if you need to call in extra. And for God's sake, get this sorted."

Feeling rebellious, Matt went back to his office and told Dilys to organise a visit to the Brevertons. "I want to interview all three of them, understand? And the sooner the better."

It took her some time, but in the end, she arranged it for early the following day. "Mrs Breverton says she'll be there at eleven tomorrow morning, after church. She's not sure about her husband, he's going up to London at some point. Says he's got an important meeting at the Treasury first thing Monday. She made a point of telling me all about it. Obviously, the small matter of a murdered teenager comes a poor second. Oh, and we're not to be late." And she left the room quickly before he could throw something at her.

The phone on his desk rang. He glowered at it, picked up the receiver and snapped, "Lambert." It was with mixed feelings he recognised Fabia's voice but, when he heard what she had to say, he pushed their differences aside, along with his encounter with Alun Richards.

"What is it she wants to tell me?"

"Best you talk to her about it I think."

"Okay. Can you hang on to her till I get there?"

There was a muttered conversation on the other end of the line, then Fabia came back to him, "She says all right, but she has to be home by one when her husband gets in for his dinner."

"Right. We'll be there in about twenty minutes." He slammed the phone down, shouted for Dilys, grabbed his coat and quickly left his office. "That was Fabia Havard," he told her as they made their way out to the car park. "She says a Mrs Pritchard came to her with some information and Fabia thinks we ought to hear about it as soon as possible. Something to do with the Brevertons."

As she was pulling out into the traffic, Dilys glanced at him quickly, a worried frown on her face. "I've just thought, sir. I know our interview with the Brevertons senior is at eleven tomorrow, but what about the daughter?"

"Isn't she going to be there?"

The worry was joined by embarrassment. "I'm not sure, see. By the time I'd finished that conversation with her mother, she'd got... got marginalised, if you know what I mean, and I only remembered when you said this Mrs Pritchard wanted to tell us something about them."

"Damn!"

"Sorry sir."

Matt ignored her apology. He was not in a good mood. First there was Rees-Jones and his bloody old boys' network, and now Fabia was getting involved again. Why couldn't this Mrs Pritchard have come straight to him with her worries? And as to not interviewing the Breverton girl, sod that, she was a friend of Amber Morgan's and she may be very useful. The devil take Rees-Jones and his cronies. He had a job to do and he wasn't about to let them get in the way.

"Okay," he snapped, "we'll just have to talk to the daughter when we can. I hope for your sake she's there tomorrow morning."

"Yes sir," she said, tight-lipped.

Soon they were pulling up in front of Fabia's house and she had the door open before they'd even rung the bell.

"Good. I'm glad you're here. Come through, we're in the sitting room."

On the settee, perched forward as if she was ready to run if necessary, was a small, grey haired woman. Neatly packed into a plain navy coat, her hands clasped in her lap, she looked up nervously as they came into the room.

"This is Chief Inspector Lambert and Sergeant Bevan, Mrs Pritchard," Fabia said. "Please, don't worry. Just tell them exactly what you told me."

"I've been thinking, Miss Havard, and I don't know if my Gwyn would want me to—"

"Please Mrs Pritchard. I'm sure your husband would feel you should help the police all you can. It's very important, you know, to find out who killed Amber." Fabia glanced at Matt. As if she's handing over to me, he thought, then despised himself for the spurt of resentment.

He sat down opposite the little woman and Dilys took a seat behind her and quietly got out her notebook and pencil, while Fabia walked over to the window and tactfully turned her back.

Matt smiled at Mrs Pritchard. "Now, in your own time, tell me just what you've already told Miss Havard."

"Well, it's like this, see." She took a deep breath then began to talk fast, as if she wanted to get rid of it all before she changed her mind. "I do cleaning for several people in Pontygwyn. Help Miss Havard occasionally if she needs me," she gave Fabia's back a quick glance. "I'm used to all kinds of people, take them as I find them mostly. But I have to say I haven't been happy at the Brevertons. Not appreciative, Mrs Breverton, very hoity-toity, and that girl of hers, thoroughly spoilt. As for him, the so-called member of parliament, well! He's as many faces as Tredegar town clock, that I can tell you." She was in full flow now. Matt listened attentively. "And the women, you wouldn't believe. It's very hard to say this of a young girl so recently dead, but she was one of his... his conquests."

Dilys dropped her pencil and bent quickly to pick it up. Matt shot her a glance, then looked away. "How do you know this?" he asked quietly, trying to make sure his tone wasn't too eager.

"I saw, well I heard, them together. That's what made me decide I couldn't go on working there."

"When was this?"

"This very week. Monday is one of my days up at the Brevertons and I was late leaving. Mrs Breverton had gone down to her sister in Swansea, who's been bad under the doctor, and I thought, while she was out of the way, it'd be a good opportunity to give the small sitting room she uses the once over –
she calls it her study. It was in a real state, something terrible. Don't know what she'd been about. She never usually uses the fireplace, says it makes too much mess, but she'd been burning something in the grate this time for sure. There was bits of half-burnt paper all over."

"And was Mr Breverton at home?" Matt enquired gently, trying to lead her back on track.

"Yes, well I was just finishing when I heard someone come in the back way, through the kitchen. It was Amber Morgan, that poor dab. I recognised her voice. She was calling out for Viz, that's what she called Vanessa, the daughter." Mrs Pritchard took a deep breath and a flush rose to her cheeks. "I knew Vanessa had gone with her Mam, and I was about to go out and tell her, but then I heard his voice."

"You mean Mr Breverton?" Matt asked.

"Yes." She drew herself up straight and looked him in the eye, her colour even deeper now. "Chief Inspector," she said, "I promise you I'd no intention of eavesdropping, I really hadn't, but I just didn't know what to do, see. The way they talked, it wasn't at all like a man should speak to a friend of his daughter, and as for that girl, well! I heard her say, 'Hallo-o' and the way she said it, all husky like, and he goes, 'What a delightful surprise Amber', and she says, 'Maybe. That depends. I was looking for Vanessa', then he goes, 'She's in Swansea with Gwen and they won't be back till this evening', and I could tell he was smiling, like, from the way he sounded, and then he says – oh dear – I hardly know how to tell you."

"Please, Mrs Pritchard," Matt said. "I know this is difficult, but it could be very important. You do want to help us find Amber's killer, don't you?"

"Of course I do, but I don't want you to think–"

"We'll be able to sort out what's important and what isn't," Matt assured her. "Please, go on."

"They must have been just outside the door. Oh, I was that scared they'd come in, I could hardly breathe, and my heart was pounding in my chest. Oh dear! Anyway, it sounded like someone leant against the door, and I heard him say, low like, 'How about we take advantage of this chance meeting?' and I could hear sounds, like they were – you know – and then she goes, 'No, not here, they might come back', and he says, 'They'll be gone for hours yet,' and there was a bit more, like; noise. Oh Inspector, I didn't know where to put myself."

"It must have been very unpleasant," Matt said. "And then?"

"Well, I think he said something about his office, and they could lock the door if it made her happier, and he sort of growls, like, and says, 'I could clear my desk, like last time', and she giggles, and then I hear their footsteps going off down the hall. I could have died I was that relieved. I crept out, grabbed my coat and got out of there, and I haven't been back, not even for my money that I'm owed, although my Gwyn says I have to go and get it. But I just can't go back there, I can't."

"Very awkward for you, Mrs Pritchard," Matt said. "I really must thank you for talking to us. Not many people would be so willing to help in these circumstances."

"So, you think I've done right?"

"Absolutely, no doubt. This has been very helpful. Thank you very much." He was interrupted by Fabia.

"Would you mind very much if I asked Mrs Pritchard one question?" Her diffidence was completely out of character. For some reason it annoyed Matt far more than the interruption.

"No, no. Feel free," he said, not meaning it at all.

Chapter 14

Fabia had deliberately detached herself from the proceedings for Matt's sake. She was well aware any interference from her would get right under his skin, so she'd listened to his questioning and Mrs Pritchard's replies, and said nothing, however much she'd wanted to. But now she had a problem. There was one thing Mrs Pritchard had said that had made Fabia sit up and take notice. She'd waited for Matt to pick up on it, but he hadn't, and she knew she couldn't let it go.

She smiled at Mrs Pritchard who was still sitting forward, ramrod straight, hands clasped tightly. "You said it seemed Mrs Breverton had been burning something in the fireplace."

"That she had. There was bits and pieces all over, half burned, spilling out onto the grate. Such a mess it made."

"Did you happen to look closely at the bits that were left?"

"Not that close," Mrs Pritchard said, but she sounded less sure of herself now. "As I brushed it all up into my dustpan I noticed there was bits of paper with letters on. And there were some bright green pieces as well, like one of those greeting card envelopes."

Fabia glanced at Matt, saw his eyes widen.

Mrs Pritchard was looking embarrassed. "I did have a quick look, just in case there was anything there she might want to keep, see?"

"Of course," said Fabia.

"It was like paper from a notebook, with lines on, and they had printing on them too, but only a bit as it was mostly burnt, just a word here and there. I wasn't being nosey," she insisted, her voice a mixture of apology and defiance. "It's just that, well ..."

"Please, Mrs Pritchard, don't worry about it," Matt said, taking over. "Did you throw all these pieces of paper away?"

"Yes. I put it all in the bin, and I put the black sack out in the wheelie by the back door."

"And this would have been collected?"

"Not yet," Fabia said. "Rubbish collection round here used to be Friday, but I think it's Monday morning now."

"Right. And who has the contract? Do you know?"

"We're old-fashioned round here," Fabia said. "It's the council. I've got the phone numbers for all the departments on my desk, as it happens." She had tried not to sound smug, but she had a sneaking feeling she'd failed. She went across to her desk. "I'll find the right one for you."

"Thanks," Matt said, shortly before turning back to Mrs Pritchard. "You really have helped us a great deal. I wish all the people we come into contact with were as public-spirited as you are."

She preened herself a little as she got up and began to pull on her gloves. "I know my duty, Chief Inspector. But I must be going now, or Gwyn will be wondering where I've got to."

"There it is." Fabia said triumphantly and handed a piece of paper to Matt, then she turned to Mrs Pritchard, "I'll see you out," she said, and ushered the neat little woman from the room.

When she got back Dilys was speaking into her mobile.

Matt glanced at Fabia and looked away again. There was an awkward little pause. Eventually, he broke the silence. "Thanks for that," he said as if the words were wrung out of him. "I really should have picked up on that business with the fireplace. Dilys is talking to the rubbish people now. If we can get hold of those bags from the Breverton's house and go through them, we might well be able to salvage some of the bits and pieces. And if they're the same as that letter of Rhona Griffiths, it could be quite a breakthrough, not that we've managed to persuade her to hand it over yet." He grimaced. "What a bunch. Given Neville Breverton's political ambitions, I'd say he was taking a risk, wouldn't you?"

"He always was an arrogant bastard. Probably thinks no-one would dare shop him."

"Well, it seems to me he's cooked his goose this time."

"I sincerely hope so," Fabia said bitterly, and Matt shot her a curious look, but she'd thought of something else and went on. "Do you remember Amber mention someone called the Bulldog in her diary? Maybe that's Neville Breverton. You must admit he looks rather like one, and there's the parliamentary connection."

"I suppose it's possible. I just didn't think it was a connection a girl that age would make, although there has been that Channel 4 series about Churchill recently." Matt ran a hand through his hair. "The more I hear about Breverton and his lot, the less I like them. We're seeing the whole family tomorrow, but I'll definitely have to have a word with him on his own now, whatever the Chief Super says."

"Charlie Rees-Jones? All he'll be worried about is his golfing and fellow Mason pal getting his knickers in a twist," Fabia said scornfully.

"That's about the measure of it. He's going to love this, isn't he?" And he gave Fabia a grin that reminded her of the old days. She smiled back, relieved he'd relaxed so much, but it didn't last. As if suddenly remembering who he was talking to, his face closed up again. "Well, we must get going."

Exasperated though she was, Fabia said nothing more as she accompanied them to the front door and watched them drive away.

* * *

Matt walked into the Cledwyn Arms just after nine o'clock, surprised but relieved to see that it wasn't very busy. He wasn't in the mood for rowdy crowds. Alun Richards was already there, out of uniform now and sitting at the bar with a pint glass, nearly empty, in front of him.

"Another of those, Alun?" Matt said as he came up. "Don't mind if I do."

"One of them and a double Famous Grouse for me, please," Matt said to the barman.

"Heavy day?" Alun asked as they picked up their drinks and made their way to a quiet corner of the room where they wouldn't be overheard.

"Somewhat. It's a shit of a case this one. For a start one of the Chief Super's friends is involved. You mentioned him earlier on, Breverton, the MP. The victim was a friend of his daughter's."

"Oh God, that's a real bugger. Rather you than me."

Matt gave him a twisted grin. "Thanks a bunch."

For a moment they sat in silence as Matt tried to decide how to approach the subject of Fabia. There seemed to be no doubt Alun believed in her and thought she'd been badly treated, and Matt, belatedly he had to admit, wanted to know the whole story. The more he thought about it, the more uneasy he felt. He should have had more faith in her. Why hadn't he asked questions before? What had held him back?

He and Fabia hadn't been working closely together for a while when he was sent off to a course in London, but they'd seen each other quite regularly, they'd still been close. Still, things hadn't been as easy between them as they had been in the past, partly because of the gossip that had surrounded their relationship, partly because both of them had been thoroughly over-worked and making time to see each other had been difficult. He'd always wanted more than mere friendship, but Fabia had held back, said she didn't want to spoil what they'd got. Ironic when in the end what they did have had been spoiled anyway, whether they liked it or not. And then he'd returned after seven weeks away to find she'd been put on indefinite sick leave, a euphemism, as he well knew, but that's what they'd called it. A few days later they'd had that terrible row, and that had been that.

Now he felt more and more certain Fabia had been set up, and that he'd let her down, but still there was this tiny niggle of doubt. Once and for all he wanted to lay the ghosts to rest, and Alun could be the person to help him do so. But now there was the problem of how to broach the subject. He despised himself for it, but he just couldn't bring himself to ask outright. How would it sound, for Christ's sake? Do you believe my ex-boss and close friend was corrupt? But in the end Alun solved the problem for him.

"So, what went wrong between you and Fabia then?" he asked without preamble, and the look he gave Matt was accusing.

"Hard to say," he said, gulping down half his whisky. "If the truth were known, the last time we saw each other we had a blazing row, and that was it."

"What was it about, this row?"

"Her taking the sick leave, as they call it. I really thought she'd fight it, stand up for herself. The fact she caved in, well, it just seemed as if she was admitting she was guilty."

"Guilty of what?"

"Of whatever it was they were saying." Now part of Matt was wishing the subject had never been broached. He told himself not to be stupid. Hadn't he come here to find out the truth?

"Shall I tell you exactly what happened?" Alun's tone turned sarcastic, "Seeing as how you don't seem to know the whole story, like."

"Well, I don't," Matt said defensively. "That drugs course took seven weeks, and by the time I got back Fabia had a week left before she was out. I knew she'd been working on a fraud case, that'd started before I went away, and I knew some high-profile people were involved, but she never told me the details."

"For fuck's sake man, you could have asked around. There's a tidy number of us would have told you all about it."

Matt downed the rest of his whisky. Why hadn't he? He could have asked careful questions of the right people, or he could have sat down and listened to Fabia. But he hadn't. He'd told himself he hated gossip. He'd closed it all off, pushed it out of his mind, accepted his promotion and got on with the job. A fine friend he'd turned out to be! And now he had to face it. Was it really that he'd been afraid he'd find out Fabia had been involved in covering up a crooked property deal? That's one thing he'd heard. Or was it that he just didn't want to get involved? He shrugged, disgusted with himself.

"I dunno," he said now to Alun, his voice full of self-mockery. "Maybe I just didn't want to run the risk of being told something I didn't want to hear." He picked up their glasses. "Same again?"

Alun looked up at him, tight-lipped. "Okay, and when you get back I'm gonna to put you straight *bach*."

When Matt got back Alun downed half his pint before saying anything. Putting the glass down carefully, he leant his elbows on the table and clasped his hands together, looking sideways at Matt.

"I'll have to go back a tidy bit, about three and a half year, I suppose. Neville Breverton was a leading light in Cardiff City Council, the coming man, tipped for selection as the Labour candidate in the next election. He was a big butty of the then Assistant Chief Constable, Vivian Sligo. I ask you, what kind of a name for a God-fearing Welshman is that? Anyway, their wives were distantly related and very close, and they were both in the same Lodge, the two men I mean."

Matt's eyebrows shot up and Alun gave him an acid little smile. "Surprise you, does it, that Breverton is a Mason? Perhaps I should say was. Wriggled out of all that, of course, when he was selected as a Labour candidate. Didn't suit his political ambitions, see. Anyway, Fabia was with the fraud squad by then, so was I, and she got a tip-off about a big property deal involving a consortium with some very dodgy connections. For instance, one of the people mentioned was Tony Vasic."

Matt's eyebrows rose. That was a familiar name, a man who was suspected of dabbling in many a shady scheme and who, so far, had got away with it. He was a thorn in the flesh of several police forces, and Gwent was no exception. So far not one of them had managed to pin him down. It was rumoured that he had powerful friends who'd protected him for years, but this too had never been proved.

"Who else was in this consortium?" Matt asked.

"That's where it got interesting. One of the names the contact mentioned was Neville Breverton. It followed he'd have been very useful. He could have made sure planning permission went through nice and smooth because of his position on the Council. What's more, although he couldn't give Fabia a specific name, the contact told her a senior police officer was also involved." He was watching Matt's face closely for a reaction, but Matt tried not to give away what he was thinking. He'd rather wait till he'd heard the rest.

Alun took another pull at his pint and went on. "Fabia thought of Sligo. She'd had a run in with him way back and she had good reason not to trust him, but it was also because of his friendship with Breverton, and anyway she had an instinct for picking out a villain, even if he was in uniform."

"And did she actually manage to prove anything?"

"Not exactly prove, but there was a hell of a lot of circumstantial evidence, and the rumour machine was going like the clappers. She told her immediate boss, that was our present chief, Rees-Jones, back then. He seemed interested at first, she said, and she really thought she was getting somewhere."

"So, what happened?"

"It all blew up in her face, and it was made very clear we had to drop the investigation. What really got to me is they seemed to have some hold over Fabia. She never told me exactly what they threatened her with, but she backed off. I'd never seen her so angry, but she still wouldn't tell me what was going on. I pushed her, believe me I did, but she just wouldn't give in. There was definitely something, or someone, that she was protecting, that's the only way I can describe it. Anyway, she said they'd poisoned police work for her. She told me all she wanted was to get right away from it all and paint, just be on her own and concentrate on a clean, honest profession. How'd she put it? Something that wouldn't make her feel grubby and ashamed of herself. Trouble was it doesn't exactly pay, the painting, however talented you are, and I think that was why she was willing to go along with the sick leave business. That way at least she's managed to live okay these last two years, until she got this artist thing off the ground."

Matt wasn't satisfied. "So how did they persuade her? It's not like Fabia to give in easily."

"I don't think you can say she gave in easily," Alun said defensively, flashing him an angry glance. "They put a hell of a lot of pressure on her, and because of that the sick leave thing maybe wasn't such a fantasy. She was definitely suffering from a hell of a lot of stress. Would have broken many a stronger woman, I can tell you; or man for that matter." He paused as if he wasn't sure whether to say any more. "I do have my own ideas on it though. I'd heard rumours of something happening when she was at Milford Haven. An affair with another officer or some such, but things like that happen often enough. I dunno. Why don't you ask her yourself?"

Matt looked at him, tight-lipped. "I might well do that."

Chapter 15

As he drove home he went over and over what Alun Richards had told him. He was angry with himself for, as he saw it now, his betrayal of his friendship with Fabia, and was willing to take responsibility for the way things were between them, but he was also angry with her for staying silent. She could so easily have explained things to him that last ghastly day – couldn't she? Why hadn't she? And then he thought back. Had he given her a chance to do so? And on top of everything else, he'd called her a coward. Looking at it with this new, cold light, he knew that had been unforgivable. He'd hurt her so badly. Guilt gnawed at him, and then anger with Fabia returned because of the guilt.

Like some ghastly pendulum on and on he swung between anger and guilt. And how on earth was he going to sort this bloody mess out, particularly in the middle of a nightmarish case and all the ghosts it resurrected? Clear as if he was seeing it right now, the picture of his sister's drowned, dead face leapt up before him. He squeezed his eyes shut for a second, opened them again and realised he'd gone straight through a red light. Christ! Forcing himself to concentrate, he drove the rest of the way home keeping strictly to the speed limit.

Matt parked his car in his usual place, in the car park of a pub called The Feathers, an arrangement he'd had with the landlord for some years now. His first floor flat was in a Victorian villa across the road from the pub. All was quiet at this time of night, the pub regulars having gone off home half an hour ago and, as Matt crossed the road, only one solitary car passed to disturb the silence.

He let himself in, and threw his coat on a chair in the hallway, which already groaned under the weight of another coat, a pile of newspapers, a copy of Blackstone's *Evidence and Procedure* and a navy-blue Guernsey jumper. Looking at this pile, he remembered how Fabia had always been surprised at his untidiness.

"How can you live with so much mess when your mind's so tidy and methodical?" she'd asked on more than one occasion. He'd found the question unanswerable, could only think that he never really thought of his flat as a home, just the place he slept and, sometimes, ate in. Now if he and Fabia – he cut the thought off before it developed, and went to the equally untidy kitchen, made himself some coffee and, to distract himself, began to go over what Alun had said about Neville Breverton and Vivian Sligo.

Matt was determined to do some digging to see if he could unearth any evidence. But when? That was the problem. Maybe Dilys could give him a hand. She had extremely trenchant views on bent coppers, nor did she have any love for the likes of Neville Breverton. Could he spare her? Not really. And there was no way he could spend time researching events long past when he had this case on his hands. But wait, maybe he could use the case itself as a reason to delve deeper. Even Rees-Jones couldn't protest if Matt told him it had something to do with Amber Morgan's death, however awkward the questions may become. And Tony Vasic, what was he up to now? He must put someone reliable onto all this first thing in the morning.

Even after he'd gone to bed, round and round it went, making sleep impossible. Finally, at two in the morning, he gave up trying to sleep and sat down with his laptop to make some notes. At four he found it impossible to keep his eyes open any longer and fell back into bed. At seven the alarm dragged him up from a sleep fathoms deep.

* * *

Dilys took one look at Matt when he walked into the office at eight and went for the coffee. She was soon back with a large, steaming mug. "There you are, sir," she said, "black and very strong, made fresh and not from the machine. Should help."

"Do I look that bad?"

"Yes, you do."

"Close the door Dilys. I want a quiet word."

She did so and came to sit opposite him, waited calmly for him to go on, and he felt grateful for her unquestioning attitude. She didn't even ask what was up.

"I want some research done, but I want it done discreetly. If anyone queries it, we can say it's to do with this case, but I want the net spread a little wider than that, and I can't spare you. I wondered if Chloe Daniels could be trusted with a job like that?"

Dilys didn't blink an eye. "Depends what exactly you want done, but on the whole, yes. She's keen, and she really enjoys working for you, so she wouldn't want to blot her copybook."

"Good. Send her in, would you?"

"Will do." She paused by the door. "This wouldn't be to do with Miss Havard, would it?"

Matt looked up at her. Not much got past Dilys. "Yes, it would, but keep that to yourself."

"Of course." But she didn't leave immediately. "I liked her. Whatever happened with that sick leave business, I really can't believe it was her fault. Be good to see the record put straight." Before Matt had a chance to respond, she left the room closing the door quietly behind her.

* * *

Matt had told Dilys they'd have to play it by ear when they got to Pontygwyn House, according to which members of the Breverton family were actually at home. He knew he'd have to interview Neville Breverton on his own at some point, but this initial meeting, if he were present, could be useful. It'd give them an idea of the family dynamics, watching the interaction between the three of them could be informative.

As he stood before the ostentatious front door of heavy oak with bright brass fittings, Matt thrust his fingers through his dark hair. He wished Fabia was working alongside him. Dilys was a good officer, but she hadn't Fabia's flair. He'd give a lot for her insight right now.

The door was opened by a small woman. She was sharp-faced but beautifully made up and her clothes were plain and obviously expensive, her hair an unlikely shade of blond which Matt was sure she'd not been born with. He also took note of the signs of strain round her mouth and eyes. Outwardly she appeared to be at ease, but Matt was sure she wasn't half as relaxed as she seemed. He hoped to find out soon enough if she was putting up a front.

"Mrs Breverton? I'm Chief Inspector Lambert, this is Detective Sergeant Bevan."

"Yes, come in." She led them into a sitting room to the right. "Please sit down, my husband will be here in a moment."

So the great man had decided to give them some of his valuable time, Matt thought as he sat down in an armchair which was one of a group gathered round the fireplace. Dilys, successfully effacing herself, chose a straight-backed chair to the side of the room. In a minute she'd take out her notebook as usual and begin making notes. He hoped they wouldn't notice. It was always easier that way.

"And perhaps we could see your daughter as well, Mrs Breverton, if it's convenient."

"Vanessa? Why would you? Oh, very well." She went to the door and called. An answering voice shouted from upstairs. After a moment Mrs Breverton came back and sat down. She leant back, her pose relaxed, but her heavily beringed hands clasped tight in her lap gave her away.

A moment later Neville Breverton marched into the room. Both Matt and Dilys rose to greet him.

"Morning, Inspector Harwood."

"Chief Inspector Lambert, sir."

"What? Oh, sorry. Lambert." He ignored Dilys who quietly sat down again.

"Sad business this, tragic loss," Breverton said, obviously feeling he must express some kind of regret. But he ruined the effect by adding, "I can give you twenty minutes, then I've got to get going; so shall we get on with it?"

"We're waiting for Vanessa, darling," his wife said with a tight smile.

"Are we now? Why's that?"

Matt decided it was time he took control and sat forward in his chair. "Your daughter was a friend of Amber Morgan's. For that reason, we feel she might be able to make a valuable contribution to our investigation."

"Do you now? I'd say that remains to be seen."

"She's very upset," his wife added.

"Of course. As a close friend of Amber's, that's hardly surprising in the circumstances." Matt watched her carefully as he spoke and noticed how her jaw clenched under the carefully made up cheeks.

"I'm not so very sure she was that close to Amber," she said, her tone icy. "They just happened to have some mutual friends."

He didn't have time to respond to this before the door opened again and a girl with untidy fair hair slouched into the room. Matt thought she would have been attractive if it hadn't been for her sulky expression and the drooping fringe which masked half her face. She glared at them then turned to her mother, who rose and put an arm round her shoulders.

"What's all this about, Mum? I was busy with my revision, for Chrissake, and this has, like, totally broken my concentration." It sounded as if she'd rehearsed this speech before entering the room.

"These two police officers are investigating Amber's death, Vanessa darling," her mother said with a pacifying tone, "and they'd like to ask us all some questions."

The girl threw herself down by her mother, thrust her hands into the pockets of her jeans and, head bent, stared at Matt through the fringe of hair. She said nothing more. Matt noticed both her parents glance at her and quickly away again. Vanessa studied her nails, picked at chipped navy-blue varnish, and then resumed her veiled stare.

Matt kept his eyes on her. "I wonder if you could tell me, Miss Breverton, when you last saw Amber Morgan?"

"Sounds as if you're going to get the handcuffs out any minute."

"Vanessa!" Her mother said, repressively.

"Not quite yet," Matt responded. "Now perhaps we could take this seriously. We are dealing, Miss Breverton, with a murder investigation."

This got through to her. She shrunk back a little, edging closer to her mother and, pushing the hair back from her face, she looked suddenly much younger. Just for a moment her lips trembled. Matt thought he could see the glint of tears in her eyes, but before she could speak her father intervened.

"That's certain, is it?"

"Yes. The post-mortem was pretty conclusive."

"Pretty conclusive?" His tone was tinged with scorn.

Matt could have kicked himself for this mistake. He added, a hard edge in his voice, "I'm certain in my own mind it's murder we're dealing with."

Breverton said no more and Matt turned back to his daughter. "So, have you remembered when it was that you last saw her?"

"The weekend before last I suppose. CJ, that's Craig Evans from down the pub, Amber and me went clubbing with some other friends."

"Where was this?"

"In Newport."

"Can you remember exactly where you went?"

"Down the Kings Head, then the Golden Monkey."

"Had you been there before?"

"'Course," she said scornfully, "loads of times."

"Is this relevant, Chief Inspector?" Breverton's voice cut in sharply.

"I believe so, sir," Matt said calmly. "Miss Morgan's movements over the last days and weeks of her life are of great importance." Once again, he turned back to Vanessa. "And did she seem just as usual that evening?"

"Yes. We had a great time. We got—" She stopped speaking suddenly. Up until that moment she'd managed to look him in the eye, defiantly, but now her eyes slid away. She began to study her nails again, carefully peeled off another layer of varnish. "We met some other mates and when the club closed we hung around a bit, then came home."

Somehow it didn't sound right. She was either lying or only telling half the truth, but Matt couldn't work out exactly which. Had she been about to say something about drugs perhaps? That'd be too good to be true. He wondered if he should push it, but decided not to. At the moment, he'd rather they were lulled into a false sense of security. Better to have them as much on his side as possible, just for a while longer, and choose his own moment to burst the bubble.

Matt turned so that he could look directly at Breverton. "Perhaps you could tell me when you last saw Amber?"

"Me?" Resting his elbows on the arm of his chair, he steepled his fingers in front of his face, effectively masking his expression. "Hard to remember, really. I'm out a lot, as I'm sure you can understand, so I don't often bump into my daughter's friends."

"On the other hand, in my experience an event like this is inclined to concentrate the mind, cause people to go back over past contacts with the deceased. Perhaps, if you thought a bit harder?"

"That may be so," Neville Breverton said stiffly, "but I'm afraid I'm very often away. When the House is sitting I spend a large part of my life at our flat in London, as my wife will no doubt tell you. If the truth were known, I can hardly bring this girl's face to mind, let alone remember when I last saw her."

"But Daddy, that's ridiculous," Vanessa said suddenly.

Her father turned to look at her. It was a look Matt had seen him use on television if the interviewer was probing too close to the mark. "In what way, Vanessa?"

"You really liked Amber. You said so." Her eyes slid away from her father's and Matt saw her clench her hands together, noticed her cheeks gradually grow pink, but she still went on. "Don't you remember giving her a lift home last Saturday, the evening you had that flat tyre?"

Chapter 16

The silence that greeted this remark was tangible. Each of the Brevertons shifted under the weight of it. Matt waited, satisfied that he'd been right about interviewing the three of them together. Neville Breverton had gone very still, his face utterly expressionless. His wife showed no sign of what she was thinking, but every vestige of colour had drained from her face causing the blusher on her cheeks to stand out unpleasantly, and their daughter leant closer to her mother as if for protection, but her eyes never left her father's face.

Matt looked at the MP, eyebrows raised in query, but Breverton still had himself well in hand. He was obviously used to thinking on his feet.

"Ah, yes. Stupid to forget." He gave Matt a practised smile. "In a life as busy as mine these things just go out of the mind. But Vanessa's right. I took the girl home, and on the way back developed a puncture. Damned nuisance, but there it is. These things happen." He was well under control now, gazing blandly at Matt, almost defying him to probe further.

Matt took up the challenge. "Whereabouts was this?"

"The puncture? Good Lord man, hardly relevant, is it?"

Matt waited.

"Church Road," Breverton snapped, "towards the top, just outside the vicarage. That vicar woman came out and asked if I wanted any help."

Matt made an effort to hide his disappointment. "And the time?"

"Half nine, ten, something like that," Breverton said, waving an impatient hand as if the question was unnecessary in the first place. "It was extremely inconvenient because there was a programme on Channel 4 about strengthening the laws on domestic violence I particularly wanted to see. You probably know I'm a junior minister in the Home Office now."

Matt would have liked to have said, "if you think that's going to impress me you can think again," but he didn't, he simply ignored the statement. "Thank you, sir. And you, Mrs Breverton, have you seen Amber recently?"

"Well obviously I see quite a lot of my daughter's friends since I'm at home more. Amber was here last Saturday, before the young all went off to Newport, but I haven't seen her since then."

"Were you happy with the friendship between Amber and your daughter?"

Gwen Breverton didn't answer immediately. With great concentration she picked at a thread on the cuff of her cardigan and Matt noticed that her hands were trembling. Finally, she took a deep breath and asked, "What do you mean?"

"Earlier you said they weren't that close," he said, his tone expressionless. "I got the impression you were glad about that; that you didn't want them to be."

"Mu-um–" Vanessa's protest was cut off by a sharp movement of her mother's hand.

"I may have thought Amber a little wild, perhaps, but that doesn't mean I disapproved of the girl exactly. And surely, now the poor child is dead, we needn't dwell on the negative aspects of her character."

Very smooth, thought Matt, but not good enough. "So," he persisted, "you had no strong objections to this friendship?"

"What is all this, Chief Inspector?" Neville Breverton intervened sharply. "My wife's relationship with... opinion of the girl is hardly relevant, is it?"

Matt turned to give him a straight look, a look that clearly said, don't give me that. "All Amber's relationships are relevant in the circumstances," he said, "of paramount importance, in fact." He held the man's gaze for a second and, just before Breverton looked away, Matt knew the man was afraid. Interesting, and a distinct advantage. It meant he might make mistakes.

"Oh, very well. I suppose you're only doing your job." He turned to his wife. "Didn't you tell me, darling, that you thought Amber... sorry sweetheart." He cast a charming smile to his daughter and then continued, "might be a bad influence on Nessa? Or was that another of the youngsters that seem to have the run of the house?"

Clever, Matt thought, very clever. He waited for Gwen Breverton's reaction to this.

"Well, I might have said something of the sort," she said, as if admitting a fault for which she felt no guilt at all. "Poor girl, she'd had a hard time one way and another. I believe her father died when she was very young, that's bound to be damaging. And Cecily has never been the strongest of mothers."

But Matt wasn't taken in. There was no sympathy in this statement, just a demonstration of feelings she felt her audience expected her to have.

"Look, this is the pits," Vanessa suddenly burst out. "Amber was my mate, my best mate. You knew that, Mum, and you're talking about her as if she was some intruder. Have you all forgotten? She's dead!" Her voice rose, but she was quelled by her mother's hand gripping her arm.

"Nessa darling, we know how difficult this is for you. I'm sure the chief inspector will let you go upstairs now." She turned her eyes on Matt with a look of loathing strangely mixed with entreaty. "Perhaps my daughter could be allowed to go?"

Before he had the chance to answer, the girl did so herself. "No! I want to stay. I want to know what's going on."

"But sweetheart–" Her father got no further.

"Dad. She was *my* friend." The emphasis was not lost on Matt. "And I want to be involved. I care about her, I want to know who killed her even if you don't."

There was a loaded silence during which Matt could just hear the scrape of Dilys's pen on paper. He decided to change tack, concentrate on the daughter. But it didn't work. Perhaps she was too frightened of her parents, her mother's arm round her shoulder controlling her, her father's hard look. For the next half hour Matt did his damnedest to break down their barriers, create a chink in the family armour, but it was no good. He felt he might have come close with the daughter, but she turned sullen and monosyllabic after her outburst. Maybe an interview with the girl on her own would be useful, trouble is he'd have to get her parents' permission, and he doubted that would be forthcoming. He decided to let them stew for a while and brought the interview to a close.

"Thank you all very much for your time," he said as Breverton ushered him and Dilys towards the front door. "If anything occurs to you that you think might be helpful or relevant, however insignificant, perhaps you'd contact my office?"

"Of course," Gwen Breverton said, her relief at their departure making her more gracious now. "My husband will be in London tomorrow, but Vanessa and I will be here."

Her husband frowned at this but soon recovered. Affable now he was about to see the back of them, he said, "Dreadful tragedy. Dreadful. Anything we can do to help – of course, of course."

As Matt stood for a second on the doorstep, he looked back across the hall to where Vanessa Breverton stood in the lounge doorway. But she wasn't looking at him. Her eyes were on her father and in them was a strange look, part fear, part triumph, part something else indefinable. Matt wondered what it meant and decided it'd be a good idea to arrange that talk with Vanessa sooner rather than later.

* * *

Matt glanced at his watch as they drove away from Pontygwyn House. It was nearly twelve thirty.

"Why don't we stop at The Oaks and have an early lunch? I could do with a pint and a sandwich. Might be useful if there are any locals in there," he said. "Then we can go on up and talk to Paul Vaughan. What time did you fix to see him?"

"Half one."

"That gives us about an hour."

Directly they walked into the pub they attracted the curious, covert glances that police men and women are so used to. He and Dilys weren't in uniform, but the news of their presence in Pontygwyn had obviously travelled to every corner of the town. There was no doubt they were recognised. Two men leaning on the bar looked round over their shoulders, raised eyebrows to each other, then turned their backs. A couple sitting in the window looked up, mouth agape in mid-sentence, then hastily returned to their lunch. Conversation throughout the room stopped for a second, then resumed slightly louder.

George Evans, behind the bar, polished a glass over and over and watched them out of the corner of his eye. Maggie came in, took one glaring look at them, and left the room. There was no sign of Craig. Perhaps his mother had gone off to warn him to keep out of the way.

When they went up to the bar George ceased his polishing, gave them a meaningless professional smile, and said, "Good morning, Chief Inspector, Sergeant, what can I get for you?" So now anyone who hadn't known who they were would be warned.

They ordered drinks and asked for the menu, George pointed out the specials board. "Very nice is my Maggie's steak and kidney, and I've got some salmon in if you fancy it."

Matt wondered idly if it was legally caught, said he thought they just wanted sandwiches, and once they'd chosen, the landlord suggested they find a table and promised to bring their food over as soon as it was ready.

They chose an out-of-the-way corner where they wouldn't be overheard. Once settled, Matt turned to Dilys, his expression questioning. "I get the idea you weren't particularly impressed with the Breverton family."

Dilys's lips twisted in scorn. "Too right. Quite apart from what we know about him and Amber, he's not what I'd call a good Labour man, not living in that mansion. My Da would swivel in his grave at the very thought."

Matt smiled. Dilys's father had been a convenor for the Miners' Union at the last pit in the Rhondda valley. In his day, it would have been more than a Labour member's seat in the House was worth to flaunt such wealth in the face of his electorate.

"Ah, but times have changed, although perhaps they're moving back again now."

"I don't know, all seems pretty fishy to me; sod the lot of them, I say."

Matt smiled, "Trouble is we're stuck with them, well, with Breverton, for now."

There was an interruption as George appeared, two large plates overflowing with sandwiches and salad garnish in his enormous fists. Once he'd gone back to the bar, having established they had all they needed, Dilys went on. "It's not just Breverton that's hiding something. Did you notice the look his daughter gave him as we left?"

"I did."

"Looked scared of him somehow, but there was more to it than that. And he's certainly a cool customer, I'll give him that. So's his wife. But that daughter, she might be useful."

"We're going to have to be careful, though. I want him lulled into a false sense of security while we do some delving into his past. Hopefully Daniels will come up with something useful."

"But shouldn't we press on now we've got Mrs Pritchard's information?"

"I deliberately didn't ask him about that, nor his wife about what she'd been burning. I don't want them knowing she's spoken to us, yet." Matt took a gulp of his beer. It was good, not the usual characterless fizz. He wondered idly if The Oaks was a free house, then came back to the matter in hand.

"And that bit about the car breaking down, for goodness sake, who does he think he's kidding?"

"I know," said Matt, "but there is the vicar. We'll be having a word with her. She might throw some light on it."

For a while they ate in silence, thinking their own thoughts, until Dilys said, her tone tentative, "Sir? I hope you don't mind me asking, but what exactly is it you want to get out of this research Chloe's doing?"

Matt didn't answer immediately, not sure how much to tell her. "For a start I want to find out more about Breverton's activities on Cardiff City Council and whether he was involved in the development at Cwmberis three years ago."

"But what does that have to do with this business?"

"We know now about his relationship with Amber, and there's such a thing as pillow talk. He might have said something which, later on, he realised was incriminating.

149

Maybe she went further than those letters, tried a bit of blackmail on him. He's an ambitious man, he might think getting rid of her was a better option than risking her talking to the wrong people. I know it's a long shot, but quite apart from that—" He paused, not sure how to go on.

Dilys sat patiently waiting, her eyes wide and honest. He smiled at her, thinking how glad he was to be working with her, with her straightforward attitude to life. There were never any hidden agendas with Dilys. "To be truthful I'm trawling for as much information as I can get about what happened two years ago, with Fabia I mean," he told her. "I want to find out exactly what went on with that fraud case Fabia was on just before she took the damn sick leave. I think there's a slim chance it could have something to do with this case, but, even if it hasn't, I still want to know, and this is a good excuse to put someone onto doing that research."

"Good idea."

"You think so?"

"Yes. I like Fabia Havard, and now I've met her I really can't believe half the gossip I've heard. I think she was probably treated very badly, I wonder if the same would have happened if she'd been a man. It's about time someone set the record straight if there was any funny business going on."

Matt could think of no response to this. He felt a mixture of guilt and shame surge up inside him. Even Dilys, having known Fabia for a matter of days, seemed to be on her side. Were there sides in this? Yes, he thought there were, and he now knew which one he should be on. The problem was how to convince Fabia of that after all this time.

Chapter 17

Up St Madoc's Road, past Well House where the Coles lived, and a few hundred yards beyond St Madoc's school grounds was a pair of ornate wrought iron gates. Carved into the granite wall and picked out in gold were the words, Bryn-y-Mor Lodge. Tall, neatly clipped conifers shaded it from the road, and rose bushes lined either side of the drive, with lawns and neat flower beds beyond. It was obvious Paul Vaughan could afford a full-time gardener.

The house itself was an attractive building, modern, long and low, built in a style reminiscent of a Spanish hacienda. But, in spite of this, it didn't look entirely out of place in this Welsh rural setting, in fact it had a smugly permanent air as it crouched, gazing out over the fields and hills beyond.

They parked the car and mounted two shallow semi-circular steps to the heavy oak front door and, when Dilys pressed the bell, they could hear a peel of music echoing through the house. She grimaced up at Matt. "Common as muck, my Nan would have said. I ask you, what kind of a doorbell does he think that is?"

The door was opened by a bald man with a broken nose and a damaged ear. If it hadn't been for his neat pinstripe trousers and black jacket, he would have been the epitome of a retired bare-knuckle fighter. His small eyes looked them up and down and, from the expression on his face, Matt gathered he wasn't impressed with what he saw. Matt took out his ID card and showed it to the man.

"Chief Inspector Lambert and Sergeant Bevan. We'd like to see Mr Vaughan, please."

The man barely glanced at the card and didn't give him a direct answer. "You can stay here," he said, and stepped aside to let them in. "I'll check with his nibs."

"Thank you," said Matt to his retreating back as the man disappeared through a door on the right.

"A Londoner, I think," commented Dilys dryly.

"And used to be a boxer, I wouldn't mind betting."

A moment later the door opened again and a man came striding out. He had show business printed all over him. From his slightly long, swept-back brown hair, his cream shirt and black leather waistcoat, striped loose-fitting trousers, to his Gucci shoes, he yelled it. But when he opened his mouth, just like his henchman, it was straightforward London backstreet boy that you heard, so much so that it almost sounded artificial.

"Afternoon. What can I do you for?"

Matt introduced them both again and explained why they were there.

"Ah yea, poor little cow." In spite of the phraseology, he sounded genuinely sorry. "She was a good kid. It was what's called foul play, was it?"

"I'm afraid so," Matt said.

"Can't get me brain round the kind of bastard that'd do a thing like that. Come in, come in. Anything I can do to help find the bugger, you only have to say."

They followed him across the black and white tiled hall to an enormous sitting room. The deep pile carpet had a pattern of beige and white swirls, and the white leather chairs and sofas and all the chrome and glass gave an impression of limitless money. In contrast to these pale shades, above the fireplace hung a vast and garishly coloured oil painting of a nude woman in a rather suggestive pose.

"Siddown, siddown," Vaughan waved a casual hand in invitation. "So, shoot."

Dilys perched primly on the edge of a massive armchair and Matt tried not to smile. Her Welsh chapel upbringing caught up with her at times, and he could feel the disapproval oozing from her every pore. That painting definitely wasn't her style. Never mind. Do her good to see how the other half lives occasionally.

"When did you last see Amber, Mr Vaughan?" Matt asked.

"About three weeks ago I think," he said, frowning in an effort to remember. "Yes, that was it. It was before I went away. Haven't been around for a while. Me and my woman have been to the States for a couple of weeks, only got back yesterday."

Matt glanced at Dilys, remembering Craig had suggested Amber might have been with Vaughan on Friday night. She gave him an almost imperceptible nod. She'd noticed and would check with the airlines.

"That was it," Vaughan went on, clasping his knees with powerful but well-manicured hands. "Last time I saw her was to give her some tickets I'd got for her and her pals for the Death's Head gig in Cardiff. I look after the group's publicity and all that. She came to collect them, the tickets I mean."

"Did you know her well?"

Matt watched as the man's eyes narrowed. It was obvious he was considering how much to say. After a moment, he got up and began to pace up and down in front of the fireplace, then he laid an arm along the mantelpiece and turned to stare down at them.

"Look, there's no point in beating about the bush. You're bound to find out soon enough, and anyway, I've got nothing to hide." He thrust his hands deep into his pockets and stood there, creating the perfect picture of bluff honesty. "At the end of last year, Amber and me, we had a bit of a thing going," he said. "Just a bit of fun it was. Not serious on either side."

"Was that how Amber viewed it?"

"Yea, sure. She was a sharp kid, that one. Knew her way around. Anyway, when my woman found out about it – that's Mel Franklin, the model you know – Vogue, Marie Claire, you name it, she's done it. Well, when she found out all hell broke loose, so Amber and me called it a day. She was a bit miffed at first, but needs must when the devil drives, eh? And Mel can be one hell of a devil at times!"

He grinned, appealing for Matt's understanding, man to man. Matt didn't respond and, after a tiny pause, Vaughan shrugged and went on. "There weren't really any hard feelings between Amber and me, not so's you'd notice. And that's all there was to it. When we were seeing each other I gave her discs, samples like, and got her tickets for gigs, arranged for her to meet the boys in the group, Death's Head, that is." It was obvious he thought they should be impressed. "All that stuff was a kind of thank you. I always like to give my girls presents, like to be generous with them."

"And Miss Franklin is happy with the situation now?"

"Umm, yeah." It was a long, drawn-out sound. For the first time he didn't sound quite so sure of himself. "Had a bit of a paddy at first, but she's cool now. Mel's all mouth."

Takes one to know one, Matt thought.

"Just blows up and blows over, end of story. Anyway, she's had her little peccadilloes, so she can hardly make much of a fuss about mine. Most of the time we understand each other, Mel and me, and she knows what

I'll stand for and what I won't. She'd better. She gets enough out of me, for Christ's sake."

His tone had become harsh and Matt wondered what was behind this. He decided to probe, "In what way?" he asked blandly.

Vaughan gave him a sharp look, then grinned, but Matt was sure he was covering up a slip of some kind. "Money, jewellery, holidays, you name it, I pay for it," Vaughan said. "She's no angel, Mel, and to be fair, she's in a stressful profession. They live pretty fast, these models, always on pills and diets and that. I look after her, keep her on the straight and narrow as much as I can. Sometimes she strays, and I have to reel her in. Still, we suit each other, most of the time."

"Is Miss Franklin at home sir?" Matt asked. "We will need to speak to her at some point."

"Why's that?"

"We'll be speaking to everyone who had anything to do with Amber. It's routine in a case like this."

"But Mel – ah well, you know your business. But I'm afraid you'll have to wait, she's gone up to town, London that is. Should be back on Tuesday if you really have to speak to her."

"We do," Matt said firmly. "I'll contact her then. Now sir, your relationship with Amber Morgan, it ended when, exactly?"

"Middle of December last year, but we were still friends. Like I said, she was a good kid, and a looker too."

"When you saw her last – three weeks ago you say – there was nothing about her that seemed unusual?"

"No. She was pretty chipper. She'd got herself a new boyfriend."

This was sounding more useful. "What made you think that?"

"She told me." He threw himself into a chair opposite them. "Said she'd found herself this new man and he was loaded and – how did she put it?" He frowned and pulled at his bottom lip. "Something about not just money this time but power as well."

"Did she mention a name?" Matt asked.

"No. I asked her, but she wouldn't tell me. Went all mysterious on me when I pushed it. I got the impression he wouldn't have wanted it known."

"And have you any idea what she meant by money and power?"

"'Fraid not, but she was certainly pleased with herself. I wished her luck. It was about time she had something go right for her. With her background, she deserved it."

Matt's eyebrows rose. This was a new tack. "What do you mean by that?"

"Look, I'm one of seven kids. I get on with most of my brothers and sisters, see some of them regular. Me old Mum's still around, still clouts me round the ear if I talk out of turn." He grinned at them, turning on the charm full blast. "I've always got me family even if my other relationships go pear-shaped. Well, Amber's own dad died when she was a nipper, that's a terrible thing to happen to a kid; then her mum ups and marries again and she and her step-dad don't get on. It happens. Okay, so he's a nice enough bloke, and he tries hard to do right by her, but he's not her own dad, and he was always going on at her to concentrate on maths and English and all that, never thought her art was up to much. And she was good, I tell you, bloody good. What's more, he mixes with all these nobby types, yer up-tight public-school crowd, so she never felt she fitted in. It's no wonder she went off the rails a bit. Like I said, she had a hard time, and now this happens. Life's just not fair, is it?"

A small part of Matt had a sneaking admiration for the performance, but he was quite sure the lovable London lad scenario was a front. He wondered what Paul Vaughan was really like and where he actually came from, because the accent didn't quite ring true. There wasn't a shadow of a doubt he'd be ruthless in business, no-one could make this kind of money without it. And Matt had plenty of experience of his type: rich businessmen, some of whom hovered on the edge of the criminal world and employed expensive lawyers to get them out of a hot spot when necessary. And something else was puzzling him. Why was a man like this living in a small town in South Wales? It just didn't seem to fit. Unless he had business interests in the area. That could be reason enough, he supposed. But surely, with the Internet and all the modern communication aids, he could run a business from anywhere in the country. Chloe Daniels, Matt decided, could add Paul Vaughan to her researches and maybe something really interesting would turn up.

Of course, Matt thought, Fabia would probably know quite a lot about him already. She kept her ear to the ground and always knew just what was going on around her, and that memory of hers, how he envied her that. He'd give a lot to pick her brains about all this, maybe he should go ahead and do so, after all it might help with the investigation and he really shouldn't pass up an opportunity to glean more information. But as he and Dilys drove back down the drive, away from Bryn-y-Mor Lodge, the misery that had been lurking at the back of his mind all morning crept up on him once again.

* * *

Their next port of call was the vicarage. Dilys parked, and Matt looked up at the attractive squat stone building of St Cybi's church. It had a comforting, solid air about it. No tall spire, just a square tower which, Matt noticed, leant very slightly to the left. He wondered how long it would take before it would lean too far. But it'd probably been like that for centuries – Pontygwyn's own Tower of Pisa. In the surrounding graveyard lichen-coated headstones were embedded in the soft earth, some at strange angles, with the occasional more recent polished granite stone amongst them. There were splashes of colour from primroses, daffodils and narcissi in amongst the gravestones, and from bunches of flowers that people had placed on the graves. The whole place had a comfortable air, giving the impression it had grown organically out of the surrounding landscape.

The vicarage next door, on the other hand, looked a little out of place. It was a small, rather boring square building of dun-coloured brick, probably built in the 1950s, the windows rather small and placed high in the walls. It must make it rather dark and gloomy inside, Matt thought.

As they got out of the car, a woman with wildly curling hair, wearing a red coat, appeared from round the side of the church. Matt noticed her clerical collar, although in all other respects she was nothing like any vicar he'd ever met. His father had been a high church, unworldly theologian. His brother had followed in his footsteps, although Matt had to admit he did have rather more contact with the real world. But this, this was something entirely different.

He stepped forward. "Reverend Temple?" he enquired. Matt introduced himself and explained why they wanted to speak to her. She was immediately serious.

"A terrible business. Well," she flapped a hand in the direction of the front door. "You'd better come in."

Chapter 18

They followed Cath Temple through to her study and, as they settled on a low, sagging sofa, Matt looked round with interest. The room felt familiar in its shabbiness, books piled everywhere, a cassock hanging on the back of the door, various pamphlets and hymn sheets in chaotic piles, and a large wooden crucifix hanging up above the desk. But one thing his father had never had in his study was a small mirror with bits and pieces of make-up on the bookshelf beside it.

He looked round at the framed photographs dotted about, some family groups, one of Cath Temple in a university gown, another of her in full vestments. Looking at the woman before him he felt sure she had her feet firmly on the ground. The plain neatness of her grey trousers and pale blue jumper were at odds with her riot of brown curls, but the face below them was intelligent, almost sharp. Nothing much would get past this particular cleric.

"That poor child." She bent her head for a moment. "It was very difficult to comfort the congregation this morning. People always want reasons, don't they?"

"You mean in your sermon? You must have had trouble thinking of a text."

Her eyebrows lifted in slight surprise. "Yes, I did. You're very perceptive."

"Not really." Matt smiled at her. "My brother's a parson, so was my father."

"Ah, I see."

Matt wondered why he'd told her that. He decided he should try to bring the conversation back to the matter in hand.

"Did you know Amber well?"

"Quite well. She didn't come to church, but that's beside the point. She used to turn up at the vicarage sometimes, just to talk. I introduced her to Fabia Havard when she told me she wanted to go to art school. She was very talented," she paused for a moment, "but she was also a very disturbed child."

"Why do you think that was?"

"Hard to tell. Several reasons I suppose, there usually are. Losing her father at such a young age, and I don't think she got on awfully well with her stepfather, but that's nothing unusual. However hard he tried, Murray never seemed to be able to get it quite right, and Lord knows he tried hard enough, poor man." She sighed. "Amber was – it's hard to find the words – call it extremely attractive, though that's rather an inadequate phrase where she was concerned. In a way, the very fact she was so attractive to men made her life more difficult."

"How do you mean?"

"We-ell," she said, as if she wasn't quite sure how much she wanted to say. The last thing Matt wanted was for her to stop now. He sat forward, clasping his hands together. "The more we can find out about the victim in a murder enquiry, personality, likes, dislikes, the better it is, so anything you can tell us about Amber will be helpful."

"It was definitely murder, then?"

"I'm afraid so." He waited, hoping she'd open up, and at last she did.

"Amber was – how to describe it? I wouldn't call it over-sexed, that's an old-fashioned, debased term, but to most men it seemed she was irresistible, she was colourful, voluptuous. And she used it. What woman wouldn't? It attracted attention, and that attention could always be taken for love. Unfortunately, I don't think she could actually distinguish between lust and love and, as a consequence, she'd had rather more physical experience of sex than was good for her at her age."

"You think these relationships she was having were more than just the usual boyfriend, girlfriend stuff?"

"Absolutely. I'm very much afraid she was using sex as a form of currency."

Matt was taken aback: this woman was full of surprises. "Do you mean she was on the game?"

"Not officially, if that's the right way to put it, but some of the men she'd been with had been very generous, and very useful to her, and I don't think she was about to discourage that generosity."

"Who, for instance?"

The silence lengthened. Crunch time, Matt thought. If he pushed too hard she might clam up altogether. He waited, hoping the quiet void would do his work for him. At last she went on, but it was only to say, "I really don't know how much I should say. It's difficult. I realise you need to know as much as possible, but I really don't feel I should speculate, and some of these people are my parishioners. I do have a duty of confidentiality."

"Would it help if I told you some of what we know already?"

"I suppose so," but she didn't sound too sure.

"We're aware of the fact she had an affair with Paul Vaughan last year." He was watching her carefully as he spoke and noticed her relax a little. "You knew about that?"

"Yes. Rather more than I wanted to in fact." She grimaced. "Amber was inclined to go into graphic detail about her conquests. I'm no prude, but there's a limit to what I really want to hear about other people's sexual activities, very much a case of information overload."

Matt suppressed a grin and decided that he rather liked Cath Temple, she was definitely not the kind of vicar that his father would have come across, why that made him like her even more was something he'd have to think about another time.

"I sympathise," he said. "So, Amber told you rather a lot about her relationship with Paul Vaughan?"

"Yes. One of the problems was that I knew... know rather a lot about him, and for that reason I really didn't think him a suitable friend."

Once more she'd succeeded in surprising him. Paul Vaughan definitely wasn't someone he'd have thought she knew well. How come? "What exactly do you mean when you say you know a lot about him?" Matt asked.

She gave him a quizzical look, smiled slightly. "Perhaps you think he's not the sort of person a vicar would know well?"

Matt grimaced, slightly embarrassed. "Maybe. My mistake." But he still waited for an answer, and when it came it wasn't at all what he expected.

"He's an ex-boyfriend of mine." Matt got the impression she quite enjoyed the effect of this statement. "Rather a ghastly coincidence, him coming to live here. I must say I got quite a shock when he turned up in Pontygwyn, but then, I suppose it's not that surprising."

"What do you mean?" asked Matt.

"Well, his family come from Newport." Matt's eyebrows rose. "Surprise you, does it? I know, that phoney London boy accent is a load of nonsense. When I knew him he was pure South Wales, but he shed that persona quickly enough – wanted to fit in in the big city music scene I suppose, silly man."

Matt decided the sooner he did a bit more research into Paul Vaughan the better. He'd put Dilys onto it as soon as they got back to the station.

"Anyway," Cath went on, "when we knew each other, in the late 80s this was, I was training to be a nurse at St Thomas's in London. My brother was doing bar work in a nightclub, impoverished student type job, and Paul was the drummer in a group that played there, that's how I met him."

"And why do you think he wasn't a suitable friend for Amber?"

Cath Temple didn't answer immediately. She bit her lip and frowned across at Matt, obviously thinking hard about how to respond. At last she spoke. "Back then, Paul was pretty hard up and it didn't take me long to realise he wasn't that particular about how he supplemented his income."

Matt's interest sharpened.

"There was nothing that serious, not then at any rate," she said, "just a spot of benefit fraud, fiddling his tax returns, that sort of thing, but he was also totally unscrupulous with women. I found out early on that I wasn't the only woman in his life and, in the end, it was me that ended the relationship." She gave him a weary little smile. "Took some doing. I was pretty keen, foolish me. But I knew it was going nowhere and I was sick of being lied to. So, there you have it. Ironic that I should be around to help Amber pick up the pieces when he finished with her."

Matt wondered if she'd told him all she could about her and Paul Vaughan, but decided not to push it. She'd already provided them with some very interesting background which would be well worth picking over. He could always come back to her to find out more if necessary. Now he asked, "Was Amber very upset?"

"You bet she was."

A re-run of their interview with Paul Vaughan played through Matt's mind. What was it he'd said? Just a bit of fun, not serious on either side, she'd just been 'a bit miffed' when he'd called it a day. This didn't match up either.

"The poor child thought he really cared about her," Cath went on. "Just as I did all those years ago. In a way I think that was the first really damaging relationship, for Amber I mean. Up until then, I got the impression her boyfriends had been in her own age group. I think he might have been the first older man she'd been with."

"The first?" Matt asked. "There were others?"

"After Paul? Yes. But she was besotted with him, and bowled over by all the money and the trappings of the pop world. I'm sure she built the relationship up into something it could never have been. I think she knew about his long-term partner – the model, you know? Melanie Franklin? But he'd given her the impression the relationship was almost over. So, when Melanie threw a wobbly and he dropped Amber, just like that, the poor child was absolutely devastated. I can tell you," she went on, "one of these days I'm going to tell Paul exactly what I think of him, and I'm really going to enjoy doing it. He can be such a bastard. Amber told me she tried to change his mind, and I'm afraid she hounded him, continually phoning up, and hanging round outside the house on the off chance of bumping into him. I tried to persuade her he wasn't worth it, but for ages she wouldn't listen."

Her anger showed through clearly, and her strength of character. As she spoke Matt got a glimpse of what a formidable woman she could be, none of the softly, softly vicar here. His respect for her increased.

"Did she know about your previous relationship?"

"Good Lord no!" she sounded horrified at the thought. "Nobody does, not even Fabia and she's my closest friend round here."

"It still seems strange to me," Matt went on conversationally, "that a man like that lives tucked away in a small Welsh town. You'd have thought he'd want to be closer to the hub of things, in London for instance."

"Well, quite apart from his family connections, and I've no idea if he sees them nowadays, he's got business interests down here, hasn't he? At least, that's what Amber implied. I can't remember exactly what—" She pressed a hand up to her forehead. "She said something about him putting money into a couple of nightclubs, and that he was also planning to set up a recording studio, on the outskirts of Cardiff I think. After all, the BBC has studios in Cardiff, so why not other media companies. He was always very shrewd when it came to money, it's probably much more economical to be based out of London, what with the way the oligarchs and their city friends have pushed up property prices in the capital, and with the internet it's not so important to be on the spot, is it?"

Matt glanced at Dilys. Her eyes wide, she looked slightly stunned by what they'd been told since they arrived at the vicarage. He gave her a slight smile, not her idea of a minister, that's for sure. He turned back to the vicar. "That would explain it, we can check up on his business dealings. But I'm getting off the point. To get back to Amber Morgan. What do you think made her change her mind, about pursuing Paul Vaughan, I mean?"

"I think it was because someone else came on the scene, it was around Christmas time, I think—" Abruptly she stopped speaking, and Matt got the distinct impression she'd pulled herself up short. Damn!

"And who was that?" he asked quietly, mentally crossing his fingers, but it was no good.

"I'm not sure. Amber wasn't specific."

"And you didn't guess?"

She said nothing, just shook her head.

"It's very important we find out the identity of everybody she had contact with," Matt said earnestly, "if only to eliminate them from our enquiries."

Matt was taken aback when she grinned at him. "Sorry," she said, going a little pink. "It's just that I've never actually heard someone use that phrase, except on police programmes on the telly of course."

He couldn't help smiling, but he was determined to bring her back on course. "Are you sure you don't know who this new man was?"

There was a loaded little silence. "No, I'm afraid not," she said.

Matt sat back and glanced at Dilys again, eyebrows raised. She took the hint and said, "There's just one more thing you may be able to help us with." She flipped through a few pages of her notebook as if she was looking for something. "Last Saturday, do you remember helping someone who had a flat tyre?"

Matt watched as the question registered. Normally he would have expected an answer to come quite quickly, but it didn't. For a long moment she sat absolutely still, not taking her eyes off Dilys's face. When she did speak, it was only to say the one word, "Yes."

"Who was the driver?"

"Neville Breverton, the MP."

"And what time was this?"

"Quite late I think."

"Could you be more specific?"

This was like drawing teeth, Matt thought. Her whole attitude had changed, the openness had disappeared completely to be replaced by a wariness she'd not shown before. What was going on here? He wondered, just for a second, if it'd be better to be upfront with her, then dismissed the idea. Maybe she'd suspected that the new man in Amber's life had been Neville Breverton and, since they'd been part of her congregation, she might feel she had a duty of confidentiality. Finally, she spoke.

"It was after eleven. I'd just shoved Mungo, my cat, outside. I always put him out last thing. I've not got round to fixing a cat door, and he has the shed to keep him warm."

"And Mr Breverton's car was where?"

"Slap by the front gate. Yes, it was definitely after eleven, probably more like twenty to twelve now I come to think of it, because I'd been watching a film on TV that ended at half eleven. Mr Breverton seemed to be having trouble with the wheel, but when I went out he insisted he was fine. He was quite brusque, so I left him to it."

Matt was delighted. He'd not really expected her to tell them much more, but what she had said was extremely useful. Tomorrow he'd set up an interview with Breverton on his own and Rees-Jones could like it or lump it.

* * *

As they drove away from the vicarage, Dilys said, "That's one of the strangest vicars I've ever come across. Who'd have thought Paul Vaughan was an ex of hers! Amazing." Her voice was a mixture of disapproval and reluctant admiration.

Matt smiled. "I could see you were a bit taken aback. I suppose she is a shade unusual. Did you think anything useful came out of that?"

"Well, there are several points, really. Do you think she was jealous of Amber's relationship with Paul?"

Matt thought about it. "It didn't sound like that to me."

"But then, you don't—" Dilys pulled herself up short, as if she'd changed her mind about what she was going to say. Matt was curious.

"I don't what?" He glanced at his sergeant and noticed she'd gone rather pink.

"It's difficult to know how to put it," she said. "It's not exactly a criticism."

He grinned at her confusion. "Spit it out, Dilys."

"You sometimes don't seem to be aware of how complicated relationships can be. Perhaps it's that you look at them more in black and white than shades of grey. I often get the impression that other people's messy lives take you by surprise."

Matt didn't know how to respond. Was he really that unperceptive? Surely not, and yet, well maybe; Dilys knew him very well, they'd been colleagues, and friends, for a long time. She could be right.

"I'll have to think about that one."

She glanced at him, frowning. "Sorry. Hope you don't think I'm speaking out of turn."

"No, not at all," he assured her, not sure if he was telling the truth. "And what else did you think about our vicar?"

"It seemed to me she wanted to protect the girl from Vaughan. She's another one who's mentioned this sexual magnetism Amber had, which could widen our field of enquiry somewhat if she really attracted men in this bee and honeypot fashion." She pursed her lips. "You know what my Nan would have said about Amber? All red shoes and no knickers."

Matt laughed aloud at this sudden digression into the vernacular, and Dilys gave him a slightly embarrassed smile. "I'm sorry, that's hardly appropriate to say about a girl who's dead, but still, that's what my Nan would have said."

"The thing is," Dilys went on after a few minutes, "given what Amber was like, she could have been meeting anybody on the bridge. Rather widens the field, doesn't it? Although she didn't actually say so, I think it's pretty certain Reverend Temple knows about the relationship between Breverton and Amber, she's just reluctant to drop him in it, probably because he goes to her church. I wouldn't have put him down as a church-going type, his wife yes, not him, but maybe it's useful to him – just goes along for appearance's sake, you know the sort of thing, all those family values politicians bang on about." Dilys frowned and Matt waited for her to continue. "Paul Vaughan's account of his break up with Amber seems to have left an awful lot out. They obviously viewed it from very different angles, or he was being economical with the truth, which is probably more likely."

"So, when we get back to the station I'd like some digging done into his involvement with those nightclubs, and the studio set up, and maybe a bit of digging into his family background, see if any of them are known to us. Whatever else, if he's got connections with the Golden Monkey crowd, we could make his life very uncomfortable for him."

"Indeed, we could," Dilys sounded delighted at the prospect. "I'll get one of the lads onto it all as soon as I can, and I'll get onto Daniels, ginger her up about that background stuff on Neville Breverton."

"I really don't know what I've done to deserve you, Dilys," Matt said.

"Nor do I, sir," Dilys replied, making him laugh again.

Matt's mobile buzzed, and he wriggled around until he could extract it from his pocket. "DCI Lambert," he said. "You have? Never mind. Get the confirmation on the blood as soon as possible, okay? Thanks for letting me know."

He turned to Dilys. "They've found the other earring. Seems it was snagged on a piece of metal reinforcement jutting out from the lower arch of the bridge. There're traces of blood on it which they're checking now, but it's pretty conclusive. It must have been torn from her ear as she fell."

"I suppose it does confirm she fell from the bridge."

"Yes, but it doesn't really help us much otherwise."

Five minutes later, his mobile buzzed again. "Yup. Nice and clear, is it? Wonderful. We're coming back in now and I'll have a look at it. Good work Pryce."

He turned to Dilys. "That's better news. They managed to retrieve the rubbish bags from Pontygwyn House and they've found the stuff from the grate in Gwen Breverton's fireplace. Bless her forever, that lovely Mrs Pritchard had put it all into a carrier bag before throwing it in the bin, so it's not been contaminated by any of the other rubbish. Some clear pieces of printing. It'll be very interesting to see what it says."

Chapter 19

Fabia came out of the post office and prepared to cross the road on her way to the bakery. As a rule, she'd have done a little window shopping in the many antique shops that had replaced the greengrocers and ironmongers of years gone by, or she'd have had a rummage in a charity shop or two. Bargain hunting was one of her favourite pastimes, and supporting these shops had that delightful by-product, the virtuous feeling you got when you spent money in them. But not today. She was far too preoccupied. Her mind was miles away, picking over what she knew about Amber's murder and wishing, uselessly, that she was more closely involved.

It wasn't until a large truck thundered past, the driver hooting frantically and gesticulating from the cab as it narrowly missed hitting her, that Fabia came to her senses. Once safely back on the pavement, she stopped to get her breath. "Stupid woman," she muttered. If she didn't pull herself together, she'd end up causing a major accident.

"You okay, Miss Havard?"

Fabia looked up and saw Craig Evans, his anxious eyes peering out from inside his biker's helmet. Quick thinking, a stroke of genius, she wasn't quite sure what it was, she just knew this was an opportunity to talk to him about Amber which she really couldn't pass up. "I'm a bit shaken up actually," she said. "Do you think you could help me into Beynon's?"

She made sure she leant heavily on his arm as they made their way into the warm, sweet-smelling bakery. Opposite the counter were a few chairs and tables where the Beynon twins – plump, rosy-cheeked, wearing identical overalls – served teas, coffee and light snacks. Fabia had often wondered how long the place could survive, with the pubs and coffee chains for competition, but so far it seemed as prosperous as ever. Relieved to see that none of the tables were occupied, she sat down and rummaged in her shoulder bag for some money, held it out to Craig.

"Would you be a dear and get me a cup of tea? I think I need something to steady my nerves. And something for yourself of course. You've been a real good Samaritan."

"Well, I–" Craig sounded doubtful, probably worried his street cred would suffer if he was seen in a place like this, so Fabia gave him what she hoped was a slightly pathetic smile. She wasn't sure how long she'd be able to keep up this act and was relieved when Craig relented, took his helmet off and placed it on a chair.

"Rightio then." He took the money and, rather red in the face, went to the counter.

Her mind raced as she waited, watching him as she did so. Just a spot of gentle probing, she told herself, nothing more. They'd been close friends, Amber and Craig, maybe she'd talked to him about her worries.

"Thank you, Craig. This is very kind of you," she said as he returned with a loaded tray – a pot of tea, milk in a matching jug, and a can of coke. He sat down opposite, looking distinctly uncomfortable while Fabia poured and he flipped open the can and took a slurp. As she helped herself to sugar from the bowl on the table – no modern paper tubes of the stuff for the Beynon sisters – she decided she'd have to move fast.

Without preamble, she said, "You were a friend of Amber Morgan's, weren't you? This must be an awful time for you."

"S'pose." He didn't meet her eye.

"Have the police been giving you a hard time?"

"Not so's you'd notice. Not about that anyway."

"What about then?" Fabia tried not to sound too interested, but when the answer came, it wasn't what she'd expected, although she told herself she should have.

"Usually it's about my bike. That dickhead – sorry – that Sergeant Pryce does go on asking where I got the money to pay for it. I told him straight, I did, my Mam's da left me some money when he died and I bought my bike, all fair and square. You was in the police, wasn't you?" It sounded accusing.

"Yes, I was, a long time ago." Best to distance herself from it since Craig obviously had no friendly feelings towards the local force.

"If you'd still been a policewoman..." He paused, chewing at his lower lip, then said in a rush, "Would you have been one of the people trying to find out who killed Amber?"

"Possibly."

Craig sat for a moment, crouched over his can of Coke which he held in both hands, elbows on the table, as he stared out through the window into the High Street. He went on staring past Fabia as he began to speak, his voice low and urgent. "I've got this mate, and he thinks he might know something that's important, about Amber I mean, and he doesn't know what to do about it. What would you tell him to do?"

Fabia was aware of how carefully she had to tread. "It would depend very much on what it was he knew."

"It's about some of the people, involved I mean."

"Involved in what way?"

"People that knew Amber. At least," he added hastily, "that's what my mate told me."

He picked up the coke can, and Fabia noticed that his hand was shaking a little. Sorry as she felt for the poor boy, nothing could diminish her urge to know exactly what was bothering him. She leant forward. "Look, anything told to the police is told in confidence. I realise you don't have much time for them, but I'm sure you want whoever is responsible for Amber's death to be caught, don't you?"

His jaw set as if he was clenching his teeth. "I'd like to get my hands on them, if that's what you mean."

"I'm sure. If you like I could arrange for your friend to talk to someone, just informally, and then they'd be able to tell him how important the information is and what to do about it. Do you think he'd agree?"

"I dunno, see. It's difficult. They're not going to believe him instead of some bloke that's important, got influence and all that. They already think I got something to do with it. Anything I say, they'll think I'm lying."

For the first time their eyes met. Fabia didn't think he realised how revealing this little speech had been. Seconds ticked by. Any minute, she expected him to get up and bolt for the door, but he didn't. Instead, his eyes welled up with tears. As he rubbed the back of his hand across them, he muttered, "I just want the fucking bastard to pay for what he done. She said he'd made promises, like, and now this. He's got to pay."

"Who, Craig?"

He stared at her, his eyes full of fear now. It was obvious he felt he'd said too much. She put out a hand to him, then changed her mind, didn't actually touch his. She had to get across how important this was without pushing him too hard.

"Look, Craig. Do you trust me?"

"S'pose." He didn't sound too sure.

"You can, you know. If you, or your friend of course, want to talk to me, that's fine. But I can't promise not to pass on what you tell me to the police. Amber has been murdered and if you know something that might help find her killer, it's very important that you tell them. No-one has the right to take away another person's life," she said urgently. "It's vital that whoever did it is caught."

"I know. But what if they think—"

"Whatever you think of the police, they're not stupid, they know what they're doing. I know Chief Inspector Lambert who's in charge of this case. He's okay, believe me. Come on Craig, how about speaking to him?"

Craig shifted on his seat and Fabia knew she was losing ground. He looked out of the window, then back over her shoulder at the two women behind the counter. A moment later, he jumped up and grabbed his helmet from the chair. "I gotta go."

"Hang on a minute." Fabia rose too. "Let me give you my mobile number, please."

"Okay," he took out his phone and Fabia quickly told him the number which he tapped in. "Please ring me if you change your mind. Please Craig, it's important. You can ring me any time, day or night."

He stood staring at her for a second, then pushed his helmet onto his head and barged out into the High Street. Fabia slumped back in her chair and, quietly, slowly and with great imagination, swore. Her resolution to keep out of Matt's way would have to be set aside. He had to be told about this conversation with Craig. He'd have to talk to the boy as soon as possible. Perhaps he'd let her sit in on the interview, she thought eagerly, but she soon discarded the idea. Hardly likely. But still – her heart lifted – at least now she had a legitimate reason to contact Matt. The first thing she'd do when she got home was phone him.

* * *

When Matt got back to his office he had a look at the pieces of paper retrieved from Gwen Breverton's fireplace. Although what had been found would be useful, there was very little of it. A few fragments of charred notepaper with the odd word still recognisable, and a piece of green paper, probably from an envelope, on which the only fingerprint they'd found was smeared and virtually useless. They'd try checking it against those of the murdered girl, but he thought it'd probably be a pointless exercise. Matt sat at his desk studying the pieces of paper, disappointed they didn't get him much further. But perhaps Dilys, or even Fabia, would have some useful ideas about them. It was while he was sitting frowning at the fragments that there was a knock at his door.

"Come in," he called, feeling ready for some distraction.

Chloe Daniels was nothing like Dilys. Tall and slim with smooth skin the colour of dark coffee and closely curled hair pulled into a clip at the nape of her neck, her eyes were bright with enthusiasm as she strode into the room. She was obviously full of news.

"I've got something really interesting here, sir, but it's not exactly through official channels, it's from my brother Gareth. He's a journalist on the Newport Evening News. I took notes, but if you'd rather talk to him direct, I can get him to come in. It does seem quite important and he–"

"Sit down." Matt smiled at her. "And slow down. Tell me what you've got, and I'll decide whether I need to see him."

"Right, sir. Well, shall I go back to the beginning?" Eyes round and questioning, she perched on the edge of her chair like an eager bird waiting for titbits.

"Probably best to do so, I think. Off you go."

"Last Tuesday, Gareth went in to work early. He says it's quiet then and he wanted to catch up on some odds and ends. Anyway, the first in always listens to the answerphone messages in case something important has come in overnight, so he did – listen to them, I mean. He said there wasn't anything much, not until the last message. You see, the reason why he told me about it was because I'd told him I was helping you with the Amber Morgan case." Matt could see warmth rising in her dark skin as she bit her lip. "I hope that was all right, sir?"

"We'll let it go this time," Matt said, wishing she'd get to the point, "but don't make a habit of talking about cases you're working on."

"Oh no, I wouldn't do that."

"Go on, then."

She wriggled on her seat then clasped her hands tight in her lap. "He said the message was rather garbled, but the caller said her name was Amber Morgan." Matt sat upright in his chair. She certainly had his full attention now. "And from her tone of voice, Gareth said it sounded as if she was very agitated, like she was really angry or maybe frightened. He noted it all down, she kept stopping and starting, sort of as if she was looking over her shoulder, as if she thought she'd be interrupted any minute, you know? And once he'd been through the transcript, he thought he'd better tell the news editor, that's his immediate boss. He – his boss I mean – was very interested, and he listened to the message and read Gareth's transcript, then said to leave it with him and he'd show it to the editor. Later in the morning, the editor came and thanked Gareth, but he told him he'd best keep the information to himself as it was a delicate matter that would need careful handling, and that was the last Gareth heard about it."

Matt frowned. It was obvious from Chloe's expression this wasn't the end of the story. He wondered what was coming next.

"Gareth says he saw the two of them, his boss and the editor, having this regular barney – it's one of those open-plan offices, but the senior staff are partitioned off with sort of glass walls from halfway up. When the news editor finally came out, he was looking really angry and Gareth tackled him, asked him what was going to be done about the message and all that, but he was told to shut up and leave the whole thing alone, it wasn't his problem any more. The thing is, he doesn't give up that easily, my brother," she said with a grin of pride and satisfaction. "He invited one of the older journalists who's been with the press much longer to have lunch, and he pumped him for information, and he says what he found out was pretty interesting."

"Okay Chloe, but what did the message say? And what did your brother find out?"

"It'd probably be best if you spoke to him yourself. Would you like me to ask him to come in?"

"No. We'll go to him. Is he still at work?" Matt asked as he got up from his chair.

Chloe glanced at her watch. "He might well be in the pub by now. I could text him to check. We could–" She paused, uncertain.

Matt smiled at her. "Come on then. I could do with a pint. Let's go and search out this brother of yours and he can tell me all about it."

Chloe was tapping away at her mobile as they left the room.

Chapter 20

Fabia slammed her front door behind her, went straight to the kitchen, and rummaged around on the table for her mobile. After a frustrating minute, she finally found it. Relieved, she dialled the number. It rang several times before a mechanical voice told her it was the voicemail of Matt Lambert and politely requested that she leave a message after the tone. She told it to piss off and dialled the station in Newport instead. Having negotiated the switchboard, she waited impatiently while Matt's extension rung and rung. At last it was answered, but it wasn't Matt's voice she heard.

"Chief Inspector Lambert's office."

"Could I speak to him please?"

"I'm sorry, he's not in the office at the moment. Can I help?"

"It's Fabia Havard here. It's very important I speak to DCI Lambert as soon as possible. Do you know where I can contact him?"

There was an infinitesimal pause on the other end of the line, then the voice, cooler now, replied, "I'm afraid he's not available at the moment. Can I take a message?"

Fabia was in two minds as to how to approach this. If whoever it was had recognised who she was, he might just be blocking her because he disapproved of what he saw as her interference. But antagonising Matt's staff would be counter-productive. Better to try the friendly approach.

"I really do need to talk to him. It's about the Amber Morgan case. I have some information for him. Would you be kind enough to ask him to ring me as soon as possible?"

"Of course, ma'am." The voice was still cool. "I'll do my best to pass the message on when he gets back."

"Thank you," Fabia said through gritted teeth. "As soon as possible if you can."

"I'll do my best."

"I realise how... well, thank you anyway."

Fabia replaced the receiver, feeling thwarted and frustrated. It was so galling! She felt that as soon as she mentioned her name all the hidden – and not so hidden – agendas attached to her past reared their ugly heads. She wouldn't mind betting her phone call would not come as a high priority with the unknown officer she'd spoken to. He might even forget it altogether. No, that was ridiculous, stupid to be so over-sensitive. But he might not even be conscious of making a decision based on rumour and half-truth. Once people made up their minds about you, created a picture of you in their mind that satisfied their own prejudices, they were inclined to react subconsciously and it was very difficult to escape the straitjacket.

What to do next? She couldn't just sit around twiddling her thumbs. That half hour with Craig must be followed up before fear and doubt took over and he clammed up completely. But, once again, she had to resign herself, there was nothing she could do. She decided work was the only answer, it would distract her, and she'd neglected it long enough. But after half an hour she gave up. Today's Fabia could immerse herself in precise, brightly coloured little drawings for a children's book on the facts of life, but yesterday's Fabia had taken over. Yesterday's Fabia wanted to be totally absorbed in the mind-stretching detail of a murder enquiry. She stood gazing out of the window as the dusk crept up over the hills, her mind working away methodically, sifting through all the information she had so far.

* * *

Rhona could feel an almost uncontrollable excitement bubbling up inside her. She stood in the middle of her attic room and a little giggle burst from her lips. With fingers to her mouth, she blocked it, and glanced fearfully at the photo of her father. His voice sounded cold and stern in her mind.

"Vanity, my girl, is a sin. Take that paint off your face immediately."

"But dearest Da," she said, walking quickly over to the photo and putting up a tentative finger to touch the unforgiving face in its cold pewter frame. "I have an important appointment, and I must make an effort, make the best of myself. You always said I should set an example, show others how things should be done." A slight cloud passed across her face, this hadn't really been the kind of example he'd been thinking about, but her doubts only lasted a second; she pushed them out of her mind. "I'm so excited. This is going to change my whole life, Da, honest. I'll not be alone any more. You know, dearest, I've been so lonely since you passed on, and now I'm going to have my very own – no, no, best not say it."

Standing in the corner of the room, opposite the photo of her father, was an ancient, rather spotted cheval mirror. Rhona made her way across and stood before it, pressed her lips together, smoothing the bright pink lipstick she was wearing. Next, she licked a finger and ran it along each eyebrow, smoothing the thin lines. She smiled at herself in the mirror, ran her hands down the flower-printed dress she wore, turned first to one side then the other.

"That will do nicely, don't you think? Just my jacket and scarf and I must be off." The giggle rose again. This time she didn't stop it as she turned and made her way down the attic stairs, still giggling quietly to herself.

* * *

Fabia was so preoccupied with her thoughts that when the phone finally rang she jumped out of her skin. She grabbed at the receiver, nearly dropped it, then clamped it to her ear, feeling relief flow over her as she heard Matt's voice.

"Fabia?" He sounded brusque, but what did that matter? "I was told you wanted to speak to me."

"I do, indeed," she said.

"I'd been planning to drop in tomorrow," Matt said, and she felt inordinately pleased at this, "but it sounded urgent. What can I do for you?"

"I've got some info for you, to do with Amber's murder."

"Have you now? Look, I hate talking on the phone." He no longer sounded brusque. "Are you going to be at home for a bit? Could I come round now?"

"Of course."

"I'll be there in half an hour or so," Matt said.

When she opened the door to him Fabia was pleased to see he was on his own. It would make things easier. The awkwardness between them was bad enough without having his neat little sergeant sitting on the sidelines taking it all in. Early though it was, she'd opened a bottle of wine and offered him a glass. He accepted it and followed her through to the sitting room.

"So, what's all this about?" he asked as he subsided into a chair. She could see he was exhausted, but made no comment. He didn't need to have it rubbed in. Instead, she told him what Craig had said.

"He definitely said 'he' should be made to pay for what he'd done, and he said he, Craig that is, would like to tackle whoever it is himself, to avenge Amber, I suppose. He implied whoever it is is important, influential, which made me think of Neville, or maybe Vaughan, and that the police would hardly listen to Craig rather than a person like that. I tried to convince him otherwise, but I don't think I succeeded. The trouble is, there's enough truth in what he said to make my denials sound a bit hollow."

Matt grimaced but made no comment.

"He said something about this person making promises to Amber 'and now this'," Fabia went on, "referring, I suppose, to the murder. I tried to persuade him to talk to you, even offered to be there, if you allowed it, of course," she'd better make that clear, "and gave him my mobile number, told him to contact me any time just to reinforce how important I thought the information was. I'm pretty sure he knows more than he told me. But there it is, that's all I managed to get out of him."

Matt sat staring into space and didn't say anything in response. Once more Fabia filled the void. "I felt truly sorry for the poor boy. I've known him a long time, he cuts my lawn occasionally and does odd jobs, so that's probably why he talked to me. Trouble is, he's no friend of the police, probably with good reason, he's certainly no angel. I think he feels he'll end up in trouble if he talks to you, maybe with whoever he'd be dropping in it, but I think he's also got it fixed in his mind that if he takes information to you lot he'll end up accused of the murder himself."

"Why on earth?"

"Think about it, Matt. There's no love lost between him and Sergeant Pryce, for one."

Matt clicked his tongue in irritation. "Okay, I'll get one of the WPCs onto it, he might respond better to a woman."

"Or I could talk to him," Fabia said tentatively. Matt frowned across at her and she felt annoyance rising inside. "I do remember the rules, Matt."

"I don't doubt it." He relented slightly. "And it's not that I mind you talking to him, it's just that if you did get some valuable info out of this kid, it's no good to us if he won't make it official, is it?"

"I suppose not," Fabia admitted reluctantly.

"Leave it with me. I'll think about it. We seem to be getting bits and pieces coming in from all directions at the moment."

"What do you mean?"

He hesitated for a moment, then said, "One of my WPCs has a brother who works at the Newport Evening News. He's come up with some information that could be very valuable." To Fabia's delight, he told her all about the message left by Amber on the answerphone, and everything else Chloe Daniels and her brother had told him.

"So, this other reporter, the one he had lunch with, told Gareth the editor of the Evening News is a close friend of Neville Breverton?"

"That's it. They go way back. And Chief Superintendent Rees-Jones was, probably still is, also a friend."

"I knew that already."

"So why didn't you tell me?"

"You didn't ask," she said, challenging him. He didn't take up the challenge.

"It's all very interesting, don't you think?" he said.

"Very," Fabia decided to stop baiting him. "So, Gareth thinks the editor suppressed the message from Amber. He may be right if its existence hasn't come through to you lot."

"Which it hasn't."

"If he phoned Breverton and ran it past him – Good Lord! This could mean Neville is much more closely involved than even I thought. The shit could well and truly hit the fan if all this gets out."

"And I have a shrewd idea that's what Rees-Jones is afraid of," Matt said. "He hauled me in and warned me to tread carefully with his MP friend. Seems to think different rules apply to his pals."

"You mean you can actually entertain the idea of your own boss being involved?" Fabia's smile was sardonic. One of the things she'd always teased Matt about was the difficulty he had in accepting that some of his fellow police officers could be as crooked as the criminals they pursued. That had made his apparent readiness to believe it of her even worse at the time. His reaction to this remark surprised her. Instead of giving as good as he got, he looked up from under his brows, pushed the hair back from his forehead with a weary sweep of his hand, and said, "I'm not the innocent abroad I used to be, nor do I think I'm always right."

"I didn't think you did," said Fabia, puzzled.

"I've learnt a thing or two recently and, well, let's just say I'm going to have to reassess a few things."

She had no idea what he was talking about but didn't think it would be a good idea to probe. It might put him off talking to her, and that was the last thing she wanted now he seemed to be opening up. This felt as if they'd slipped back in time, discussing a case almost as they used to all those years ago. Fabia went back to the matter in hand, praying that he wouldn't clam up on her.

"Of course, we're jumping way ahead of ourselves here. Tell me again exactly what the message from Amber said."

Matt got up and began to pace up and down the room, his hands thrust deep in his pockets. "The most important bits were that someone she knew well, who lives in Pontygwyn, is abusing a woman. This same person has a much-respected position in the community, and if what he's doing came out it would ruin him. She, Amber, wanted to talk to a reporter because she said it was the only way to stop this abuser. She implied it would put his advancement in his chosen career under threat. Now, I have it on good authority that one of Breverton's current hobby horses is violence against women, which is hardly surprising given the high-profile abuse is getting at the moment; politically it'd be useful to him to be seen to be pro-active on that."

"That's interesting. It's definitely not a subject I'd associate with him."

"No? Well, it seems he's on some Commons committee or other investigating police attitudes and rates of prosecution, etc. She didn't give any names, but Gareth thought the whole scenario matched up with the position Neville Breverton holds, and she said it sounded as if Amber herself was the abused woman. What if Amber asked for too much money, or threatened to talk about their affair, and he got violent?"

"Yes, but you don't know for sure she was referring to him. And it doesn't really match with what Mrs Pritchard overheard."

"No, but it could have been a sudden falling out. The encounter Mrs Pritchard heard was on Monday morning, and she only heard the beginning of it. Amber was murdered some time during the night between Wednesday and Thursday. They could have ended up having a row on that Monday morning, he could have lost his temper, threatened her. I don't know. I'll have to think about it." He stopped his pacing and threw himself back in the chair.

They sat in silence for a while, both brooding on their own thoughts, then Fabia thought again of Mrs Pritchard. "Have you managed to retrieve the bits and pieces from Gwen Breverton's fireplace?"

"We have. There isn't an awful lot there, just one smeared thumbprint – we don't know whose – on a piece of the bright green paper, probably an envelope, and three scraps of lined paper with words printed in capitals."

"Just like Rhona's. What words?"

He half closed his eyes in an effort to remember. "One piece has the words 'his women' on it, followed by a full stop, and then the two words, 'likes them'. Another has a few letters, barely distinguishable, and the last bit has 'spill the' on it, that's all."

"As in 'spill the beans' perhaps?"

"Possibly, but there's no way of telling."

"Not an awful lot to go on," Fabia said sympathetically.

"No, but it's better than nothing."

Not long afterwards Matt pushed himself up from his chair, saying that he'd better get going as he had a load of paperwork to do. Fabia didn't press him to stay. He'd already told her much more than she thought he would, and discussed the case with her far more freely than she'd dared to hope.

On the doorstep he turned back, a frown on his face. "Fabia, I want to talk to you about the—" but Fabia's attention was distracted. Rhona's front door had opened very slowly, her sharp face peered out and she looked down the road, away from them.

"What on earth is she up to?" Fabia whispered to Matt. He followed her gaze. It was still the back of Rhona's head presented to their curious gaze. A moment later the rest of Rhona slithered out. She shut the door with extreme care and crept down the path to the gate. It was obvious she'd taken great pains over her appearance. She wore a full skirted dress with a pattern of pale pink and yellow flowers, over this she'd added a short, white fake fur jacket, and a bright pink chiffon scarf kept her tight brown curls under control. On her feet were precariously high heeled sandals. In the dusk Fabia could have sworn they were pearlized candyfloss pink. If she'd been about to take part in a production of Grease, she couldn't have been more suitably dressed.

"What on earth?" Fabia exclaimed as they watched.

"God knows, but she's certainly put some effort into it," Matt said.

It was at this moment, just as she closed her garden gate, that Rhona turned and caught sight of them. She stumbled on the spindly heels and nearly fell, the expression on her face one of shocked consternation. "Well, I must say!" she exclaimed, and even in this light they could see the colour flood her cheeks. "The two of you standing there so quiet. What are you staring at me for?"

"Matt was just saying how smart you look, Rhona," Fabia gabbled, and added lamely, "Going to a party?"

Rhona's lips worked. "That's none of your business. And a person doesn't like to be spied upon." A second later, a strangely disturbing little smile crept around the edges of her mouth. There was an air of barely suppressed excitement about her. "No, not a party. I'm meeting someone, someone special, and that's all I'm going to tell you." She nodded several times and then, with a quick smoothing down of her skirt and a pat to the chiffon scarf, she teetered off down the road.

Fabia and Matt stood there in shocked silence, not quite knowing how to react. Fabia felt laughter rising up inside her, valiantly tried to suppress it, and lost the battle. A gale of slightly hysterical laughter bubbled out in spite of her efforts to suppress it. But it didn't last long, a moment later, all desire to laugh suddenly left her. She turned to Matt, "I wouldn't mind betting she's meeting some man or other, which might well explain the contents of that letter, don't you think?"

Chapter 21

Craig made his way up Morwydden Lane, glad of the lack of street lighting. Two of the lamps had been vandalised and the remaining one was up the church end, and that was nearly home. He should be okay. He tightened his arm across his chest and there was a rustle of plastic from the wrapped bundle hidden under his coat. Nice pair this evening, one five-pounder, one a bit heavier. Lovely fish, they were. Should bring in a tidy bit of dosh. The restaurant out past Cwmcoed Farm would pay good money for wild salmon, and ask no questions.

Craig trudged on, thinking about Amber, feeling the misery tighten its grip round his throat. That's why he'd gone down to get the salmon – he thought it might take his mind off things, but it hadn't. Stupid to think it would. Anger rose inside him again. Who'd done this? Taken his best mate away from him? If those bastard police ever found out, and he doubted it the way they fucked about asking questions of the wrong people most of the time, but if they did – well, whoever it was better watch out. Craig's fists clenched and once more the tears rose, threatening to overwhelm him. He swallowed painfully. Amb would have laughed at him, told him not to be such a wimp. But the thought brought on a shuddering sob and the tears finally escaped to roll unheeded down his cheeks.

He wiped an arm across his face and quickened his pace, wishing he'd risked bringing the bike, but the noise would have attracted attention. Nearly home now, just coming up to the church and the street lamp outside it. His heart thumped as he heard a burst of laughter from the pub, voices calling goodnight, footsteps retreating up towards the High Street. He ducked into the corner of the vicarage garden, crouched under a rhododendron bush. For a while he stayed there, hidden by the foliage, waiting. The footsteps and voices slowly died away and, at last, silence reigned once more. He was just about to emerge from his hiding place when he heard another set of footsteps, but it was only one person this time, coming from the direction of the church, quiet, urgent, hurrying.

Craig heard the lychgate hinge creak and peered cautiously out through a gap in the branches. Just before the person disappeared round the corner, in the light from the pub windows, he recognised who it was. He frowned. What was this about? Not a regular churchgoer, Craig was pretty sure of that, and anyway – he glanced at his watch, the glowing numbers told him it was just after nine. What had been going on in the church at this time of night on a Sunday evening?

After about five minutes he decided it would be safe to emerge. Quickly he dashed across the road and round the back of the pub, letting himself in as quietly as he possibly could. All was quiet back here, there was no-one around in the kitchen. Craig pushed his package right to the back of one of the large fridges in the pub kitchen, then made his way up the back stairs to his room, closed the door behind him, leant against it and breathed a deep sigh of relief. Tomorrow, early, before Mam and Dad were up, he'd retrieve the salmon and take them down to that poncy restaurant, then he'd go and order a wreath for Amber.

* * *

Cath had made a habit over the last few days of going into the church when she had a free moment and saying a few quiet prayers for Amber and her family. She made herself pray, too, for Amber's killer, but this she found a little more difficult. Forgiveness, she told the Lord, was not one of her strong suits. But still she felt she must try to do what her faith and her training told her should be done.

In the middle of Monday morning she'd finished a pile of paperwork, sent off a few e-mails, and found herself at a loose end. Her next appointment wasn't until one o'clock. Knowing this would be the only quiet moment in her day, she decided to pop over to the church for fifteen minutes.

Taking the keys from the hook in the hall reminded her she'd found the side door unlocked the evening before. She must mention it to Rhona. Maybe she, or one of her team, had left it open after cleaning up the day before. The insurance was crippling enough already, without having to confess to the insurers that the church had been left open.

She walked across the vicarage garden and, looking around, decided she must ask Craig Evans to come and cut the lawn. He could probably do with a little extra cash to help with petrol for that bike of his, and it wasn't just the grass that was looking shaggy after its winter rest – the flower beds could certainly do with tidying. She knew her concentration on mundane gardening matters was a reaction. If she made herself think about everyday things, it took her mind off the horrors surrounding them. But it didn't last long. Soon thoughts of Amber intruded once again.

Still she lingered a little as she let herself out of the gate and into the small graveyard. It was a quiet, gentle place and she loved its peaceful atmosphere, and the feeling it always gave her of reducing the small worries of life to manageable proportions. Sadly, her present preoccupation could hardly be called small. Sighing, she pressed on to the church door. No time to waste. She only had a few minutes to spare.

As she stepped into the cool gloom she trod on something slippery and nearly fell. She flung a hand out to steady herself against the heavy oak door and, heart beating fast, glanced down. In this light she could see nothing. Frowning, she turned to flick on two of the lights and looked down again to see what it was. A bright silky scarf lay at her feet. Cath bent and picked it up but didn't recognise it. She stuffed it in her pocket.

An uneasy feeling of being watched crept over her. She dismissed it, telling herself not to be fanciful, or that maybe the owner of the scarf was still around.

"Hallo?" Cath called tentatively, but her voice simply echoed back at her from the ancient stones. St Cybi's was a very old church, some of the building going back as far as the eleventh century. There had probably been plenty of potential for the creation of restless spirits in its history. Maybe that was the answer. Cath gave herself a little shake and told herself firmly that she didn't believe in such things.

The main entrance, with its thick wooden double doors, was at the opposite end to the altar and tucked back below the organ loft. It was almost always kept locked, except when there was a big wedding. The door which was used most of the time was the one in the side porch through which she'd just entered. To Cath's right was an alcove with a small library of books to borrow, and some to buy. Opposite were shelves stacked with hymn and prayer books, above them a notice board, and next to it a small cupboard where extra hymn sheets and stacks of baptism cards were kept. It was all so very familiar to her, everything was exactly as it should be. But Cath still felt uneasy as she walked along behind the pews, looking around as she did so, her footsteps echoing in the gloom. The door had been locked so there couldn't be anyone else here and that was that. But in spite of herself, she turned and went back to check the two collection boxes by the door. They were both untouched. That put paid to that idea. Back she went along to the centre aisle and looked down towards the altar. On it the brass candlesticks gleamed in a shaft of sunlight full of dancing dust motes streaming in from a high window. Nothing was out of place. She sighed with relief and turned to look towards the dark doors below the organ loft. The two lights she'd turned on hardly penetrated the gloom here so, at first, she couldn't quite work out what it was that seemed out of place.

Her heart began to beat faster again as she made her way towards the back door, past the carved stone font which stood to one side. She'd only taken a couple of steps when she realised there was a pile of clothing spread out on the stone flags below the organ loft. Quickly she went round the font and flicked two switches on the wall. Light flooded the area and, as it did so, shock hit her like a punch in the stomach. For a second, she stood rigid, staring at what her eyes recognised but her mind tried desperately to shy away from.

Sticking out from the pile of clothes were two thin, white legs, the feet thrust into pink stiletto sandals. To one side an arm, covered in some furry material, stuck out at a strange angle, palm uppermost. At the other end, in deeper shadow, was a head of brown curls, stained now a darker colour, and a pool of the same dark colour lay across the cold stone flags of the floor.

* * *

"There you are, sir!" Dilys exclaimed as Matt walked into the office. "I've tried half a dozen times to get you on your mobile. "

"Sorry. It's been playing up. What's going on?"

"There's been another one," she said cryptically.

"What?"

"Another death. Reverend Temple phoned. She's found a body in the church, says it looks as if she fell from the organ loft. It's that woman from down Morwydden Avenue."

Matt stopped dead. For an unbelieving second, an icy chill of fear gripped him. It wasn't possible. Surely? "Which woman?" he snapped so sharply that Dilys blinked.

"Rhona Griffiths." Then understanding dawned. "Oh Lord! I'm sorry sir. I'd forgotten Miss Havard lives next door."

She was gazing at him in open-mouthed consternation, but Matt, guilty relief surging through him, waved a dismissive hand. "Come on, you can give me the details in the car. Is the team on its way?"

"Yes. I've contacted Dr Curtis, and the SOCOs left fifteen minutes ago. Same team. Could be suicide but in the circumstances–"

"Absolutely. Well done Dilys."

As they left the station, into Matt's mind came a picture of Rhona in her pink dress and fur jacket walking jauntily off the evening before, heels clicking on the pavement as she went. Surely, given her mood then, she wouldn't have done away with herself, she'd seemed positively elated. Had she had a date with a murderer? But why should this be murder? It was more likely an accident. Dilys echoed his thoughts.

"It looks like an accident, or I suppose it could have been suicide. Reverend Temple said Miss Griffiths had a key to the church because she was in charge of all the cleaning. The vicar thinks she must have fallen from the organ loft while she was dusting yesterday. But she'd have had to be leaning right out to overbalance. More likely she jumped. Let's face it, she was a bit doolally tap."

But she was very religious, thought Matt, surely committing suicide would, in her eyes, have been a great sin. And to do so in a church would have been even worse for someone like Rhona? On the other hand, Dilys was right, she had been a bit touched, as his mother would have called it; definitely an interesting study for a psychologist. But there was no point in speculating. He'd just have to wait and see what they found at the scene.

It took them a good deal longer than expected to get to St Cybi's church as they were delayed by an accident between Newport and Pontygwyn. By the time they parked behind the two police cars already outside the church, it was nearly three-quarters of an hour since they'd left the station. Matt, irritated by the delay, glared at the small crowd of people who'd gathered on the opposite pavement, murmuring to each other and stretching for a better look. There was a constable standing by the lychgate, also glaring at them.

"They've been collecting over by there since I arrived, sir," he complained to Matt as he and Dilys came up the path. "Don't know what attracts them, I really don't."

"The ghoul mentality. You'll find it in every community, I'm afraid. Are the rest of the team inside?"

"Yes, sir. And the vicar wants to speak to you, urgent like."

"All in good time. Come on, Sergeant," he said to Dilys, "let's get on with it."

For Matt, old churches always had the same smell and atmosphere. As he stepped through the porch he was pushed straight back into his childhood. A familiar feeling welled up in him, a mixture of resentment and apprehension. He stopped for a second in the doorway, reluctant to go further. This case had so many unpleasant resonances for him. Amber's death with its disturbing connections, and now this taking him back to childhood Sundays. Week after week, they'd trailed reluctantly into church in his mother's wake to hear his father preach sermons few people could understand, to have their every move watched by parishioners all too ready to criticise the vicar's children, and to feel the burden of knowing he didn't believe as the rest of his family did, but was unable to admit it. With an effort, he thrust these thoughts aside. He couldn't afford to be distracted by personal problems. There was a job to do.

Following in Dilys's wake, he joined the group at the back of the church where, just below the organ loft, Dr Curtis was crouched down on the tiled floor by the pathetic bundle that had been Rhona Griffiths.

"Afternoon," she said curtly.

He watched as, with infinite delicacy so much at odds with her brusque manner, she lifted the matted hair from the face. Only one of Rhona's half-open eyes was visible. It stared out at him. Her cheek was spattered with blood and her tight brown curls were soaked in it. He felt a wave of pity shudder through him, followed by sharp anger at the waste of it all. Face grim, he ran his eyes slowly over what could be seen of the rest of the body, and finally came back to her right hand. He bent down to look more closely. It lay palm up, the fingers curved inwards. The nails were torn and there were flakes of some brownish substance under them. He bent forward to get a closer look. Yes, it was a dark mahogany brown. He got up and went round to look at her other hand, but there was nothing like it here, no flakes of anything, no tearing. The forensic team would, no doubt, find out what this substance was and tell him in due course, but it didn't stop him speculating.

"Chief Inspector," a voice called from immediately above him. He raised his head to see one of the SOCO team gazing at him from above. "Could you come up a moment, sir? There's something I think you should see."

"Get me some gloves, Dilys, would you?" Matt said as he searched round for the stairs. There was a narrow door behind the font which was ajar. He walked towards it, pulling on a pair of latex gloves as he did so. Here, a narrow flight of stairs curved upwards, cold stone on one side, wooden panelling on the other. A young woman in a disposable white suit was studying the treads carefully.

"Okay for me to go through?" Matt asked.

"Yes, sir. I've finished here."

All the same, Matt took great care as he went up, pulling his jacket close so as not to let it brush either side of the narrow stair, and stepping with as little pressure as possible on the wooden treads. In the organ loft, which sloped down in broad, shallow steps either side of the surprisingly large instrument, by a dark wooden rail were two more of the team.

"Afternoon, sir," said Glyn Pryce. "Getting quite an unfortunate reputation for itself, Pontygwyn is," he added.

"The village of doom," said his companion in a theatrically deep voice. "Bring us your women and we'll deal with them."

"I'd suggest less of the comic turns and more concentration on the job," Matt snapped at him. He knew gallows humour was part of their way of coping, but he wasn't in the mood.

"Sorry, sir," the man muttered, reddening.

"Okay Pryce, what have you got?"

"Over here, sir." He made his way down to the front of the organ and Matt followed him.

Chapter 22

On the organ loft side, there was plain wood panelling, although Matt had noticed the side facing the body of the church was elaborately carved. Pryce was standing by the panelling.

"These marks, sir. I missed them earlier on. What do you make of them?"

Matt bent to look more closely at the wooden rail. Most of it was satin smooth from year after year of devout polishing, but where Pryce indicated Matt noticed scratches in the glossy surface, and they looked new. He bent to look more closely. Three grooves, one very faint. He walked slowly along, studying the rail, but there were no similar marks. Turning, he came back, his eyes never leaving the rail until he'd studied its whole length.

"I know it's speculating, but I'd say these were made by someone's nails. And they're fresh. Did you notice the victim's fingernails, on the right hand?"

"Yes," Evans said. "That's what made me have another look up here."

"Well done. I'll send the photographer up, we want a record of these, every detail."

"And there's another thing, sir. We found this earlier too."

In front of the organ was a plain wooden stool, no cushion, just polished wood smoothed by many an organist's seat. Pryce was pointing at one corner, there were dark marks, something sticky, and some of the same substance had dripped on to the floor below. It looked like blood.

"What I thought, at first, sir, was that the lady fell and hit her head, became dizzy maybe, and toppled over the rail? But then, I don't think so; somehow, it's too high."

"You're right. I don't buy that either. Well done, Pryce. Get the SOCO team up here and have them go over it again. I want a fine-tooth comb job, okay?"

"Will do, sir," said Pryce, sounding pleased with himself.

Matt thought he knew how the grooves had been made, but he wasn't so sure about the blood on the organ stool. Did she jump or was she pushed? The old music hall phrase played out a rhythm in his mind. He made his way carefully down from the loft and walked across to Dr Curtis, who was busy putting her equipment into a battered but capacious leather holdall.

"I've finished here," she said. "It'll be okay for the lads to move her now."

"What was the cause of death?" Matt asked.

"How on earth do you expect me to answer that question at this stage?"

"I know you've probably got a pretty good idea."

"Maybe, maybe not."

"Come on, Doctor," Matt said, irritated. "What did you find?"

"Severe fracture of the skull. Back of the head smashed right in, which is probably what killed her. Broken femur in the left leg, probably other bones broken as well. Almost certainly massive internal bleeding. She came down with a hell of a whack, and these stone flags are decidedly unforgiving."

"What about the time of death?"

"You know I can't possibly say yet," she snapped, then relented a little. "She's dead some time, rigor's well established, although the temperature in here has to be accounted for."

"One thing. There're some marks up there, on the corner of the organ stool, looks like blood. Did you notice anything on the body that could account for it?"

"No, but I've hardly started. You really do seem to think I'm some kind of miracle worker. As I said before," her voice sounded as if she felt she was talking to a child with a decidedly low IQ, "you'll have to give me a chance to get her back to the mortuary. When I've finished the PM all the details will be in my report."

Matt knew he'd have to be satisfied with that. "Thank you, Doctor," he made himself say, but couldn't resist adding, "I need another quick PM. If this is murder, we could be dealing with some lunatic who's going to make a habit of it. I don't want Pontygwyn turning into the village from hell. As it is, the press is going to have a field day. An attractive teenager followed by a harmless spinster. What more could they want?"

"I'll do my best. For once, you'll just have to possess your soul in patience." She picked up her bag and stomped out of the church. Matt watched her go, wishing he could work with a pathologist who wasn't the human equivalent of Eeyore.

Matt stood silent while, with infinite care, the body was lifted on to a stretcher covered with a black plastic body bag. A moment later, it was zipped up and he could no longer see the smashed remains of Rhona Griffiths.

Dilys came and joined him. "Should we go over and talk to the vicar, sir?"

"Yes. I suppose we should."

"There's a WPC with her, but Pryce said she seemed pretty together about it. Shocked, of course, but apparently she was an A&E nurse before she was ordained, so death probably isn't quite so disturbing for her as it is for most people."

"I don't know so much," Matt said curtly. "It's pretty familiar to people in our job, but that doesn't mean it's easy to deal with. You just have to develop coping mechanisms."

Dilys shot him a questioning glance, but he didn't elaborate as they made their way out of the church and round to the vicarage. The front door was open, but Matt knocked anyway and waited for Cath to appear, the WPC following in her wake.

"Oh, it's you," Cath said, sounding relieved. "Come in. I thought it might be one of that crowd across the road. I was going to give them a piece of my mind."

"There's a police constable keeping a weather eye on them. He'll make sure they don't bother you."

"Good." She led them through to her study. "Can I get you some coffee or tea or something?"

"That'd be very nice."

"I'll do it," said the WPC. "I know where everything is from when you made ours."

"Bless you," said Cath, and sounded as if she meant it. "This is a dreadful business. Poor, poor Rhona. What can have made her do it? I had no idea she was that unhappy, which makes me feel very guilty. She was one of my most regular parishioners, and she worked like a Trojan keeping the church clean. Granted, she was a bit odd at times, and could go in for some rather malicious gossiping, but still, I'm sure her heart was in the right place."

Matt wondered if Fabia would agree with her. What was it she'd said of Rhona? A nosey old bag, always snooping into everything whether it was her business or not. Maybe it was a case of curiosity killed the cat, Matt thought bleakly.

"You believe she committed suicide, do you?" he asked.

"Didn't she? I've been going over and over it in my mind. She couldn't have overbalanced. The organ loft rail is far too high."

The WPC came back with their coffee on a tray. Matt leant forward and picked up a mug with a design of Tintern Abbey on it, spooned in sugar and wondered how to put what he wanted to say. "There is, of course," he began slowly, "the possibility that someone else was involved."

Cath Temple looked at him, horror in her eyes. "You mean, murder? Oh my God! Not another one. Are you sure?"

"Not as yet."

"If she was deeply religious, surely suicide would have been out of the question for her?" Dilys pointed out.

"I suppose so," Cath said, "but murder, what on earth is going on here?"

Matt treated the question as rhetorical. "Obviously we'll know much more when the forensic and scene of crime reports come in," he said. "Until then, I have to keep an open mind." He sat forward in his chair. "I need you to give me some idea of timings. I actually saw her leaving her house about eight o'clock yesterday evening, I was next door talking to Fabia Havard. Did you by any chance see Miss Griffiths later than that? Perhaps you could outline exactly what happened and when."

"I'll do my best." She spoke, hesitantly at first, then with more certainty. She said she'd gone across to the church about ten in the morning, described treading on the scarf in the porch. "I don't know why, but from then on I had this feeling something was wrong, the scarf felt so sort of slimy under my foot, I nearly fell over when I trod on it. Maybe that was why. I don't know."

Matt interrupted her. "Where is the scarf now?"

"I gave it to one of your men."

"Good. And then?"

"It was when I turned towards the font. At first, I thought it was a bundle of clothes, but then I saw her legs." She took a shuddering breath and Matt wondered if she was as much of a stoic as Dilys had suggested.

"Take your time," he said gently.

"I'm okay. It's just remembering how pathetic they looked, sticking out from under that floral skirt, with those ridiculous shoes still on her feet. And I remember the way one eye looked up – sorry." She took another shuddering breath and wiped a hand across her mouth. "I checked if she was still alive, but of course she wasn't. I already knew it really. Then I said a quick prayer while I knelt there, it seemed the right thing to do. After that I locked the door and ran back here to phone you lot."

"When was the last time you were in the church, before this morning?"

"Last night, just before nine I think. I was looking for my blasted cat and I noticed the door was ajar. Rhona must have ..." The colour drained from her face and a look of abject horror came into her eyes. "Oh my God!"

"What is it?" asked Matt, his interest quickening.

"I saw the door wasn't closed properly. I knew Rhona was due to do some cleaning late yesterday afternoon, so I just assumed she'd forgotten to lock up after her. I looked round the door and called out, but there was no answer, so I came back here and got the key, then locked up as usual. The thing is," she swallowed hard and looked near to tears, "do you think she was in there? Maybe if I'd found her then I could have saved her. She might still have been alive."

"I doubt it. From what the pathologist told me, I think death must have been instantaneous. There's no way of knowing, as yet, if she was in the church when you locked up, but there's very little chance you could have done anything to help her."

"Oh dear," Cath got up and began to pace about, "this is a terrible business. I must phone and speak to the bishop, let him know what's happened, and the archdeacon too, I suppose." She frowned, chewing absent-mindedly at a fingernail. "If Rhona was murdered, the church will probably have to be reconsecrated. I'm not sure of the exact form. This isn't a situation I've ever had experience of before."

"I'm sure you haven't," Matt said soothingly.

"Do you know when you'll be finished in there?"

"Probably by tomorrow morning."

"That soon. Well, thanks."

"Don't thank me. That's just the way it goes."

But she hardly seemed to hear him. "Do you need me anymore?" she asked anxiously. "I do rather need to make a few phone calls. The bishop will have to be told as soon as possible, and the churchwardens."

"We'll leave you to it then," Matt said, getting up from his chair. "We'll probably need to talk to you again, but that should be all for now. Will you be here for the rest of the day?"

"Yes, and most of tomorrow, unless there's some kind of emergency." She grimaced, realising what she'd said. "I don't think we need any more of those, do we?"

* * *

When Fabia caught sight of the police constable standing by Rhona's front door, she strode round to ask why he was there. By dint of a mixture of flattery and pulling rank, she managed to find out all she wanted to know. Shocked and disturbed she went back inside; she needed someone to talk to. She rang Cath, but the phone was engaged, and she was sure Matt would be with the SOCOs at the church. She'd just have to wait. Fabia thought back to last night and Rhona creeping furtively out of her front door, dolled up like a Christmas fairy. She'd seemed so excited, elated even. Fabia was positive she was off to meet someone. And then what had happened? Another killing wasn't beyond the bounds of possibility. Was Pontygwyn playing host to a serial killer? And if so, who would be next?

Fabia told herself speculating would get her nowhere. Just because Amber was murdered didn't mean Rhona had been too. She got up and went over to the window, looked next door to where the constable stood. Nothing else was happening out there yet. Just as she was about to move away, Matt's car pulled up outside Rhona's front gate. Fabia hurried from the room and out of the front door. By the time Matt emerged from his car, she was beside it.

"It's true then, about Rhona?"

"I'm afraid so."

"Suicide or murder?" Fabia asked, coming straight to the point.

"Not sure yet."

"This is terrible, Matt."

"You think I don't know that?" he snapped, glaring at her. He dropped his voice and went on. "We're pretty sure it's murder. Dilys suggested she might have seen or known something Amber's murderer found threatening. You said before she was in the habit of snooping around, spying on people."

"Yes. I'm afraid it ran in the family. Her father was just the same. Mrs Pritchard once told me he owned this incredibly expensive telescope, state of the art stuff at the time. He was always talking about studying astronomy, but the rumour was that he pointed it down rather than up and used it to spy on his neighbours. You see that dormer window up the top there with the glass sides?" she pointed up to the roof of Rhona's house. "That's where I understand he used to keep it, and I imagine you can see a hell of a lot from that vantage point." As Fabia spoke she saw Matt's eyes widen, knew that the same thought had occurred to both of them. "Why didn't I think of that before? She could have—" But Fabia was now talking to Matt's rapidly retreating back.

Chapter 23

Matt found Dilys directing operations in Rhona's sitting room. "Have you looked in the attic yet?"

"No, we've only just started on this floor, and there's the next floor up yet."

"Come with me."

"What's up, sir?"

"I'm not sure, it's just something Fabia said."

He took the stairs two at a time. On the landing they found a narrow door. It was locked. Dilys had Rhona's keys and tried one then another. On the fourth try, they were successful. The door creaked unpleasantly as it opened and revealed a narrow staircase. They made their way up it into the large gabled room. Matt paused to look around.

The floor was uncarpeted and the room obviously a repository for unwanted furniture. There was a stack of dining room chairs in one corner and two ancient Lloyd Loom armchairs, their paint dull and chipping, in another. In the middle was an ancient three leaf dining table, and backed up against it an old, sagging two-seater settee. All the furniture was covered in a thick film of dust. And yet, to the right of the window, tucked under the eaves, was an old tan leather suitcase with not a speck of dust on it. It was square cornered with stitching round the edges, expensive in its day, but battered and faded now, and either side of the handle were brass locks, polished and gleaming. It definitely had an air of being cared for.

Matt made his way to the window embrasure, but before he got there he was distracted by a framed photograph on a small shelf to one side of it. Some fresh flowers, daffodils and irises, stood on the shelf in a cut-glass vase, and before it were two small candle holders designed to hold night lights. The candles in them were half burnt down. On the other side was a free-standing brass crucifix of a particularly ugly design. It had obviously been polished quite recently.

Matt's mouth twisted in distaste as he studied the face in the photograph. It was of a man, unsmiling, his dark hair plastered close to his head. He had prominent ears and wore an expression of thin-lipped disapproval. The humourless, rather cruel eyes stared back at him. The photograph, like the candlesticks and the suitcase, looked as if it had been well cared for and dusted regularly.

"He looks like a teacher we had at school," Dilys said as she came up beside him. "Really nasty, he was. Got the sack for beating some poor kid half senseless. Dead weird isn't it, with the flowers and all. Wonder who he is?"

"Her father, I'd say. There's a strong likeness."

"Didn't she mention him when we interviewed her?"

"Yes, she did, several times, her dearest Da," Matt said, distaste in his voice. It would definitely be helpful to know more about Rhona's father, and her background generally. Fabia came immediately to mind as a source of information. Perhaps he'd drop in later, once he'd finished here. He tried to ignore the buzz of pleasure the thought gave him. Concentrate on the matter in hand. The telescope.

It stood in the dormer window on a custom-made stand, a magnificent instrument, all black metal and gleaming brass. Matt rummaged in his pocket for a pair of gloves and pulled them on, then he carefully lifted the end and put his eye to the lens, making sure he didn't come into contact with the metal. Gradually things came into focus. It was certainly a strong one, some seventy-five times magnification, and with the glass sides to the dormer, its position was perfect. A pigeon on a rooftop in Parc Road gave him a beady-eyed stare then flew off towards Gwiddon Pond. Matt followed its progress before swinging back along the length of the River Gwyn until he came to the bridge. The detail was amazingly clear. It would be a simple matter to pick out people on the bridge, and very easy to recognise them. Is that what had happened?

"This is an extraordinarily good instrument, Dilys. Have a look."

Dilys, who'd also pulled on a pair of gloves, took his place. "I'm not sure I'll be able to focus it properly."

"You won't have to. It's all set up. You realise what this means of course."

"What are you getting at?"

"Well, think about it. What a gift to a person who likes a good snoop into their neighbours' activities. It's a perfect way to keep an eye on everyone. She could gaze straight into people's bedrooms, watch them walking in the park, rowing or fishing on the pond. The range is fantastic. She'd be able to see into most of the gardens and houses on the opposite side of Morwydden Lane, those in this end of Parc Road, the activities in that warehouse, or whatever it is, between here and the High Street, and into some of the top floors of the High Street shops nearest the bridge. As to the bridge itself, clear as daylight." Matt could feel excitement mounting. "I think that's why she's dead. I think she saw Amber meeting somebody. Maybe she even saw whoever it was kill Amber."

"Isn't that rather a lot of speculation?" said Dilys.

"Maybe," Matt snapped, irritated, "but it fits, doesn't it?"

"But why didn't she tell us?"

"Would you, if you were going to try and make some money out of it?"

"No, I don't suppose I would, but nor would I put Rhona Griffiths down as a blackmailer."

"Well, not for money, perhaps, but there are other things she could have asked for."

Standing in the middle of the room, Matt looked round again, and once more his eyes came to rest on the leather case with its gleaming locks. He walked over to it, tried to lift the lid, and wasn't surprised to find it locked.

"Let's have that bunch of keys," he said to Dilys. "There were several smaller ones on it. We might come up lucky."

She handed them to him and he sorted carefully through them, looking for a small enough key to fit the locks on the case. There were only two that looked remotely possible. He tried the first one, but it wouldn't even go in. He tried the second. It went in smoothly enough and turned just a little way, then met resistance, but he kept trying. After a little manipulation there was a grating click as the key turned. The other side was easier. Dilys leant over his shoulder as he flipped the latches back and, very carefully, lifted the lid.

The case was full. There were stacks of what looked like hymn sheets and the like, some theatre programmes, none of them for recent productions, and several bundles of letters. A shoe box which, when Matt carefully lifted the lid, revealed another stash of letters, some with blue and red airmail markings round the edge, and several old-fashioned photograph albums. Matt closed the lid.

"Get a couple of the SOCOs up here to go through this lot, would you? With a bit of luck, it could tell us a great deal about her. No, on second thoughts, get Roberts onto it. It's right up his street, methodical stuff like this."

When Police Constable Roberts arrived, Matt told him what he wanted. "Make a record of absolutely everything, it doesn't matter how ordinary you think it may be, but anything that looks even remotely unusual or out of the ordinary, or relevant to the case in hand, I want to know about it immediately."

* * *

Knowing Matt and his team were next door made settling down to work impossible for Fabia. She tried to do some housework, but when she found herself standing, gazing blankly into space, while the hoover roared away on the same spot, she gave up. Striding determinedly out to the kitchen, she checked the cupboards and made a list of odds and ends she didn't really need, then tore it up. The last thing she felt like doing at the moment was trudging up to the High Street just for the sake of shopping that she could do any time. When she found herself at the window, gazing next door yet again, she decided a brisk walk was the only solution. She threw on her coat, wrapped a scarf round her neck against the chilly wind, and strode out of the house. Turning determinedly away from Rhona's, without even a glance next door, she strode off towards Parc Road.

Several times since that dinner with Alun Richards and the others – hard to believe it was only last week – she'd found herself thinking back, unable to leave the past alone. And it wasn't just Matt she'd been thinking about, it was Peter Harrison too, and the rest, that whole ghastly debacle. How long ago had it all begun? Ten years, if she went back to the very beginning.

Fabia sighed, stopped and looked around. Pontygwyn provided magnificent views to the east and north. From here, she could watch the blue and mauve shadows of clouds creating tumbling patterns across the lower slopes of the Brecon Beacons, moving with the wind over the patchwork of fields, and beyond to the distant hills. Down towards the end of the park, where the river disgorged itself from Gwiddon Pond, she could see the dun-coloured brick of Cwmcoed Farm nestling in the dip, and ribboning past it the road turning northeast towards distant Hereford. But the beauty of this countryside she loved so much was not having its usual calming effect. Matt's reappearance in her life, and Neville Breverton's involvement in the case, had brought back too many dark memories. Stupid to think she could have buried it all so easily. All she'd done was to clamp the lid on the cauldron for a while. Now it was thrown open again, getting the lid safely back in place wasn't going to be easy.

Ten years. Way back then, she'd just been made Inspector, the youngest female Inspector Milford Haven had ever had. That was when Peter Harrison had arrived.

"He's coming in from the Met" they'd been told by their chief superintendent. Pulpit Jim, they'd called him. Jim Evans, Chief Superintendent of police and part-time Baptist preacher.

"Harrison has had a great deal of experience with the new systems," he'd said, "and he's coming down here to bring us up to date, teach us how to be more efficient. I want your full cooperation, mind. I hope that's understood."

But she didn't think he'd meant quite the kind of cooperation she'd provided.

Peter had been dynamic, exciting, and incredibly attractive. Let's face it, Fabia thought now, I fell like a ripe plum straight into his hands – and his bed. She'd had no idea he was married, his wife and two children still in London. And even if she had known, would it really have made that much difference? she wondered bitterly. Fabia walked on, head down, lost in the past, no longer aware of the view.

It hadn't been long before the bubble burst, only three short months. Of course, they'd been discreet, but not discreet enough. Inevitably, someone had told Pulpit

Jim what was going on. Fabia still felt a sickening lurch of the stomach at the memory of the repercussions. Not only was it just the sort of behaviour to get him preaching morality; what she hadn't known was that Peter had a dual role. He'd also been brought in to ferret out some rotten officers in the drug squad; to clean things up. As far as the bosses were concerned, their relationship had completely undermined that part of his job.

Even now, anger rose inside Fabia over the injustice of being blamed for the whole affair. Overnight Peter cooled off and, from then on, virtually ignored her. There'd been no way he was going to allow their relationship to jeopardise his career. And as for Pulpit Jim, he'd made a real meal of it all.

"You have a straight choice, Inspector Havard." She could still hear the distaste in his voice and knew, as a woman, he would hold her entirely responsible. No doubt he'd preached many a sermon condemning the Jezebels of this world. "Either you leave the force now, or you accept this transfer to Cardiff and we forget about the whole sorry episode. Your disgraceful behaviour will not be referred to again by anyone, ever, and that includes you. I cannot allow the actions of one promiscuous young woman to destroy all the good work we've done here. Let that be an end to it."

If only it had been the end of it. Not for her. For months, years she'd waited for a phone call from Peter, seen him round every street corner, tensed at any mention of his name. It hadn't been until nearly three years later that she'd almost accepted his betrayal, and meeting Matt had finally helped her push Peter out of her mind. But then the whole affair had blown up in her face again.

Sick leave! What a farce. Fabia threw back her head, looked up into the wind, felt it grab at her hair. At last, she was rid of all that, she'd finally resigned. But a small voice in the back of her mind couldn't be denied. There was no way the wind could blow away the nightmare memories.

Of course, it wasn't the end of it, not now Matt was back in her life. It remained to be seen whether that was a bad or a good thing, but she had to admit, she wasn't optimistic.

Fabia stopped her steady trudging. It'd be lovely if she could just stand here, looking out across the hills, and consign the past to their ancient embrace. She gave a twisted smile, told herself not to be fanciful. She wasn't far from the farm now, must have walked nearly a mile and a half. Time to stop this brooding and go back.

Chapter 24

When Fabia got back, Matt's car was gone, although there were still two others parked outside Rhona's, and the police constable stood on guard by the door. She picked up the Newport Evening News from the mat as she walked in, carried it through to the kitchen and threw it on the table. First, a much-needed cup of tea, then she'd sit down and read it. There was bound to be something in there about Amber's murder. Of course, Rhona's death wouldn't be reported yet, but it wouldn't be long before the press pack descended.

As it happened, she didn't even get as far as filling the kettle. Her attention was arrested by the main photograph on the front page of the paper. There was Neville Breverton smiling out at her, dressed in a dinner jacket under a velvet-collared overcoat, his hand lifted in greeting to the photographer. Beside him was a woman Fabia found vaguely familiar.

Tea forgotten, she leant her hands on the table and read the headline. "Local MP Says His Piece for Women". Quickly she spread the paper out, sat down, and began to read. It was a report on a speech Neville had made at a dinner the night before.

"In his capacity as a Junior Minister in the Home Office with particular responsibility for violence in the home, Neville Breverton MP was invited to speak at a fundraising dinner last night for the charity, Full Stop. He is seen (above right) arriving at the Guildhall with Lady Rosalind Masterton QC, Patron of the Charity."

So, Neville had been in London last night. This put a completely different complexion on things. Fabia wondered if Matt knew. And there was something else. The fact that his speech had been given pride of place on page one did rather indicate his friendship with the editor was a strong one. Usually the front-page news was much more locally orientated. What happened in faraway Westminster was felt to be of little relevance here, in fact, since the advent of the new Welsh Assembly, people were inclined to resent coverage of national politics.

Fabia ran her eye down the page. At the bottom was a piece about Amber's murder, but there was little there that Fabia didn't know already. It was obvious Matt was keeping things very close to his chest, not giving the press any more information than was absolutely necessary. The reporter fulminated for a while about the safety of the streets, but said nothing useful, simply ending with advice to readers to contact the police if they had any information they thought might be helpful.

Her eyes travelled back up to the photo of Neville with his smug smile. Suddenly something that had been lurking at the back of her mind since Saturday pushed itself to the fore. "Oh, bugger!" she said aloud. That was it. Why hadn't she remembered before? Could these last two years have affected her powers of observation so badly? She felt an impotent anger with herself. She must put this right as soon as possible. Fabia grabbed the phone and, yet again, dialled Matt's number.

* * *

Late that afternoon PC Chloe Daniels knocked on Matt's office door. "I was just about to get going, sir," she said, face pink and eyes bright with satisfaction, "but I thought you might like to know what I'd come up with so far."

"Let's have it."

"This is the list of planning applications. I went back four years like you said: who was involved, who benefited, directors of the companies, etc. Then I did some research into local party funds. I think you'll find that bit by there quite interesting in the circumstances. As to the membership of the golf club etc, that was a bit more difficult, but I managed in the end, and the information about the Masons, well—" The pink of her cheeks darkened a little. "I asked my brother about that, sir. I hope you don't mind. I remembered he'd done a piece on the influence of the Masons in local government. Don't worry, I didn't tell him why I wanted to know, but I can usually get what I want from Gareth if I go about it the right way."

Matt smiled in spite of himself, "You obviously have your methods, constable."

"Yes, well, you said it was important. And here are the details on the last case Miss Havard was investigating before she was transferred from the Fraud Squad. Seems odd, really, her being taken off the case so suddenly, particularly as she seemed to have turned up quite a lot. It was that Cwmberis development – Vasic and his son. Apparently, at one point, it was thought the land had been contaminated, heavy metals, but nothing was ever proved. Old man Vasic's dead now, but the son, Tony, is still involved in several projects locally, some of them decidedly iffy. He's not come our way again yet, but it's rumoured he's got some very dodgy friends."

"There's no doubt about that. It's making anything stick that's the problem."

"Isn't that always the way, sir?"

Matt looked up at her eager face and wondered if she'd ever lose her enthusiasm for the job when she realised how very true that statement was. He hoped not.

"Good work, Chloe."

"Thank you, sir. Is there anything else I can help with?"

"Not at the moment, but what you've done so far is excellent. I won't forget this."

"Thank you, sir," she said again, and left the room positively glowing.

Matt got himself another cup of coffee, he seemed to be living on the revolting brew at the moment, and sat down again. He rubbed at his eyes and prepared to go through the information Chloe had put together, but before he could start reading, his desk phone rang. He grabbed at the receiver, "Lambert," he snapped.

* * *

It wasn't until much later that evening that Matt arrived on Fabia's doorstep. As soon as she opened the door to him, she could see he was in a bad way. He looked exhausted, drained of energy, his shoulders sagging and his eyes bloodshot.

"I'm sorry, I couldn't get away until now."

"No problem," she said, a little brisk. "You look knackered," she added, relenting a little.

He followed her into the kitchen. "It's a nasty one, this, and now we're getting it in the neck because there's been a second death. You know the score."

"You bet I do. Have you eaten?"

"No, but there's no reason why you should feed me," he said stiffly.

"Shut up Matt. Let's try and pretend we're friends, okay? I've got a piece of steak I didn't fancy which could do with eating up."

"Well, if you're sure." He sounded so awkward she almost laughed, but instead of answering she pushed an open bottle of wine across the table to him, and pointed to a cupboard. "The glasses are in there. There's lettuce and some watercress in the fridge, make a salad, and you'll find half a baguette in the bread bin."

Matt fetched the bread, tore off a chunk and began to chew at it absent-mindedly while he searched for the salad. As Fabia cooked she went on talking, wanting to fill the silence as much as anything else. "I've got some odds and ends to tell you. Of course, you might know some of it already—"

"Fire away."

"It seems Neville Breverton was at a dinner in London last night, some charity do, and it's covered in the Newport rag, photo and all. I doubt very much he could have been home earlier than three in the morning, if then."

"Dilys picked up on that one and had the same thoughts. But it doesn't alter the fact he was involved with Amber."

"I suppose not. Have you got a time of death on Rhona yet?"

"No. Pat Curtis is doing the PM tomorrow morning."

"Was it murder?"

"Probably."

"Poor little dab of a woman," Fabia said sadly. "I'm afraid I wasn't very nice to her these last few days." For a while she concentrated on her cooking, then lifted the steak onto a plate and put it down in front of him. She sat down opposite and poured herself some wine.

Matt ate in brooding silence for a moment, slicing into the succulent meat and chewing away rapidly. After a few minutes he looked up, shamefaced. "Sorry. I hadn't realised how hungry I was."

"Don't worry, you go ahead," Fabia said, twirling her glass slowly and watching the light play on the wine inside, thinking as she did so how good it was to have Matt sitting in her kitchen. She gave him a tentative smile. "It feels a bit like that first case we did together, the Glynmor gang, remember? I think I was your sole source of food for about three weeks."

He said nothing, hardly seemed to have heard what she said, just went on eating. The smile on Fabia's face faded. She felt snubbed. Anger niggled, but she pushed it aside. Better to change the subject. "Did you have a look at that telescope of Rhona's?"

Now he did look up at her, frowning slightly. Fabia got the impression his thoughts were returning from a long way off. She wondered what he'd been thinking.

"Telescope?" At last he answered her question. "Good Lord yes, it's the most fantastic instrument. She could have spied on the whole of Pontygwyn with that – well nearly all of it – and it's in pristine condition, obviously been well looked after and used regularly. The focus was spot on. Have you ever been up into that attic of hers?"

"Not recently. Has she still got that shrine to her father up there?"

"Yup, gave me the creeps. He didn't look a particularly pleasant chap."

"He wasn't. You should have heard my Auntie Meg on the subject. He was still alive when she lived here and she used to tell me the most awful horror stories about him. It's no wonder Rhona is... was like she was."

Matt pushed his plate away. "That was delicious. Just what I needed. Thank you so much." And the smile he gave her across the table was completely natural. Fabia's heart gave a jolt, for a moment he looked so much like his old self. But this was no good. Nothing could come of trying to turn back the clock. It had been her, after all, who'd held back from getting too involved before. There was no mileage in sitting here mulling over past mistakes. She shrugged dismissively. "I'm glad you enjoyed it," she said.

"Okay," said Matt, rubbing a hand across his eyes, "as you suggested we've picked up that nearly new stuff from the vicar. Luckily the sale isn't until tomorrow evening, so it was still all there. You were right, the fabric matches. We'll be following that up."

"I know it's tenuous, but it does rather point in one direction, doesn't it?"

"But making it stick, that's going to be the problem, unless we turn up some more evidence, and a motive, for that matter. We've got that message Amber left, but we need more."

Matt slumped down in his chair, his legs thrust out in front of him. The silence drew out and neither spoke. It lengthened to uncomfortable proportions, and then both spoke at once.

"Fabia, I wanted to talk to you–"

"What's next? Have you–"

Both smiled, embarrassed. There was another awkward pause. "You first," said Fabia.

Matt leant forward, cradling his glass in his hands, gazing down at it. She wondered what was coming next. When he finally spoke, it wasn't at all what she expected.

"I had a drink with Alun Richards the night before last. He told me you and some others get together occasionally, for old time's sake, and I... and, well, I wondered why on earth we don't."

Fabia felt a spurt of anger bubble up inside her. That had to be a question he could answer for himself. Surely, he should know why? "For Christ's sake, Matt, you–"

"I know, I know," Matt said quickly. "What I mean is, what does Alun know that I don't? Sorry," he interrupted her protest, "that didn't come out right either. I mean, it's my fault I don't know exactly what went on before you left. I should have made it my business to find out at the time. And now you've actually resigned, I just couldn't – oh God, Fabia, I just–"

"Believed all the scuttlebutt and didn't bother to come to me and ask what really happened?"

"After that row we had?" Matt protested, glaring at her. "I assumed you wouldn't want to talk to me."

"Assumed!" Fabia almost shouted. "How difficult would it have been to find out? I thought you cared about me, Matt. You told me you did. What's worse, I thought you knew me. And yet you were willing to walk away, make no effort to patch things up. How do you think I felt about that?"

He didn't reply, just continued to look at her under frowning brows. Below his eyes, deep shadows stood out in his white face, his dark hair flopped down over his forehead and he didn't bother to push it back. His broad shoulders were hunched, he looked completely defeated. Her anger evaporated. Poor Matt. She couldn't help feeling sorry for him.

She leant across the table and touched his hands with the tips of her fingers. "Look, let's take this wine into the sitting room and try to clear away some of the cobwebs. I'll tell you the full story, if you really want to know. And you can tell me how you're feeling. I've been thinking about Bethan too these last few days, and I do have some idea of how difficult this case must be for you."

"Nothing I can do about that," he said, his eyes bleak, "and you'd better make coffee, got to drive back."

Fabia grimaced. "True, the last thing you need is one of your PCs pulling you over for a breath test."

Chapter 25

Once settled in the sitting room, neither spoke for a while. Earlier on Fabia had lit a fire to cut the chill in the air and in a vain attempt to cheer herself up. It had died down and she bent to sort it out, not satisfied until the flames were licking up around the logs she'd added to the smouldering remains.

Matt sprawled back in an armchair, his chin on his chest, his coffee mug nursed between his long fingers. He watched her as she prodded at the wood. Fabia felt his eyes on her and wondered what he was thinking. Still kneeling on the hearth rug, she twisted round to look at him. "Can you honestly say you know nothing of what went on?" she asked him.

"Well, not nothing."

"Didn't you go to someone and ask about the reasons for the sick leave?"

"No. I thought there was every reason for you to feel incredibly stressed, so I suppose I put it down to that. I hardly wanted to add to it by giving you the third degree, particularly not after that row."

"Oh Matt, isn't curiosity part and parcel of being a police officer? How could you stop yourself asking around?"

"You know I hate gossip, and anyway, I thought you'd prefer it if I just kept out of things."

Fabia sighed, understanding but exasperated at the same time. She tucked her legs up under her and leant back against the settee. "You'd better start by telling me what you do know."

Matt stirred, seeming uncomfortable with this direct approach, and Fabia's exasperation increased. "For goodness sake, let's talk about this once and for all. No-one's completely impervious to gossip. Surely you must have picked stuff up, if only in the canteen."

"No, not then." His tone cooled. "And I wasn't about to sit in the canteen earwigging the chit-chat, you know that's something I never do."

"Don't be so bloody self-righteous," she snapped. "You're making yourself sound like a total prig."

"Thanks a bunch!"

"I'm sorry, but that's how it comes across." Then she added, her voice quieter but cool as well. "Perhaps it's just that you didn't care enough to find out."

Matt said nothing, just glared at her. In the end, she relented. "I appreciate you don't like gossip. And people knew we were close friends, so there's always a possibility they clammed up when you were around."

"Probably."

"But I'm amazed you didn't ask, say, someone like Alun Richards."

"I knew you were involved in a fraud case that started up just after I went off on that course, but by the time I got back it was all done and dusted. It wasn't until I asked Alun about it this week, when we met for a drink, that I found out any details."

"You could have come and asked me." It was a cry from the heart.

"That's what he said." He held a hand out to her, but she didn't take it. His shoulders sagged. "What can I say? I'm truly sorry, really I am."

"Water under the bridge now," she said, trying to dismiss it, but knowing she couldn't. "What did Alun tell you?"

"He said Neville Breverton was a city councillor at the time, in Cardiff, and he was the front-runner for selection as Labour candidate. I suppose that must have been for the by-election a few years ago."

"Yes, it was."

"He told me Breverton was a close friend of Vivian Sligo, the then ACC. That they were both Masons and also belonged to the same clubs, golf and all that, and that their wives were related or something."

"Cousins."

"You got a tip-off about a dodgy property deal involving old man Vasic and a few others. It was rumoured the land was contaminated, but Breverton had made sure planning permission went through nice and smooth. He said it was also rumoured that a senior police officer had some kind of financial involvement. Is that right so far?"

"The bare bones, yes."

"Alun said you went to Rees-Jones, who was then your immediate superior, and soon after that the whole thing went pear-shaped. Alun told me you said they'd poisoned police work for you, made you feel grubby and ashamed of yourself, though why you should he can't imagine." He paused and took a deep breath. She waited, dreading what would come next. "And he told me he thought they'd got some hold over you, that's why you gave in so easily and took the sick leave."

Fabia made a small sound of protest and he stopped. His eyebrows were raised, his face anxious, and she could tell he was asking for reassurance, but she said nothing.

"The last thing he told me was that he'd heard something about you having an affair with a fellow officer when you were at Milford Haven, and he thought that might have had something to do with... well... why you let them get the better of you. That's about it."

Strange, Fabia thought, how she'd not thought about Peter much for months, and yet today he'd hardly been out of her mind. She looked at Matt, wondering now why she hadn't made him listen to her side of the story at the time. Looking back, she realised it wasn't so much to do with the row they'd had, it was that she hadn't wanted to tell him about Peter. At the time, she'd been afraid it would make him think less of her. Matt could be such a puritan at times. And quite apart from this, she'd convinced herself it was best they should go their separate ways. After all, she, of all people, had known only too well that having a relationship with a fellow officer was asking for trouble.

But now she wondered if she'd made the right decision. Quite apart from anything else, it had deprived her of a good friend – and deprived him of one as well, she supposed. And she knew now that she'd loved him, back then. She just hadn't had the courage to take the risk, too afraid that a relationship with Matt would turn out just as disastrous as the one with Peter.

Gazing into the patterns made by flames licking up round the wood in the fire, slowly she began to speak. Without emotion, but not sparing herself any of the details, she told Matt about the affair with Peter and all the repercussions. He listened, slumped back in his chair, his fingers steepled in front of his face masking his expression, making it difficult for her to tell how he was reacting.

"But what has all this got to do with Breverton and Rees-Jones?" Matt asked finally.

Fabia rubbed her hands wearily over her face and went on. "Unfortunately, rather a lot. The more I delved into that building project, the more obvious it became it was dodgy, and that both Neville and Sligo were involved.

Trouble was the evidence was all circumstantial, or merely hearsay, and a couple of the contacts I had weren't exactly model citizens, although I'd have sworn they were telling the truth this time. The whole thing was bloody dynamite."

She could feel the old mixture of frustration and anger welling up inside her, giving the lie to her conviction she'd put it all behind her. It was still there, deep down, a festering wound that had never healed. Stupid to think otherwise. She sighed as she went on.

"At that time, I thought Rees-Jones was on my side. I took the whole thing to him, and at first he supported me, but not for long. I'm not saying he's dishonest as such, I just think that, for him, the reputation of the force came before the career of one officer, particularly a female officer. He was willing to sacrifice me for what, to him, was the greater good. So, it all blew up in my face. Sligo insisted the investigation was to be dropped, Rees-Jones went along with him, and it was made clear if I didn't do so too, my affair with Peter would be resurfaced, thus ruining not only my career but possibly his as well."

Matt frowned down at her. "So why didn't you fight? You're not the sort to give in to blackmail."

"If it'd been just me I might have." She shook her head. "But it was Peter as well–"

"For Chrissake, Fabia, he'd left you to carry the can. You owed him nothing."

Fabia sighed wearily. "It wasn't for him," she said, "it was for his wife."

Matt made a disbelieving sound, but Fabia went on, not allowing him to interrupt. Now she'd started, she might as well tell him the whole story.

"Don't get me wrong, I'm not some lily-white idiot whose guilt over her adultery suddenly got the better of her." Her tone was scalding, allowing herself no mercy, but then she spoke more quietly. "It was complicated, Matt. The poor woman was dying, some sort of cancer. I found out through someone Peter and I had both worked with. If

I'd fought – no, I couldn't have done that to her, poor woman. Anyway, what I said to Alun was right. At the time all I wanted was to get the hell out of there, and the sick leave business seemed the best way to do it without losing out too much financially. Back then, I had no idea I could make any kind of living out of my painting, so I thought that was the best solution." Fabia sighed as she looked up at him. "So, there you have it."

Suddenly Matt gave her a twisted grin. "I should imagine the Brevertons are shitting bricks wondering whether or not you'll rake up the past now."

"I'll not do that unless I have to, but I'll be damned if I'm going to sit back and let Neville get away with this as well." She sat forward, eager again. "One thing I heard from one of my contacts at the time – and you have to remember this is all rumour – is that Neville had had an affair with an under-age girl. Her father kicked up a fuss, but Sligo fixed it for him and the whole thing was swept under the carpet. Neville owed Sligo, with a vengeance, so maybe he paid him, in cash. What do you think?"

"For God's sake, Fabia!"

Feeling slightly light-headed with relief that it was all out in the open, she grinned at him. "Just a theory, but one that's plausible. And now we have all this. Okay, maybe he didn't kill Amber, but he certainly had motive enough. Maybe he got someone else to do it for him. It's worth investigating, isn't it? I'm quite happy to see the bastard sweat a little while you rummage around."

"We don't know for sure that he didn't kill her himself. I know this London business complicates things, but if he thought Amber was going to go to the tabloids about their affair, if all that speculation of yours has a grain of truth in it, he could well have felt she had to be silenced."

"On the other hand, just because he's had to do with a few bent business deals doesn't make him a murderer," Fabia said, playing devil's advocate.

228

"Like you said, maybe he paid someone else to get rid of her."

"To be honest, I think that's a bit farfetched, don't you?"

"Wouldn't you say that depends on how ambitious he is?"

"He's certainly ambitious, but so's Gwen. There've been times when I wouldn't put murder past her."

Matt's eyes widened. "Now, that's an angle I hadn't thought of."

For a while they sat in the flickering firelight, absorbed in their own thoughts. Fabia felt drained, but somehow content. Although she didn't expect their friendship to return to its old easy ways, she was relieved there was no longer that dark barrier of unspoken questions between them. Of course, they'd never work together as they used to, now that she wasn't a colleague, but perhaps there were advantages to that. At least, now she was no longer his superior, they could meet as equals, and neither was she constrained by the rules of police procedure. She almost smiled at the thought. A free hand? Now that was certainly a delightful prospect. But best not to say anything about that to Matt at the moment. She didn't want him panicking about what she might or might not do.

Matt stirred, pushed himself up out of his chair and glanced at his watch. "God, it's nearly half twelve. I must get going. I've got to be back in the office by seven." He smiled at her, tentative, a little embarrassed. "I'm so glad we've, you know, cleared all this up. It's been a weight on my mind for so long."

"Me too," Fabia said quickly, not wanting to continue this particular conversation, not at the moment. It'd take more than one evening for the pain of the last two years to be washed away. She followed him to the door. "What's first on the menu tomorrow?" she asked briskly.

"After the briefing and setting up the usual routine vis-à-vis Rhona Griffiths, almost certainly a disagreeable interview with the chief. He's bound to hold me entirely responsible for a second death," he said bitterly. "And later on, we're seeing Amber's mother. We've finally managed to fix a time. The poor woman is still sedated, but her doctor says she should be up to it now."

"I must drop round and see her. What time will you be there?"

Matt gave her a sharp look. "Half eleven, that's the arrangement. Why do you want to see her?"

"She's a friend of mine, Matt. I want to know if there's anything I can do to help." Her eyes wide and innocent, she asked, "What else would I be going round there for?"

He obviously wasn't happy with this answer but said nothing. Fabia smiled at him as she opened the front door. He reached out a hand to her, bent as if to kiss her goodbye, but she stepped back. She wasn't ready for that kind of intimacy yet. She didn't know if she ever would be. This had to be taken slowly.

Chapter 26

Fabia woke early the following morning and, in that no man's land between waking and sleeping, felt an unexpected upsurge of pleasure at being alive. For a moment her mind groped around for a reason, and then she remembered the evening before. The painful splinter of misunderstanding between her and Matt didn't feel nearly as sharp any more. She got up and stretched, smiling to herself, but it wasn't long before thoughts of the events of the last few days sobered her mood.

She pushed the curtains back. The morning promised to be bright and sunny, the daffodils and narcissi were nodding in a gentle breeze and the apple tree rained pink and white blossom on the lawn. The weather obviously wasn't aware of the tragedies being played out in Pontygwyn. Fabia dressed quickly and, after a breakfast of black coffee, flung on her coat and left the house.

All was quiet, except for a solitary police constable on duty by Rhona's front door. Fabia lifted a hand in greeting and, as she did so, wondered what Matt was doing, whether he'd set out for his first call of the day. For a second, doubts crept into her mind about what she was about to do, but she pushed them aside, got into her car, and drove determinedly round to Well House.

The woman who answered Fabia's knock was Mrs Greaves, the Coles' next-door neighbour. Fabia had met her a couple of times, but didn't know her well.

"Oh, Miss Havard," she said, her expression a mixture of relief and disappointment. "I thought you might be that chief inspector. Murray left a message to tell him Cecily still isn't up to seeing him, but I thought he might have come anyway."

"I doubt he'd do that."

"Maybe not, but still, it is important he speaks to her isn't it?"

"Yes, but he'll probably ring and make another appointment."

"I suppose so." She didn't sound too sure. "Do come in. Murray had to go out and didn't want the poor love left on her own, that's why I'm here."

Fabia walked past the woman into the hall. "How is Cecily?" she asked.

"As well as can be expected, still sedated, but she's awake. She'd probably like to see you, you being a friend and all, but would you mind if I go and ask her if it's okay?"

In a very short time she returned. "Cecily says she'd like to see you, come on up."

Fabia followed her up the stairs and into a large bedroom. The curtains were drawn almost completely across the windows, making the light in the room dusk-like and rather oppressive.

"Here's Miss Havard to see you, love. I'll pop home now, but I'll be back later this morning." She closed the door firmly behind her and Fabia sensed her relief at getting away for a while.

Fabia made her way across to the bed where Cecily lay, her mousey hair untidy on the pillow, her body curled foetal with the covers drawn tight up to her neck. Her face was waxy pale, the eyes enormous and red-rimmed. She looked like someone suffering from some debilitating illness. Not, thought Fabia, that she'd ever been the most colourful person – more inclined to blend into the background than make her presence felt. Not for the first time, Fabia wondered where Amber had got her spectacular dark looks. Must have been from her father, as this frail woman was nothing like her daughter had been. A wave of pity swept over her as she sat on the edge of the bed. She put a hand out to touch Cecily's fingers where they clutched at the covers under her chin.

"I had to come to say how very sorry I am about Amber, and to see how you are," she said. "If there's anything at all I can do, you only have to say."

The pale blue eyes gazed up at her. Cecily's lips moved as if preparing to speak, but no sound came out at first, then she said, sounding as if it took a great effort to articulate the words, "Thank you Fabia. I really need to talk to you." She said nothing else for a long drawn out moment, then went on, "But I feel so... so confused. I can't remember what it was..." Her voice trailed away as her eyelids slid down. Fabia waited, but before Cecily spoke again, the bedroom door opened, and Murray Cole walked in.

Fabia was shocked at his appearance as well. Gone was the usual assertive charm. He looked diminished, just as Cecily did. In a way, the distressed state he was obviously in made her think better of him.

"Murray," she said, getting up and going over to take his hand, "I'm so sorry about all this. You must be having a dreadful time, the two of you. I was saying to Cecily, if there's anything I can do."

"Thank you. It's at a time like this one realises who one's true friends are." He drew her over to the window and said in hushed tones. "Cecily is completely distraught as you can probably see. Dr Cook has sedated her, but she doesn't seem to be able to rest at all, and her mental state really has me worried. Half the time I can't understand what she's talking about. It's terrible to watch her suffer so, just terrible."

"I'm sure it is."

Fabia looked over her shoulder at the woman in the bed. She'd pushed herself up from the pillows and was looking across at them, extreme anxiety in her face. Her lips moved soundlessly, and a moment later Fabia heard her own name. She went back to the bed, took Cecily's hand.

"What is it dear?"

"Amber, my baby, where's Amber?"

Fabia's heart went out to her. She put an arm round Cecily and felt her flinch, as if she'd been hit, then she clutched at Fabia's sleeve.

"Don't let them send her away. Please, please, don't let them send her away."

"Cecily, my love." Cole was on the other side of the bed, his eyes full of concern. He straightened the cardigan his wife was wearing, gently doing up the top two buttons, then he picked up a small bottle, shook some pills into his palm and took up a glass of water from the bedside table. "Take these. The doctor said you should take two every four hours. They'll help you sleep."

Fabia watched as Cecily swallowed the pills down, realising there was no point in trying to find out what it was she'd wanted at the moment. It'd have to wait until she was more coherent. She glanced up at Cole, shrugged and smiled, "I'll leave you alone now. But please don't hesitate to give me a ring if there's anything I can do, anything at all."

"You're very kind," he said over the top of his wife's head as he settled her back on to the pillows.

As she went down the stairs to the front door, Fabia wondered how long it would be before Cecily was in a fit state to see Matt. In that drugged state, there was little he'd be able to get out of her. But at least now she knew she'd been right on one point. She must tell Matt. She thrust her hand into the bag over her shoulder for her mobile and selected his number.

* * *

"That's useful." Matt sat holding his mobile to his ear while he leafed through some papers on his desk. "I'll follow it up. And thank you for feeding me last night." He knew it sounded stilted, but there were still barriers that had to be negotiated. He wondered how long it would be before he could feel completely at ease with Fabia again. His guilt over the past wouldn't leave him easily and, until that was resolved, he supposed there'd still be this shadow hanging over their relationship. "I've got a desk piled high with junk," he said, "and no time to sit and sort it all out. Plenty of info coming in, but nothing I can act on yet, and a whole load of loose ends with not enough time to tidy them up. Other than that, I've nothing to do." He heard her laugh and had a sudden urge to go round and see her. "Will you be home later on today?"

"I should be." He thought he could hear caution in her voice. "My agent's moaning about deadlines, and since it's the first really good commission I've had, I really must get some work done."

"I won't come round if it's not convenient."

"No, no. I'll probably be glad of the break."

"If you're right and trying to interview that poor woman is a waste of time, I'll cut it short and come at about one. Oh no, I can't then. How about early evening? Would that be okay?"

"Sure." Now he was almost certain she was laughing at him. Rescue came in the form of a knock and Dilys's head appearing round the door. He nodded and flapped a hand at her. She came the rest of the way in, followed by Chloe Daniels, who closed the door quietly behind them.

"Got to go, Fabia. I'll see you later." He ended the call with a regretful sense of relief. "You two look full of news," he said.

"It's mostly Chloe that's done the work," Dilys told him. Chloe Daniels' cheeks flushed up in gratification. "She's turned up some tidy bits and pieces. Trouble is, some of them might not go down very well with him upstairs."

"I see. Have a seat and fire away."

Chloe Daniels settled in a chair, her face glowing with enthusiasm. "You know I pointed out that contribution to Labour Party funds in the run-up to Neville Breverton getting elected?" Chloe said. "Well, I've got confirmation now that it came from the Vasic clan, perfectly legal, but still, it establishes a connection. That's one thing. And there's this about Paul Vaughan's involvement with the Golden Monkey." She leant forward and handed Matt a piece of paper. "Gareth got it for me. This here is the holding company, they've got three nightclubs, the Golden Monkey in Newport, Club 59 in Cwmbran and the Blue Banana in Caerphilly. It seems Vaughan stepped in and rescued the company when it was facing some financial problems, and now he's the major shareholder. Now, this is a list of directors. You see that name by there? He's been up for dealing in class A drugs in the past, but he got himself some fancy London lawyer and the case was dropped, and down here, we have our friend Tony Vasic."

"Nice colleagues our Mr Vaughan's got," said Dilys dryly. "Interviewing those kids about their involvement with the Golden Monkey doesn't seem nearly so urgent now, that part of the investigation has gone way beyond that."

"You could say so, maybe set it aside for another time?" suggested Dilys.

"Good idea," Matt said.

But Chloe hadn't finished. "And then there's this," she went on. "I came across it by chance, thought it might be useful." She pushed a newspaper cutting across to Matt. It was a report in one of the tabloids, dated the day before, of one Mel Franklin, famous model and budding singer, and beside her was a dapper man in pinstripes. She was holding up a hand as if to shield her face from the cameras. The man was scowling into the lens. The report said he was her solicitor. Another photograph showed Paul Vaughan getting into a car and glaring at the camera as he did so. "She's up on a charge of possession, cocaine, and the reporter implies she's dropped her boyfriend in it, says he got her onto drugs and he's the one who supplied her."

"That's that relationship down the drain then," Dilys said, her tone acid. "He certainly made no mention of anything like this when we saw him.

"Well he wouldn't, would he?" said Matt. "Maybe he didn't even know she was going to drop him in it, would have stopped her otherwise."

"He denies knowing anything about it," Chloe said. "Says she's so drugged up she doesn't know what she's talking about, and he's been trying to get her off the drugs, not put her onto them. Anyway, he's not been taken in for questioning yet."

"It'd be worth our having another word with him, now we know about this; for future reference if for no other reason. Maybe he did the same sort of favour for Amber Morgan. I'd like to speak to whoever's in charge of the case against Mel Franklin. Fix that up, Dilys, would you?"

"Will do."

"Is that all, then?" Matt asked, raising a quizzical eyebrow at Chloe.

"Just one more thing." She paused for effect, her eyes bright with zeal. "It turns out Neville Breverton's connection with the Evening News isn't with the editor. Apparently, he's big butties with the owner of the paper, they were at school together and have been close as," she crossed two fingers, "ever since, so that's tidy, isn't it?"

"Good God, this whole business is so bloody incestuous."

"Par for the course, sir," Dilys said wryly, "after all, this is South Wales." Matt grinned at her as she went on. "You asked me to have a word with the sergeant who heads up the domestic violence unit. There's no record of our friend being reported at any time, but that doesn't mean anything really, only a tiny percentage of hitters ever come to our attention."

"We'll just have to go about it another way. Good work, Chloe, and I'm sure I don't have to remind you, this is strictly between the three of us."

"No, sir."

"You've done very well. I won't forget this." When she'd left the room, Matt turned to Dilys, frowning. "She is completely safe, isn't she?"

"Safe as houses, I'd say. Anyway, she's not going to blot her copybook where you're concerned. Can't you tell she's taken a shine—"

"Piss off, Dilys," he said amiably. "I think I'll put Chloe on to Craig Evans, let her have a quiet word and see if anything else comes of it, he might open up to her."

"Why not ask Miss Havard to have another word with him? You said she was willing to do so."

"I could, I suppose." But he wasn't at all sure he wanted to involve her even more. It went against his old habit of never bending the rules. But Chloe's researches weren't exactly by the book, were they? Maybe he was getting to be more of a rebel. Fabia had always said you had to be to get results. Exasperated, he ran his hand through his hair. He didn't want to believe it, but he was beginning to think she'd been right all along.

And now he had two murder investigations on his plate. Which one should he concentrate on? The answer was obvious. Both, since he had a very strong feeling they were connected. "You're right, we should chase up the Evans boy, find out what it was he was going on about

238

when he met Fabia. I really don't want him to clam up completely, but I'd prefer to keep it official. It's getting the balance, that's the problem. We'll try Chloe first and keep Fabia in reserve."

Dilys gave him a curious look and he was sure she was dying to ask about Fabia but, much to his relief, she didn't.

"I'll arrange things with Chloe."

He changed the subject. "Did you check on Neville Breverton's movements?"

"I managed to speak to a friend of mine who's working on security at the House of Commons. I used to be at college with him. He checked, and apparently Breverton was in the House all day, went straight to the dinner from there, and left about midnight. The security was pretty tight, as per usual, so there were plenty of people who saw him there. He stayed in the flat the Brevertons have in Dolphin Square overnight. One of the security men there saw his car return about 12.30, and he left at crack of dawn Monday morning. So that looks like he's out of the picture so far as Rhona Griffiths is concerned."

"Unless she was killed a bit later Monday morning, but Pat Curtis thinks she'd been dead for well over twelve hours when the vicar found her." Matt grimaced, then brightened. "Okay, so maybe we won't get him for murder, but we might well be able to rock his boat on the contributions to party funds, and his dodgy friends, ex-Assistant Commissioner Vivian Sligo included. The old bastard was retired with a golden handshake before anything could rise to the surface, but that doesn't mean we can't stir things up a bit now. I owe that much to Fabia at least."

Dilys's eyebrows lifted, questioning, but Matt didn't elaborate. As he got up and shrugged on his jacket all he said was. "As far as I'm concerned this is payback time." Slightly embarrassed at his own vehemence, he glanced up at Dilys and surprised a look of complete understanding on her face. She grinned at him. "Go for it," she said.

He gave a rueful laugh. "There's not much I can get past you, is there? Come on, we'll get out to the Coles' now, see if Mrs Cole is up to being interviewed."

"I checked on that conference Mr Cole was at," Dilys told him as she followed him out of the room. "It's all legit. It wound up after lunch on Thursday, so he would have set off for home about mid-afternoon I suppose, which tallies with what he's already told us."

"I thought it would. We mustn't forget to ask him about the phone call Rhona made, and have you found out what church do Cecily Cole was at that afternoon?"

"Doing the flowers for a wedding on Thursday morning."

"Thursday? Do people get married on a Thursday?"

"Seems like it."

"Right. Let's go." Matt stopped suddenly as they went through the main office and Dilys nearly cannoned into him.

"Get someone to check if Mr Vaughan is at home, or if not, where his office is. I'd like another word with him as well, see if we can squeeze anything out of him about this drugs business. If he was supplying Amber and her friends, it might well be relevant. We don't want to get locked into one idea too soon and then end up with egg on our face. And after that, we tackle that bloody MP again. This time we're going to put the wind up him, no mistake." And sod the chief, Matt thought.

Chapter 27

In spite of the message from Cole, Matt and Dilys drove up to Well House at lunchtime on the off chance they might finally manage to interview Cecily, but without success. Cole told them she was still sedated and, although outwardly helpful, added little to what they knew already. Yes, he had arrived home early on Thursday evening; no, Cecily was not at home at the time; yes, he had had a phone call from Rhona Griffiths.

"She wanted to speak to my wife, and when I told her Cecily was out, she proceeded to go on and on about some set to she'd had with Amber."

"When did she say this was?" Matt asked.

"God knows. Sometime last week. That woman, well, one doesn't want to speak ill of the dead but–" He paused, obviously reluctant to go on.

"Anything you have to say can hardly harm her now," Matt said. "Please go on."

"I suppose that's true. I'm sorry to say it, but in my opinion she was dangerously unbalanced. Her preoccupation with the young, and with Amber in particular – all I can say is her attitude was thoroughly unhealthy, a mixture of fascination and repulsion. She was always phoning Cecily, or stopping her in the street, to complain about Amber's clothes, her behaviour, her language, and she had the temerity to suggest that Cecily was not a fit mother. I have to say, I was very angry about that. There was nothing about our poor Amber that she didn't find to complain about. It really was very unpleasant." He frowned at Matt, hesitant again. "I have to say, I wouldn't be surprised if you find she had something to do with Amber's death."

Matt and Dilys remained determinedly silent, waiting for him to go on and reluctant to stem the flow. "I'm not saying she was directly responsible," he added hurriedly, "no, but I can't help thinking she had something to do with it."

"In what way," Matt asked.

"God knows, it's just a feeling – a suspicion," he said.

"But that doesn't explain the attack on Miss Griffiths herself," Matt said.

"I suppose not, if there was one." He sighed, shook his head. "I'm afraid I think she did away with herself, and that would follow, wouldn't it?"

"Perhaps it would." Matt was not about to tell him they were almost certain Rhona had been murdered, not until the full report came through from Pat Curtis. He thanked Cole for his time, stressed once more how important it was they speak to his wife, and asked that they should be allowed to do so later that day. Cole assured them he understood and promised to contact them as soon as his wife was sufficiently recovered. Matt thought ruefully that it would take longer than a few hours or days for that to happen.

From the Coles', they drove on up St Madoc's Road to Brynymor Lodge to tackle Paul Vaughan. But this call was also unproductive. Vaughan was in Cardiff, they were told by his pugilistic henchman, and not expected back until the following day. When asked where in Cardiff, he said he didn't know, just some business he had to do.

Where was he staying? He didn't know that either, that was the boss's business. Annoyed and frustrated, Matt gave in, leaving a message that it was imperative he speak to Mr Vaughan as soon as possible the following morning, with a caveat that he'd search him out in Cardiff if necessary.

"Where now, sir?" Dilys asked as they drove back down the driveway.

Matt checked his watch. Half past twelve. There was always a chance Neville Breverton would be home for lunch.

"Have you got that list of contributors to Labour Party funds that Chloe put together?"

"Yes." She tapped her briefcase. "In here."

"Good. Let's go on up to Pontygwyn House and rattle his lordship's cage."

"Are you sure, sir?"

Matt glanced at her. "I thought we'd been through this, Dilys," he said, frowning. "I know it's unorthodox and rather throws out the rulebook, but can you think of any other way of putting him on the spot?"

"I suppose not, oh hell, let's go for it."

Matt gave her a twisted smile. "Seems you and I have changed our spots, Dilys. Fabia would laugh like a drain."

* * *

"This is most inconvenient, Chief Inspector," Gwen Breverton said over her shoulder as they followed her into the sitting room. "Given my husband's position, I would have expected you to make an appointment. Quite apart from the fact that he has a great deal of work to do this afternoon, I really would like him to be able to finish his lunch in peace."

She stood before them, her hands clasped tightly in front of her, her jaw clenched.

"It's not always possible for us to make appointments, Mrs Breverton, things come up in an investigation that have to be addressed urgently," said Matt firmly. "We'll wait."

She flinched slightly but still stood hesitating with her arms crossed protectively. Matt waited, his face expressionless. In the end she sighed, threw her hands up in a gesture of frustration and said, "All right, but you're going to have to make it quick. He's a busy man and I really don't know what more he can tell you about this business."

He didn't comment, just said "Thank you," and watched as she left the room.

"She's scared," said Dilys once the sound of Gwen Breverton's footsteps had faded away. "Definitely scared."

"Which is all to the good, but I wonder what exactly she's scared of. That her husband had something to do with the deaths, that his affair with the girl is going to come out, or that his past is going to be raked up? There's plenty of dirt there. When you think about it, it could be any or all of those. But at least it means we may be getting somewhere. The cracks are beginning to show. If his wife's got the wind up, then she must think we can shake him. That's fine with me." His jaw set and he began to pace up and down the room.

Dilys watched him. "Are you having doubts?"

"No. I'm pretty sure of my ground. I don't think he's going to risk the affair becoming public property."

"Maybe it's just that you're not used to bending the rules," Dilys suggested tentatively.

Matt looked at her, then grinned. "You may be right. Fabia always teased me about being wedded to the rule book. She was always pushing her luck, told me I should try it more often. She used to say it was exhilarating."

Dilys grimaced. "I have to say, I don't agree with that."

"No, but you're a law-abiding soul, just like me."

They were interrupted by a rumble of voices followed by the door being pushed open. Matt had been wondering

244

how Breverton would decide to play it. The MP's first words answered the question. He'd decided to go on the attack.

"What is all this, Chief Inspector? I'm a very busy man. I thought we'd gone through all that needed to be said. Does Charlie Rees-Jones know you've come back to pester us?"

His wife, who had come into the room at his heels, seemed to have gained confidence from her husband. Her haughty expression was accentuated, and she glared at them over her husband's shoulder. She'd obviously decided to follow his lead.

"I doubt very much that he knows anything about it," she said, raising her eyebrows disdainfully.

Matt chose not to respond to this and simply said, "Thank you for giving us some of your valuable time, sir."

Breverton seemed taken aback by the bland courtesy. He frowned then glanced at his wife, his expression accusing, as if it was her fault he'd been wrong-footed, then waved a hand at them. "Sit, sit, and let's get on with it."

"You might not know that there's been another death," Matt said as he settled himself in one of the large armchairs.

"What?" This seemed to come as a surprise to them both.

"Miss Rhona Griffiths was found dead in St Cybi's church early yesterday morning. She'd fallen from the organ loft to the floor below."

"Good Lord!" Breverton said, and his wife's eyes widened. "She was always a bit unstable, poor old biddy. Suicide no doubt?"

"We don't know for certain yet. We're still waiting for the post-mortem report. But that isn't what I came to talk to you about." Matt glanced at Gwen Breverton, then turned back to her husband. "This is quite a delicate matter, sir. You may not want your wife to be–"

"Delicate? What are you going on about?" The bullying tone was still there, but he didn't sound quite so sure of himself. Matt waited, his expression questioning. In the end, it was Gwen who spoke first.

"My husband and I have no secrets from each other, Chief Inspector."

Matt said nothing. He didn't particularly care whether Gwen Breverton stayed or not, but he wanted it to be their decision, not his. In a way it might be better if she did stay. It might undermine her husband. The seconds ticked by. Breverton, slumped in his chair, arms crossed, stared at him over the top of his glasses. "Yes, well. Okay, Gwen, off you go."

"Neville!"

"Come on, old girl. I'll tell you all about it later." Matt very much doubted that he would. "This is official business, my dear, probably confidential." He raised his eyebrows at Matt.

"You could say that, sir."

Gwen Breverton rose from her chair, smoothed down her skirt and, with great dignity, stalked from the room. They heard her cross the hall and mount the stairs, her footsteps tapping out her protest. When silence reigned once more, her husband turned back to Matt, his eyes steely.

"Okay, Chief Inspector. What is this all about? And do try to remember who you're dealing with. I will have no hesitation whatever in putting in an official complaint to your boss – who is a very close friend of mine, I'll have you know – if I feel the least necessity to do so."

"That's understood, sir. It's not Rhona Griffiths I wanted to ask you about. It's Amber Morgan." Matt decided not to beat about the bush. "We have reason to believe you had a very close relationship with her, in fact that the two of you were having an affair. Is that right, sir?"

Neville Breverton eyes narrowed, his lips thinned, and he clenched his hands together. The clock on the mantelpiece ticked noisily in the silence. For quite some time nothing was said. Matt waited, watching every twitch of the man's body, every line of his face.

"Who's been feeding you all this nonsense?" Breverton barked out at last.

"We've found Amber Morgan's diary. We also have evidence of some anonymous letters she'd been sending to various people in the neighbourhood, your wife included, in which she makes reference to a relationship."

Some of what Matt said obviously came as a surprise to Neville Breverton. Matt was pretty sure he wouldn't have known about the letter to his wife. But he seemed to have decided to bluff it out. "This is ridiculous," he blustered. "Gwen never said anything to me. I'll ask her now." He began to push himself out of the chair.

"Hold on a moment, Mr Breverton. That isn't the only evidence we have." Thank goodness, thought Matt inwardly. "We also have a witness to one of your encounters with Miss Morgan, and we have reason to believe you weren't entirely honest with us about the evening you had the flat tyre, after you'd taken Amber home that Saturday night."

"You'd better be careful what you say unless you want to be up on a disciplinary charge. How do you fancy going back on the beat, Chief Inspector?" His colour had deepened and Matt thought, as he looked steadily across at Breverton, that he resembled a particularly unpleasant bull terrier, a cornered bull terrier. But bluff as he may, there'd be no escape if Matt had anything to do with it.

"Mr Breverton, this witness has given us a signed statement. What's more, you told us you were outside the vicarage at 9.30 that night, the vicar told us she spoke to you no earlier than 11.30, a discrepancy of two hours. And we have the evidence of Amber Morgan's diary. Now, shall we start again?"

Eyes half closed, Breverton's eyes flickered from Matt to Dilys and back again, and then he forced a smile. "Now look, Lambert, this is hardly relevant to that poor girl's death."

"I don't know how you work that out, sir. It could be highly relevant. If this had got out, to the tabloids, say, you might well have had to – what's the phrase? Consider your position?"

"But for Chrissake, man, I'd hardly do away with the poor girl..." He was frightened now. Matt felt a wave of satisfaction. This is for you, Fabia, he thought.

"Look, I'll be honest." His tone had changed. Come on, we're both men of the world, he seemed to be saying. Matt felt his contempt for the man was increasing as Breverton went on. "Amber and I did have a little fling, nothing serious you understand, and I treated her extremely well."

"You mean you gave her money?"

"No – well, yes, but only as a gift. I was very fond of the girl, and she of me I believe." He leant forward, gave Dilys a sideways glance, then lowered his voice as if to keep the conversation between him and Matt alone. "You have to understand, a man in my position has a great deal of stress to contend with, and my wife is, er, isn't as, er, forthcoming... I'm sure you understand what I mean. I meant the girl no harm, no harm at all, and if the truth were known, you might say she seduced me, the little minx." His smile didn't quite come off.

Matt decided to go along with him for now.

"How long did this relationship go on?"

"Three, maybe four months. You can imagine, now you know about this, how very upset I was to hear of poor Amber's death. I cared about the girl, I really did."

"I'm sure you did, sir." Like hell you did, you randy old pervert, he thought. Now to widen things out a bit. He turned to Dilys. "Do you have those records I asked you to bring, Sergeant?"

Dilys bent and opened her briefcase, handed him a piece of paper, her face completely expressionless.

"I'd like to go on to a completely different subject now, sir, if I may." He watched Breverton carefully and caught a look of relief in the man's eyes before he managed to mask it. "Can you tell me if this is an accurate record of contributions to local Labour Party funds in Cardiff at the time of the last by-election?"

Breverton's eyes widened and he sat forward. This wasn't what he'd expected. "What's all this about?" he growled, and snatched the piece of paper from Matt. He scanned down it. "I suppose. I don't know off-hand. I left all that to the treasurer."

"We are reliably informed that it is. You see the third name down, sir?"

"Vasic?"

"Yes. He was the developer on the Cwmberis project, was he not?"

In the silence that followed this question, the clock on the mantelpiece ticked away, measuring the seconds as they passed. Out in the garden, a solitary blackbird could be heard singing its heart out, and somewhere in the recesses of the house, female voices could be heard. Matt waited, feeling now that he had the upper hand.

"I really can't remember," the MP said finally, and thrust the piece of paper back at Matt. He was definitely rattled. His fingers tapped rapidly on the arm of his chair, but, with the other hand, he made a dismissive gesture as if sweeping away all this nonsense. "It's a long time since I've had anything to do with that kind of development."

"But weren't you involved in pushing for planning permission for the project when you were on the Council?"

"Not directly, no. Anyway, what's this got to do with the matter in hand?" He pushed himself forward aggressively, making a point of looking at his watch. "I can only give you ten more minutes, so, get to the point?"

This was crunch time. Matt knew he was about to take a hell of a risk. He had to trust to Neville Breverton's fear of his relationship with Amber coming out into the open, and the hold that gave him over the man, in order to get away with what he was about to do. But he'd gone too far now, no drawing back, and who was to say it wouldn't succeed?

Looking Breverton in the eye, Matt held his gaze and said very slowly and quietly. "I believe planning permission for that housing project was fast-tracked by you, at the request of several of your friends, Vasic amongst them. In return they made some generous contributions to your campaign fund. All of you were members of the same Masonic lodge, weren't you?" Breverton began a rumble of protest, but Matt ignored it and kept going. "A great deal of money was made by all concerned, in spite of the fact the land has subsequently turned out to be contaminated by heavy metals and the houses are now unsellable. Although it's almost certain the developers, Vasic included, and some in the planning department, knew about the contamination, no-one has ever been prosecuted, nor have any of the buyers been compensated. An investigation into this fraud was blocked two years ago. The police officer heading up the investigation was forced to take sick leave and, subsequently, resigned from the force. One of the people responsible for her being sacked – that's what it amounted to – was my boss, and your friend, Chief Superintendent Rees-Jones, but the main mover was the then Assistant Commissioner, Vivian Sligo."

"You must be mad to tell me all this," Breverton hissed at him. "Don't you realise what this could mean to your career?"

"My sergeant is still here, sir, and she's taking notes," Matt said quietly.

Breverton flashed a venomous look at Dilys who still sat quietly, notebook on her lap, pen in hand. "She's taking a risk, isn't she?"

Matt glanced at Dilys who sat impassive, her face totally expressionless. "She doesn't seem to think so. Now, sir. I know about your affair with Amber, and I'm fully aware of how much you'd hate it to become public, but at least she had passed the age of consent. I gather that hasn't always been the case with your conquests. I believe a few years ago you had a spot of trouble over sex with a minor? But that was sorted out by your friends as well, wasn't it, sir?"

"You bastard!" Matt felt a wave of satisfaction. Breverton hadn't denied it. "I'll get on to Charlie Rees-Jones. You'll be out of the force before your feet can hit the ground."

"There's no need for that, sir. I have the statement of the witness to one of your amorous encounters with Amber. I also have Amber's diary, and the admission you've just made. I would not advise you to mention anything about the subsequent part of our discussion today to anyone at all, until I've decided exactly what I am going to do about all this. I can assure you, the officer in charge of that investigation at the time is going to be cleared of all blame, that is certain."

"Gwen said we should watch out for that Havard bitch," he muttered, then seemed to realise how revealing this comment was.

Matt got up. "Thank you for your time, sir. I'll be keeping you informed of the progress of both investigations, and anything further on the Cwmberis development. We'll see ourselves out."

"This isn't the last you'll hear from me, Lambert," Breverton spat at him as Matt made his way to the door, "not by a long chalk."

Matt turned and looked at him, allowing all the contempt he felt for the man to show in his face. "I'm sure it's not, sir. In fact, I'm counting on it."

Chapter 28

Fabia was halfway through a late lunch when she heard a motorbike roar to a stop outside. She put down her knife and fork, got up and made her way quickly along the hall to the sitting room. Through the window she saw Craig hurrying up the path, removing his helmet as he did so. As she went to open the door, she wondered if Matt had followed up on what she'd told him about the conversation in the bakery.

"Morning, Craig, I'm glad you've come round." There were many questions she wanted to ask him, but all she came up with was, "I was planning to ask you to have a go at my garden."

"Fine, but–" He gulped. It was obvious Fabia's garden was the last thing on his mind. "Can I have a word, like?"

"Of course." She stepped aside and ushered him in. "Is it about your friend?"

"Sort of. Well no, not exactly. To be honest, that was me."

Fabia smiled at him. "I thought it might be."

"But, miss, now it's all changed, 'cos now I know what I thought before was wrong, see. I'd got the wrong person fixed in my mind, and now it's all changed." His hands, clutching the rim of his helmet, passed it round and round, but she didn't think he was aware of the action. "It's important. It's to do with Miss Griffiths."

"Hadn't you better speak to Chief Inspector Lambert, then?" Deep down, Fabia hoped he'd say no.

He did. "No way!" The fear was clear in his voice. "I'd rather tell you about it. I don't want no more to do with the police, not if I can help it."

Fabia was about to say that he may have no choice in the matter, but she bit the words back when she'd taken a closer look at him. What she saw was a youngster barely out of childhood, acne and nascent beard struggling for supremacy on his face, fear in his eyes. Since he seemed to trust her, surely she should try to find out as much as possible from him.

"Come along into the kitchen," she said. "I'll get you a drink, and then you can tell me all about it. Will coffee do, or do you want tea?"

"Tea thanks, miss." He sank down in a chair, his whole body sagging in relief.

Fabia put the kettle on, got down two mugs from the cupboard and searched in the fridge for milk. She made herself move slowly, no hurrying, no urgency. The last thing she wanted was to frighten Craig off.

Craig put his helmet on the floor beside him. As Fabia pushed the mug across to him, she asked, "Do you take sugar?" He shook his head. "So, what did you want to tell me?"

Now she'd asked the direct question, he seemed to hesitate. He took a gulp of his tea, then placed the mug slowly and carefully down in front of him. It could have been a valuable piece of crystal the way he handled it. Looking up at her under his brows, he chewed at his bottom lip. Fabia waited patiently, no point in rushing him. At last he began to speak.

"I was coming back from... from a walk, like; Monday night, about half-past nine. When I got up by the top of

Morwydden Avenue I heard some people coming out of the pub. I didn't want them to see me." He paused a moment, obviously realising this demanded some kind of explanation. "My Mam didn't want me to go out, said I had to do some work, but I'd slipped out to... to meet a mate."

He wouldn't look her in the eye and Fabia was sure she wasn't getting the whole truth, but made no comment, she didn't want to put him off.

Craig went on. "I ducked down under them bushes, you know, where there's a break in the fence by the church, so's not to be seen. I was just about to come out, there was no-one around anymore, when I saw someone come out of the church, sort of furtive like."

Good Lord! she thought, and asked, as calmly as she could manage, "Who was it, Craig?"

Taking a deep breath, he told her.

* * *

Fabia was desperate to get hold of Matt. She'd tried his mobile but, yet again, all she'd got was the voicemail. She'd phoned the station and managed, after a long wait and a great deal of foot tapping and muttering, to talk to a total stranger who'd treated her like some geriatric troublemaker. And when she'd told him who she was, the brisk and dismissive treatment she'd received had made her so angry she'd slammed the phone down. What to do? Nothing but wait for Matt to get back to her. She'd just have to hope and pray he'd manage to come round as he'd promised.

But could she afford to wait? What if he didn't get her message? Or if he did, what if it wasn't until much later, or tomorrow even? What she'd found out for herself, and what Craig had told her, it all added up to one thing. Maybe she should have handed it all over to the unknown, and extremely irritating officer she'd just spoken to. At least then it would have been out of her hands. But that, if the truth were known, was just what she didn't want. She wanted to be in on this, for Amber's sake if nothing else. She grimaced ruefully to herself. Was that really the truth? Yes, maybe, but she was also desperate to be involved, to get back to the exhilaration of the chase.

* * *

Silence reigned as Dilys started up the car, turned right out of the gate, and made her way down the road towards the centre of Pontygwyn. Matt jabbed Fabia's number into his mobile, held it to his ear. Nothing happened. He tried again. Still nothing.

"Damn. This bloody thing's playing up again. Never mind. Back to the station. I want to check up on how far Roberts got with the contents of that suitcase. With any luck, he'll have turned up something useful."

"Isn't he off duty now?" Dilys asked.

"Is he? Well he's had time to go through most of it. I know he's methodical, but surely?"

"He's got things on his mind. Their baby's due any day now."

"Of course, I'd forgotten about that. Let's hope he handed over to someone else before disappearing off home."

It was halfway down Pontygwyn High Street that a large Mercedes convertible sailed past and turned up St Madoc's Road.

"Stop!" Matt ordered. "That was Paul Vaughan. We could catch him now before going back. Turn into the Spar car park and we can go round that way."

They arrived just as Vaughan was mounting the steps to his front door. He turned to see who it was, then waited for them to approach. "So, what can I do for you this time?" His tone was far from friendly.

"We'd just like a quick word, Mr Vaughan," Matt replied. "Can we come in?"

"Can I stop you?"

Matt didn't bother to respond to this.

"You'd better make it snappy," Vaughan growled. "I haven't got any time to waste."

They followed him across the tiled hall, and into the cream and white lounge. He took up a position with his back to the fireplace, legs astride, arms crossed, and glared at them. Gone was the studied charm of their first encounter, he wasn't bothering with any of that this time. Perhaps he'd had enough of the police in London these last few days, thought Matt.

"When we last spoke to you, you mentioned your girlfriend, Mel Franklin. We understand she's been arrested for possession of cocaine."

"'S'right, silly bitch, and she's my ex-girlfriend now." Matt could see his jaw clench. "Anyway, what's it got to do with you?"

"She told the police in London you supplied her with the drug. Is that true?"

"That she told them some fairy story, yes. That I supplied her with the stuff, no."

Matt said nothing in response to this. Just waited to see if Vaughan would elaborate, but he didn't. In the end, Matt gave in. "Can you prove you didn't?"

"Look, mate, I've been through all this with your pals in the Met and I'm not about to go through it again with you. They've got nothing on me, whatever that stupid little slapper chooses to say, so you might as well accept it just as they've had to."

"And you didn't supply Amber Morgan with drugs either?" Matt asked blandly.

"Ah-ha. So that's where you're heading is it?" He seemed completely unperturbed and in control. If he was guilty he was certainly a good actor. Not by a flicker of an eyelid did he indicate any kind of uncertainty. "No, I didn't. Nor do I allow anyone in any of my clubs – I'm sure you've checked up on which ones I have an interest in

– to deal in drugs or take drugs on the premises. Anyone who tries it gets kicked out and banned, understand?"

Matt found it hard to believe a word, but there was nothing he could do about it at the moment. "Just one more question, sir. Did you ever see Amber take drugs of any kind?"

"No. Now, I'd be grateful if you'd bugger off and leave me in peace."

"I think that's all we need from you at the moment," Matt said, trying to retrieve something from this confrontation, "but I might want to speak to you again."

"Not if I see you first. You can find your own way out."

Matt gave in. There was nothing else to do but retreat with as much dignity as possible. As he and Dilys made their way to the front door, he noticed Vaughan's troll-like guardian watching them from a doorway the other side of the hall. A talk with him might be a good idea at some point, but not now. Now the most important thing was to find out if Roberts had turned up anything useful from Rhona Griffiths' suitcase.

Back at the station they found Roberts had had to rush off after a phone call from his mother-in-law. His wife was in labour and he was needed.

"He said to tell you he's finished with the suitcase, sir," Chloe Daniels told Matt. "He's left a list on your desk. Nothing startling, just sad, really. A whole lot of photograph albums, theatre programmes and such like, and some letters, very flowery and dated about twenty years ago. It seems Miss Griffiths had a pash for some chap who went off to South Africa and left her, poor old dear. Some of the letters were written by her and had obviously been returned. And there's a pile of stuff about her father, newspaper cuttings and copies of sermons, stuff like that. Nothing relevant to the matter in hand is how he described it. Would you like me to go through it all again? A second opinion, so to speak?"

"Not now, Chloe. If you've got time tomorrow, you could have a quick look through." Matt went to his desk and picked up the sheaf of papers Roberts had left for him. He leafed through it, but a quick glance didn't produce anything of real use. He'd had a niggling hope that Rhona had hidden the poison pen letter somewhere in the suitcase, but it had been a forlorn hope. Why should she keep it? No doubt, she'd disposed of it just as Gwen Breverton had hers, burnt or maybe flushed down the pan. But still, he had this prickling at the back of his neck. Fabia would call it a hunch.

He pulled a report of the door to door enquiries that had been made so far towards him, began to leaf through it, and was interrupted by a knock, followed swiftly by Glyn Pryce appearing round the door.

"Message for you, sir," he said. "Miss Havard called wanting to talk to you. The lad who took the message, well I'm afraid he didn't take it too seriously."

Matt scowled at Pryce. "Why the hell not?"

Pryce looked embarrassed. "Said he thought she was, like, trying to interfere or some such."

"I'll deal with him later," Matt said grimly. "When did this message come in?"

"Couple of hours ago. She tried your mobile but said she couldn't get through. Do you want me to get her for you?"

"Leave it with me." He reached his hand out for the phone and chose Fabia's number. It rang and rang. In the end, he gave up, but he was feeling edgy. What had she wanted? What's more, what was she up to? He got up and threw on his coat, glanced at his watch. Nearly five. That meant she must have phoned about three. His sense of urgency increased.

"Dilys," he called out, "I'm going out for a bit. Won't be long."

"But, sir, what about that meeting with the chief super?"

"Oh, bugger. What time's he expecting me?"

"Half five."

Matt dithered. He really couldn't miss seeing Rees-Jones, not if he wanted to keep the man sweet until he had all the information he needed. He wanted to be able to present him with a fait accompli, not allow him the chance to wriggle out of facing the truth. But what about Fabia? He'd have to put Dilys on to it.

"Could you give Fabia Havard a call and tell her I'll be round later, and not to go out until I get there?"

Dilys gave him a curious look but simply said, "Okay."

Matt felt a rush of gratitude for her unquestioning attitude. "Phone me on my mobile and tell me what she says."

"Is your mobile working now?"

"I'll try it out." He punched in Dilys's number and a second later a muffled tune, vaguely resembling one of Bach's Brandenburg concertos, could be heard.

"Seems it is," said Matt as Dilys delved in her pocket.

Matt rushed out of the station and got into his car, telling himself as he went that there was nothing to worry about. But the edgy feeling persisted. He knew Fabia. She couldn't be trusted not to go it alone. But, surely, she wouldn't now that she was no longer in the force? He wasn't convinced. The sooner this meeting was over the happier he'd be.

Chapter 29

As the day had worn on, Fabia's restlessness had increased. She desperately needed something to do but couldn't settle to anything. Now it was late afternoon and still there was no sign of Matt. She kept thinking about Cecily; felt she really should do something to help her. The poor woman needed all the friends she could get at the moment. The walk up to Well House would be good exercise, it'd blow away the cobwebs and help her think straight, clarify the tumble of thoughts that had been plaguing her.

She glanced next door as she went down the path, and said good evening to the constable, a different one this time, stationed outside Rhona's door.

"Nice afternoon for a stroll." He sounded envious.

"Yes. I thought a walk would do me good," she told him. "Just going to see Mrs Cole up at Well House."

"That's the murdered girl's Mam, isn't it?" he asked.

"Yes, poor woman."

"Needs her friends at a time like this, I should think," he said.

Fabia smiled, lifted a hand in farewell, and went on her way. As she strode up Morwydden Lane towards the High Street she went over and over what had been on her mind. From whatever direction she approached it, what Craig had told her and what she'd seen for herself, it still came round to the same thing in the end, however unacceptable. But how to prove it? As always, that was the problem.

When she arrived and knocked on the Coles' front door it was opened, once again, by their neighbour. Fabia wasn't surprised. Cole was a creature of habit and Tuesday evening was one of the rehearsal nights for the Pontygwyn Male Voice Choir. Even at a time like this, she couldn't see him missing that. Telling Mrs Greaves that she'd see herself up, and suggesting she take the opportunity to pop home while Fabia was with Cecily, she strode purposefully up the stairs and knocked gently on the bedroom door.

As before, Cecily was curled in bed. The curtains were half closed, filling the room with the same gloomy shadows. Fabia walked across to the bed. "Only me, Cecily," she said. "I thought I'd drop back and check up on you."

The washed-out blue eyes gazed up at her. "Fabia!" There was alarm in her voice as she pushed herself up on the pillows, and tried to see round Fabia to the door. "Where's Murray? Does he know you're here?"

"I didn't see him when I arrived. Mrs Greaves let me in." She reached across to the bedside lamp and turned it on. Cecily hardly seemed to notice, although the glow picked out the dark shadows under her eyes, and the fear in them as well.

"That's all right then," Cecily said, sounding greatly relieved.

"What is?"

"Murray doesn't like me to have visitors, in case I get upset again. He hates it when I get upset. So long as he doesn't know you're here, that's all right."

"I'm sure, at a time like this, he understands."

"No. No." She was becoming agitated. "He hates it. It makes him – worried." Fabia was sure that wasn't the word she'd intended to use. "He doesn't like to see me cry," Cecily finished lamely and, as if the word had prompted them, tears filled her pale eyes. "Oh Fabia, what am I going to do?"

Fabia sat down on the bed, took one of Cecily's thin, white hands and held it between both her own. "I don't know, my dear. There's nothing anyone can say to make things easier for you I'm afraid. But it will become bearable in time, I'm sure it will." What else could she say? She'd never had a child. How could she know the agony of losing one, and in such a terrible way?

"I know Amber was wild, and I know she could be very difficult," Cecily spoke in a rushed undertone, as if she didn't want to be overheard, "but she was so talented, Fabia. You knew that, didn't you? She loved visiting you. She said you understood, about her art. She was talented, wasn't she?"

"Yes, very. One of the best untrained artists I've ever come across."

"Yes, yes, and so bright and lively. My dark angel, I used to call her when she was a child – my dark angel. She looked so like her father. Huw would have known how to handle her, he was an artist too, you know?" Cecily sat up eagerly, obviously wanting to talk about her daughter, as if doing so might bring her back. "He wouldn't have tried to tie her down, make her conform. He probably would have joined in her wild schemes." Tears were crawling down her pale cheeks, but she hardly seemed to notice them, and still she spoke in the rushed undertone. "Murray just didn't understand. He tried hard to do so, but he likes things to be predictable and, sort of, run to a set timetable. And he likes people to do as he says which, of course, Amber never would. I'm afraid I've been a great disappointment to him."

"Oh, surely not." Fabia reached out a hand to touch the poor woman's arm and was shocked to see her flinch. "What is it?" As she spoke, the cardigan Cecily was wearing slipped off her thin shoulder, almost down to the elbow, and through the thin material of her nightdress Fabia saw that her arm was covered in a fuchsia purple bruise.

"Cecily!" she exclaimed, before she could stop herself. Too late a pale hand came up to grab the cardigan, drag it back to cover the bruise, but Fabia was on her feet, leaning over to look at Cecily's back. The bruising travelled across her back and there were familiar marks under the ears which Fabia only saw when, very gently, she lifted the fair hair away from Cecily's face.

"No, no, Fabia, leave it. Don't, please don't!" But her protests were too late, Fabia had seen all she needed to see. She'd seen bruising and marks like these before, many times in fact, during her time in the police.

"Cecily, who did this to you?"

"No-one," she said breathlessly. "I fell. It's nothing."

"Was it Murray?" Fabia asked.

"No. No, of course not." She sounded terrified now. "I tell you I fell over, stupid of me." Cecily said, her voice a frantic whisper now. "It doesn't matter, really it doesn't." And then she let out a little shriek and cowered back.

Fabia hadn't heard the door open. She didn't realise he was there until she heard his voice. "Good evening, Fabia. How nice of you to visit us again. But I think it's time for you to go now. Cecily is tired, and she needs her rest, don't you, my dear?"

This was a different Murray Cole. All the charm and caring wiped away to be replaced with a look of cold contempt. He stood halfway across the room, his eyes travelling from one woman to the other, as if calculating his next move.

His wife didn't answer his question. She cowered back, whimpering now and staring with terrified eyes at her husband as he made the rest of the way to the side of the bed. Fabia felt his hand grip her elbow. The fingers were steely as he pulled her unceremoniously to her feet.

"Would you please let go, Murray?" she said as calmly as she could.

"No. Not yet." He pulled her towards the door and she went, unresisting, not wanting to agitate Cecily any more, or to make things worse for her. When they were out on the landing, Cole, keeping his grip on Fabia's arm, leant back into the room. "You settle down now, dear. I'll be back to deal with your pills as soon as I've seen Fabia out." He closed the door firmly and propelled his captive irresistibly down to the hall.

Fabia's mind was racing. Should she try to pull away from him? No, she was sure that would only make things worse. Instead, she went with him, desperately trying to think of some way to distract him sufficiently to loosen the excruciating grip on her elbow. The lower part of her arm was beginning to throb and her heart beat heavily in her chest. She made herself breathe slowly and deeply as she tried to dredge up the techniques of her self-defence lessons.

"It's not like you to miss a practice, Murray," she said as calmly as she could, thinking perhaps a pretence at normality might help.

"You must have a strange idea of me to think I'd go out singing at a time like this, Fabia." He opened a door and pushed her into a small room that looked like a study. Bookcases lined two walls and there was a desk in the window with a computer on it, along with filing trays and other office paraphernalia. Closing the door behind him, he stood against it and looked coldly at Fabia where she now stood in the middle of the room, her back up against the desk. She rubbed at her arm to try to bring some life back into it.

"Now you can tell me what the hell you're doing snooping round here yet again," he asked. "Isn't one visit a day enough for you?"

"No, not when a friend is in distress," Fabia said, still trying to sound as calm as possible. "And I wasn't snooping. I was listening to Cecily talk about Amber—"

"Crap!" The crude word sounded all wrong from Cole. "You were digging for information. Your sort can never leave well alone, can you? Once a copper, always a copper, is that it?"

"Perhaps," said Fabia, with a flash of anger. But that was no good. She must keep calm, find a way out of this. "Anyway. I must get home now, I've friends arriving this evening." She hoped the lie would worry him. It didn't.

"I don't think so, Fabia." His tone was matter-of-fact, as if he was disagreeing with her choice of wallpaper design, but when he spoke again the tone was very different. "You're not going home. I've disposed of one inconvenient middle-aged woman, I can dispose of another."

Fabia felt a chill crawl over her skin. She looked quickly round the room. There was only the one window behind her. The door, her best means of escape, was blocked by Cole. She looked behind her. Anything on the desk she could use as a weapon. Nothing. Stupid, stupid woman! Why couldn't she have left well alone, or told Matt of her suspicions and let him deal with it? Thinking of Matt made controlling the rising panic inside more difficult, so she thrust him from her mind. Must concentrate. She'd been in tight corners before and got out of them, she could get out of this one. Just keep calm, talk to him, that was best. What was it she'd often told new recruits? The arrogance of many criminals was often their downfall, and appealing to their vanity could produce results. She'd just have to keep him talking until she could decide what to do. But all she found herself asking was, "Why Amber, Murray? What harm could she do to you?"

He stood staring at her. Every vestige of charm had left him now. The expression on his hawk-like face was as cold as the bird's would have been.

Fabia felt anger rise inside her. The arrogance of the man! For a moment the anger blotted out her fear. "Did she find out you were beating her mother, was that it?"

Immediately she knew that was the wrong thing to say. The blaze in his eyes warned her she'd gone too far. Her heart beating fast, she braced herself. She gripped the edge of the desk. Waited. But he didn't move.

"You're all the same, you independent women. You think you know it all. Cecily is my wife, and I am master in my home and I have every right to chastise her." He sounded like some Dickensian patriarch. "She knew what would happen if she didn't obey me. I will have order in my house. Surely a simple timetable is easy enough for anyone to follow? But no, after a gruelling drive I arrive home to an empty house, no meal on the table, nothing! And as for that child from hell!" The throbbing anger and disgust in his voice echoed round the room. "She dared suggest she'd report me to the police. Me, who'd done so much for her. Me who, in spite of her defiance, her disgraceful disobedience, had treated her as my own."

He was breathing heavily now, but made an effort to calm himself, passed a hand across his face, then went on more quietly. "When she was younger she was controllable, but once she got involved with people like you, leading her astray, encouraging her to defy me, that's when the rot set in. Art school for God's sake! A crass waste of time and money. She would have ended up as useless a specimen as her father."

Fabia couldn't stop herself protesting. "But she was so talented." It was another mistake. His eyes came back to rest on her face.

"Don't talk nonsense, woman." He said calmly, and this very calm was far more frightening than his agitation had been. "When she stopped me on the bridge that night I told her she'd have to leave. There was no way I was having her back under my roof. And do you know what she said? She actually had the gall to tell me it was I who would be leaving. She actually threatened me! Said she had to protect her mother from me. Can you believe it? Of course, her falling into the river was an accident, but a fortuitous one, don't you think? And entirely her own fault. She should not have defied me. She brought it all on herself."

He pushed himself away from the door and took a step forward. "And now you're in the way, just as Amber was, just as that stupid woman Rhona Griffiths was, dressed up like a Barbie doll and thinking I'd make love to her." Disgust throbbed in his voice.

"But why kill Rhona?" Fabia asked frantically, trying to distract him, but it didn't work. Fabia braced herself as he strode towards her.

Chapter 30

Dilys was considering calling it a day. She'd been at work since seven in the morning. It was definitely time for home, a hot bath and some mindless TV, she thought. She tidied up the mess on her desk, switched off her computer, and was about to put her coat on, when she heard footsteps pounding up the stairs and someone shouting, "Sarge! Sarge!" A moment later Chloe Daniels erupted into the room.

"What is it, Chloe? Calm down."

"In the suitcase – I've found–"

"Sit down. Get your breath back, then tell me."

Chloe subsided into a chair, took a few deep breaths, and as she did so waved a large manila envelope under Dilys's nose. "Look! Look–" She took another deep breath, "inside that."

Dilys took the envelope from her and very carefully shook out several pieces of lined paper, the sort with a margin and two holes punched at one side. They were covered with small, neat copperplate writing, so small that it was difficult to read. At the top of the first page was a date and a time, underlined, ruler straight.

"Not that page," Chloe said, leaning over her shoulder. She'd recovered her breath. "The next one, halfway down. You see the date? Thursday 3rd April. That's the day the girl was killed, and she's put a time too, 11.15 p.m. Now read what she's written."

"She?"

"Rhona Griffiths. Yes, yes! Read it," Chloe urged.

Dilys read aloud. "*I saw them on the bridge. They were just below that street lamp, so I could see quite clearly with your lovely telescope, Da. It was frightening, but exciting too, and it was just as well I was there to witness her disgraceful behaviour. I'll be able to protect him, Da, won't I? Everyone must know he had good reason. I think she was threatening him, pushing her face up near his and shouting. How dared she! No respect, and him her step-father and a man of standing, importance. Then ...*" Dilys read on to the end of the page, disbelief and consternation in her face. "Lord God almighty!" she said when she got to the end. "Where did you find this?"

"In the lid of that suitcase. The lining was a bit loose, and it had come away on one side, so I felt around it and realised there was something behind it. I eased it away, the lining I mean, and this fell out. Roberts must have missed it."

"How the hell? Well, I suppose he was preoccupied, what with his wife and all, but the chief's going to go ballistic. We've got to get hold of him, the chief I mean." Dilys thrust her hand into her pocket, scrabbled for her mobile and clicked away until she came up with Matt's number. "Just pray that damn machine of his works," she said to Chloe.

* * *

An early dusk was creeping across Gwiddon Park as Matt slowed to cross the bridge, turned right into Parc Road, and drove along past the playing fields where some schoolboy rugby players, plastered in mud, were just finishing a game. He hardly noticed them as he turned left

269

into Morwydden Lane. The meeting with Rees-Jones had gone on and on, but he'd finally managed to escape. He'd not heard from Dilys and presumed she'd managed to pass his message on to Fabia. If she hadn't, surely she would have let him know.

Matt parked outside Fabia's house and his phone rang. At least it's working, he thought, looking at the screen. Dilys. As he listened, his eyes widened in disbelief, swiftly followed by grim satisfaction.

"This is just what we needed. I'll never be rude about hunches again. I'm at Fabia's. Did you manage to get through to her?"

"No. I tried to let you know, but there was no response."

"Damn! Still, I'm here now. I'll just pop in and speak to her, then I'll be back. Tell Chloe well done." He pressed cancel and got out of the car.

Outside Rhona's door the constable stamped his feet, obviously bored and feeling the growing chill of the evening. As he walked up Fabia's path the man spoke.

"Evening, sir. If you're looking for Miss Havard, she's gone out."

Matt felt a cold chill of apprehension. "Do you know where?"

"Said she was going to visit the dead girl's Mam, neighbourly like. Good of her, I thought."

Matt stared at him, fear creeping down his back. Right into the lion's den. How could she? But she wasn't to know, or was she? After all, it had been her hunch. Oh God Fabia, what are you up to? He punched Dilys's number into his phone. It seemed to go on ringing forever. Come on, come on! At last he heard her voice.

"I might be over-reacting," he said, "but get a team out here pronto, four or five, and come yourself."

"To Miss Havard's?"

"No. To Well House. Haven't got time to explain. I'll see you there." He turned to the constable next door.

"What's your name?"

"Watkins, sir."

Ah yes, the youngster in the organ loft, the one with the gallows humour. "Right, you can come with me." They both climbed into Matt's car. "We're going up to the Coles' place. Might be a false alarm, but there could be trouble."

"How come, sir?"

Matt smiled grimly to himself. "Call it a hunch, Watkins."

* * *

Fabia had fought hard. Dazed now, half-conscious, through the throbbing pain in her head, she desperately tried to think clearly. Her wrists were strapped together behind her, her shoulders ached abominably. He'd used some kind of strong sticky tape. Used it to silence her as well. She could feel it across her open mouth.

He'd gone out of the room now, left her lying on the floor by the desk. There'd been a high-pitched voice calling. Cecily. That was it. A long time ago she'd been upstairs, sitting on the edge of the bed talking to her. If she could make enough noise Cecily would know she was still here, down in the study. But then she would have heard enough noise already and she hadn't come down, or had she? Fabia couldn't remember. She tried to lift herself. It was a mistake. Her head swam, and she felt herself falling, down, down, back into that dark place again.

She had no idea how long it was before she came to again. The room was darker now, just a sliver of light shining in from the cracks round the door. Slowly, her eyes became accustomed to the gloom and she realised she was still on the floor by the side of the desk.

Why, oh why had she been so stupid? Curiosity, and that old feeling that had got her into trouble before, the conviction that if she didn't solve a problem it would stay unsolved. Matt would be so angry. He'd always told her she'd go too far one day. Well, he'd been proved right. Thinking of Matt made tears spring to her eyes. She blinked them away. No good breaking down now, mustn't give up, must try to think.

Head still throbbing, but not quite as groggy as she'd felt before, she made herself take deep, steady breaths. One, two, three. There was a sharp pain in her side. A cracked rib, perhaps. But her head cleared a little, in spite of the pain, and the ache in her arms wrenched behind her back. She flexed her legs, only to discover that her ankles were strapped up too. So, little chance of getting up from here. She tried to wriggle into a more comfortable position, but the movement made her head throb and swim, and the pain in her side stabbed again. She gave up, but only for now, she told herself.

There was a disgusting taste in her mouth. Very carefully she slid her tongue between her lips. It touched the sticky tape. That's what it was. More deep breathing. One, two, three ... Footsteps! Oh God! He was coming back. Clamping down on the panic, she forced herself to go limp. Better if he still thought she was unconscious. In her mind was some vague idea that that way she could take him by surprise. She had to believe she was going to get out of this. She had to.

Opening her eyes fractionally she saw a triangle of light appear as he opened the door. He didn't turn the light on in the room. Slowly he walked up to her where she lay beside the desk. He put out a foot and kicked at her. Pain radiated up her back from the point where his shoe made contact. She knew she'd grunted, but kept her eyes closed tight, feeling tears squeeze themselves from below her lids. Nausea rose in her throat, she swallowed it down. Don't move. Play dead. Dead? Don't like that word. What was he going to do now?

Earlier, he'd talked about a well. This was Well House, he'd said, and did she know why? Because, down in that secluded spot in the corner of the garden was an old well, hidden by long grass, nettles and brambles. He'd muttered away, seemingly uncaring whether she heard or not, as if he was organising things in his own mind as much as anything else. Everyone thought the well had been capped, that it was safe, but he knew better. All he had to do was clear away the brambles and there it was. And down she would go, never to be found again. All muttered into her reluctant ears while she was trussed like a chicken.

The kick had obviously been a test, which she seemed to have passed. He must think she was still unconscious. He bent and picked her up, settled her over his shoulder like a sack of coal. She never would have thought he could be this strong. Christ how it hurt! She mustn't moan or cry out. Mustn't make a sound. Please, God help her. Her breathing was restricted by the pressure of his shoulder on her stomach and her head swam and throbbed, swam and throbbed... the black void came up to envelop her once more.

* * *

Matt knocked on the front door of Well House. No response. He knocked again, harder. Still no response. He stepped back and looked up at the first-floor windows. No lights on, and none on the ground floor either. He banged again, this time with his closed fist. Nothing.

"Go round and check if the back door's open," he said to Watkins as he lifted his hand once more, but now they could hear footsteps approaching. Watkins came quickly back to stand beside Matt.

The door opened to reveal Cole. There was no light on in the hall, but it wasn't completely dark yet and Matt could see he was frowning, but when he saw them, his face cleared and he smiled. As he did, a cut on his lip began to bleed a little.

"Good evening, Chief Inspector," he said, his voice a little muffled as he dabbed at the cut with a handkerchief he had in his hand. "Sorry to keep you waiting. I've just been trying to deal with this, annoying how lips bleed, isn't it?" He held the door half open, stood in the gap, a questioning look on his face.

"How did it happen?" Matt asked.

"Stupid really. I bent over and hit the corner of the kitchen table. What can I do for you?"

Matt made no comment, but he didn't believe him. "Could we come in and have a word, Mr Cole?"

"Well, it isn't really convenient at the moment. I'm in the middle of trying to persuade my wife to eat something. She's very distressed, but she must eat. I'm sure you'll understand. Perhaps tomorrow?"

He began to close the door. Matt put his foot out to stop him. "I'm afraid this is rather urgent, sir." He put up his hand to push at the door, but it was held firmly. The man wasn't going to give in that easily.

"Chief Inspector," he was no longer smiling. "Please, don't insist. Haven't we been through enough already?"

"I understand how distressing this must be, but it won't take long."

"No. You can't come in now." From the tone of voice, he obviously expected them to back down. "I'll see you tomorrow morning if you insist, but not now, Cecily—"

"Mr Cole, this is a murder enquiry and I have reason to believe you may be able to help…"

"—with your enquiries?" He gave a humourless bark of laughter. "Really? You can't be serious." There was contempt in his voice, but maybe a tinge of fear now. Matt tried to follow up this advantage.

"I'm afraid I am. And I insist that you let us in."

Cole stood hesitating, glaring out at them from the gap between door and door jamb. Into the silence came a sound of muffled knocking from somewhere inside the house. Irregular but distinct. They all noticed it at the same time. Cole's head went back slightly, he called over his shoulder, "Coming Cecily," but his voice didn't sound right.

The knocking had stopped. Matt glanced at the young constable, nodded towards the door, and then pushed at it with all his strength, assisted, after a second, by Watkins. Cole staggered back but recovered himself.

"How dare you!" he shouted, his voice shrill. He came at them but Matt sidestepped him. He was sure the noise had come from the back of the house, it had been faint, but definitely on the ground floor, he was sure of that.

Watkins was struggling with Cole. The man was strong, but Watkins was young and built like a prop forward. For a second, Matt hesitated. Should he try to help or should he investigate the noises? Then it was all over, Cole was on the floor, his arm up behind his back, cursing them in that shrill, almost unrecognisable voice.

"My handcuffs please, sir," Watkins gasped.

Matt took them from Watkins' belt and helped him clip them on to Cole's wrists, then made his way quickly to a door at the back of the hall, and opened it. The knocking had stopped. The curtains in the room were closed, it was very dark, but in the shaft of light from the door he could see a body lying on the floor. Feeling sick with dread, he went to kneel beside it.

Chapter 31

It was nine in the evening at the end of a very long day. Everyone else had gone home, but Matt sat in his office with the phone clamped to his ear.

"I've told him to expect you," Alun Richards was saying on the other end of the line.

"Was that wise?"

"I think so. He said his wife's away with the kids, so tonight would be a good time. He doesn't want them to be there when he meets you. Look, the man's been plagued by this ever since he left the force. He feels he let himself down, but what's more, he feels he let Fabia down as well."

"So why didn't he say something at the time?" As soon as the words were out of his mouth, Matt realised what a stupid thing it was to say.

"You should be able to answer that for yourself," Alun's tone made it obvious he thought the same. "For a start, he was just a lowly police constable – only been in the force a couple of years."

"You're right. Sorry."

"Anyway, he's ready to get it off his chest, that way he can stop feeling guilty about it all and everything's tidy. I get the impression there was no love lost between him and Sligo."

"I know how he feels," Matt said.

"Yes, well, time for you to set things straight then."

"You're right. I'll go now."

"Okay but, maybe you and I can take Fabia out for a celebration meal some time?"

"I hope so," said Matt.

"Cheer up," Alun told him. "She's tough, is Fabia. She'll pull through."

"You didn't see her – okay, you're probably right," said Matt, but he could help dwelling on the sight of Fabia, bruised and bleeding on the stretcher as the paramedics pushed it into the ambulance. There was no knowing yet how long it would be before Fabia would be fit enough, if ever, to go out for celebratory meals.

Later on, Matt had spoken to the doctor at the hospital and been told they weren't sure how severe her internal injuries were. The outer bruising was obvious, and they knew she had some cracked ribs, but there were more X-rays and tests to be done. She was in ICU for now and hadn't yet spoken. They'd know more tomorrow. The doctor had told him he'd have to be patient. Matt wasn't good at waiting, but he had no choice. And at least now he had something useful to do, something for Fabia.

* * *

Matt had no difficulty finding the house. It was small and semi-detached in a row of almost identical houses, not far from Newport's main shopping centre. As he went up the path, he noticed a child's bike lying abandoned on the patchy lawn, with a football and one solitary scuffed trainer lying beside it. A little effort had been made on the garden, a few rose bushes that needed pruning and some clumps of daffodils on which the flowers were now wilting, but it was obviously not a priority. In the gloom of light provided by a nearby street lamp, the place looked depressing and neglected.

He rang the bell and waited. After a moment, he could see, through the half-glazed door, the outline of a man. The door opened a couple of inches. A large, moon-like face looked out at him through the space.

"Steve Hughes?" Matt said, questioning.

"Yes?" The tone was not welcoming.

"Chief Inspector Lambert. Could I have a few words?"

The door was opened further. "Oh yea, Alun told me you'd be along. You might as well come in."

He was a big man, running to fat, his beer belly protruding over the top of grubby jeans, his shirt gaping to reveal his navel. In his hand he held a can of lager. He waved it towards a door on the right. "Through there. D'you want one of these?"

"No, thanks," Matt said, guessing that the man had had quite a few himself already. "A cup of tea would be good, if that's possible."

"I'll put the kettle on, milk and sugar?"

"Just milk, thanks," Matt said.

He lumbered off down the hall and Matt went through into the room indicated.

There was evidence here of a man alone in the house: a plate containing pizza crusts on a coffee table, a sports channel on television talking to the empty room, several used mugs and empty lager cans dotted about the place. Matt grimaced then pulled himself up. There were times when this wasn't unlike the state of his own flat.

Steve Hughes came into the room carrying a steaming mug. "Have a seat," he said to Matt. As he handed him the mug, some of the tea slopped on to the carpet. He didn't seem to notice, just reached out and pressed the mute button on the remote. The figures on the screen continued to run soundlessly around the field.

"So, what did Alun tell you then?" he asked.

On his way in the car, Matt had wondered how to

approach this interview. He'd known it would depend, to a certain extent, on what sort of man Steve Hughes was, so he'd made no rigid plan. Now he was here, sitting opposite this man who'd let himself run to seed, who lived in a house that showed little evidence of love and care, and who gave all the signs of having given up on himself, Matt felt it was going to be even more difficult than he'd anticipated. He sat forward, elbows resting on his knees, his mug held between his hands.

"First of all, thank you for agreeing to see me. It could be very useful."

Steve shrugged but said nothing in reply.

"Alun told me you had some information you wanted to pass on to me, something you learned when you were still in the force. He told me that, at the time, you didn't feel able to make this information public as you feared for the effect it would have on your job prospects and your family, but when he told you about Superintendent Havard's resignation, you decided it was time to speak out, even if it wasn't publicly. Does that about cover it?"

"Just about. She was good to me, the Super. I liked her, a real tidy sort she was, and they well and truly shafted her. It was a disgrace, what they did."

"So why haven't you spoken out before?" Matt asked, unable to stop himself.

Hughes rubbed a large hand over his face, dragging the skin either side of his mouth down. The action made him look even more lugubrious than before. "It's like this, see, back then – when we were working on the Cwmberis development case – I was cannon fodder. A lowly PC with no clout whatever. I hadn't been in the force long, but long enough to know speaking out against my superiors would screw things up for me good and proper, and probably hardly affect them. What's more, it was made very clear I was to keep my mouth firmly shut."

"Made clear by whom?"

"Bloody Vivian Sligo, that's who." The bitterness in

the man's voice reverberated round the room.

"Why didn't you go to Fabia Havard with what you knew?"

"I tried to, but they'd sent her off on sick leave by this time. I did try to get in contact with her, but she seemed to have gone to ground." Matt couldn't believe he'd tried very hard, but didn't say so. "That was when the rot totally set in, it screwed the job for me. Never really enjoyed it after that, so I got the hell out, been doing private security work ever since. Pays the bills."

"So, what's made you want to speak out now?"

The answer didn't come immediately. Hughes got up and wandered out to the kitchen, came back a moment later with another can of lager, threw himself back down in the chair. He looked broodingly across at Matt. He opened his mouth to speak, then seemed to change his mind, and shut it again. Matt waited. At last, the man spoke.

"It's been on my mind, like, ever since I left, eating away, never seems to leave me alone. Guilty, I suppose I felt, and Eiluned – that's the wife – when I told her about the Super resigning and that, she said for God's sake speak out, do something. Got a mouth on her big enough for a male voice choir, that one, but she's right. She says," he gave Matt a rueful grin, "I've been hell to live with lately, with this on my mind and all, and it's about time I sorted it once and for all. She's taken the kids and gone off to her Mam, said to let her know when I'd sorted it and then she'll consider coming back."

Matt raised his eyebrows, "A strong-minded woman."

Hughes' face relaxed for a moment into a rueful grin. "You could say that."

"So, what is it exactly you have to tell me?" Matt asked, making an effort to hide the impatience.

Hughes lumbered up out of his chair once more and went to a cupboard below a shelving unit. He opened it and took out a small flat leather folder with a zip round the edge, opened this up and took out several pieces of paper.

Silently, he handed them to Matt.

"They're just photocopies. I took them because I wanted some kind of insurance against being dumped in it by Sligo and his pals, just in case they decided to shaft me like they did Superintendent Havard. What I suppose I should have done was handed them over to her. Stupid but, like I said, I was too worried about my job. Now it doesn't matter quite so much."

The first was a report from the County Council Health and Safety Officer and it took only a quick leaf through it for Matt to realise it condemned the land at Cwmberis as toxic, contaminated with heavy metals, and outlined how much it would cost to de-contaminate it and make it safe to build on. The second was a letter from a private engineering firm disagreeing with the Health and Safety report and giving a much lower cost for de-contamination, but in the small print at the bottom, in the list of non-executive directors, was a familiar name – Neville Breverton. The third was a letter from Neville Breverton to Vivian Sligo thanking him for his help with "that little embarrassment" and telling him he would show his appreciation in more concrete terms at a later date. The last was an e-mail from Sligo to Breverton saying the Havard woman had been dealt with and they could now relax, no further worries. Matt's eyes widened as he read, and he couldn't stop himself grinning. None of these bits and pieces would stand up in a court of law, any good barrister would shoot them down in no time, but this was enough for him to use on Fabia's behalf. Okay, Charlie Rees-Jones, he thought triumphantly, put this in your pipe and smoke it!

"How the hell did you get hold of all these?" he asked in amazement.

"I've got a friend who worked in Health and Safety, the two reports came from him, but I didn't tell you that, understand?"

"Okay."

"And the other two, let's just say I managed to get copies of them before Sligo got rid of the originals."

"How on earth?"

"I'd rather not say, if you don't mind."

Matt decided not to probe for now. He could always try to find out at a later date. All he said now was, "Risky, wasn't it?"

"I had to protect my back," Steve said defensively, and Matt couldn't but agree with him, however much against the rules it may have been. He was so grateful to have been handed the information, he could hardly start criticising its source.

"Can I keep these?" he asked.

"As far as I'm concerned you can do what you bloody well like with them. I want nothing more to do with it. If you manage to do some good for Miss Havard, that'll be fine by me, and tell her..." He paused. Matt wondered what was coming next. "Tell her I'm sorry. I should have come forward before."

"I'll do that, and don't worry," Matt said, "I think she'll understand."

* * *

For once, Matt didn't mind a summons from Chief Superintendent Rees-Jones. Oh boy, this he was really going to enjoy. He knocked on the door and walked in.

"Good morning, sir."

"Morning, Chief Inspector." The older man looked as if he'd not slept much. He gave Matt a stiff smile and held his hand out. "Congratulations on a job well done." Matt wondered how much that had cost him. Okay, he thought, that's how we're playing it, is it? It didn't make any difference. He was still going ahead with what he'd planned.

"Thank you, sir," he said, shaking the proffered hand.

"Sit down. I'll get some coffee in," his boss said.

When a young, extremely attractive WPC brought in a

tray with two mugs, cafetière, milk jug and sugar bowl, accompanied by a plate of chocolate digestives, and placed it on the desk, Matt wondered if this was the norm, or maybe just on special occasions.

Rees-Jones sat back. "Do the honours," he said to Matt, waving a hand in the direction of the tray and smiling again. Matt almost laughed as he got up to pour the coffee. This was getting ridiculous. But then, it must mean the old man was rattled. Fine, about bloody time too.

"So, have you managed to get him to confess to both murders?"

"We're getting there. At first, he was denying everything, and when we showed him the torn coat Fabia Havard found in the sack of nearly new clothes, he denied it was his. But he's intelligent enough to know that we can prove his ownership forensically. After we pointed that out, he admitted he owned it, but said he hadn't worn it for ages. He insisted that if we found traces of lichen from the bridge, that was because he'd walked that way before, which is right, of course, but we're hoping the forensics team turns up a bit more than that."

"And what about the contents of the suitcase?"

"It was when we started on that, that he began to open up," Matt said. "He completely changed his tune."

"So, has he confessed?" the Chief Superintendent asked hopefully.

"I don't know if that'd be the right word – boasted more like. He's now talking as if he was entirely justified, in both cases. His step-daughter defied him, tried to stop him returning home because she'd found out he was hitting her mother. He says she lashed out and he pushed her away from him, and that was the point at which she overbalanced and went over the parapet into the river. He categorically denies hitting her or pushing her into the water. As far as he's concerned, it was self-defence, and her death was entirely her own fault. We pointed out that the girl was small, and a man of his size and strength could hardly feel physically threatened by her, but he won't accept that at all." Matt bit into a digestive and discovered he was hungry. He couldn't remember the last time he'd eaten. Since they were on offer, maybe he'd help himself to another one in a minute.

"As to Rhona Griffiths," he went on, "she threatened to make public what she'd seen through her telescope unless he agreed to meet her at the church. She was besotted with him and seemed to think he'd agree to a relationship under duress. He's adamant she had to be dealt with, that she brought it all on herself, and again, he says her fall from the organ loft was her own fault, but I think we'll be able to establish she wouldn't have fallen if he hadn't had a hand in it. Why they ended up in the loft I don't know yet, but perhaps he'll tell us in the end." He helped himself to another biscuit. "We now know he's been drugging his wife to keep her quiet, otherwise I think she would have contacted us days ago. There's no knowing how long it would have been before he decided she too had to be disposed of. I believe, from what Mrs Cole has told us, that she was about to tell Fabia Havard of her suspicions when he surprised them together. I've not been able to check up with Ms Havard. The doctors haven't allowed us to speak to her yet. That's about it, the rest you know."

"A nasty business."

"Very."

The chief superintendent smiled yet again. "Well, congratulations, and tell your team well done." He rose from his chair, but Matt didn't move.

"There is something else, sir."

Rees-Jones subsided slowly back into his seat. "Oh?" he said warily. "And what's that?"

Chapter 32

Matt did his best to keep his voice neutral. It would not be a good idea to let his boss know how much he was enjoying himself.

"During my investigations into both murders I've had to interview Neville Breverton a couple of times, and I also asked for research to be done into his background as, at one point, we thought he might have murdered the girl."

"But that's—"

Matt interrupted him firmly. "He was having an affair with Amber Morgan." There was a splutter of protest from Rees-Jones, but Matt ignored it. "He's admitted to it, sir. Amber was responsible for an anonymous letter to Mrs Breverton threatening to tell the tabloids about it, which seemed motive enough for us. But when we found he couldn't have been responsible for Miss Griffiths' death, we began to doubt his involvement in the first murder. The thing is, during our researches into his background, and because of my close contact during this investigation with Fabia Havard – she knew both victims very well sir, as you know – I've had occasion to go back and review the Cwmberis development case."

"What on earth for?" He sat forward aggressively, his

eyes narrowed. "That case came to nothing, and it obviously has nothing to do with the Amber Morgan case."

"I know, sir, but initially we thought they might be connected. And I'm sure you agree that the Cwmberis investigation shouldn't have – come to nothing that is. There was a strong case to be answered." Matt said. "Miss Havard should never have been forced to take sick leave. All that did was imply she'd had some kind of involvement with the fraud."

"Nonsense. I seem to remember she was suffering from a great deal of stress, which was hardly surprising, it was a very difficult case," the chief superintendent blustered.

"As you say, it was hardly surprising, but that was partly because she got no support whatever from anyone else, in fact it was assumed by all those who did not know the details, including myself I'm ashamed to say, that Superintendent Havard," it gave Matt great delight to give Fabia her full title, "had been involved in activities – how shall I put it? Activities that did not befit her rank or station, perhaps that's the best way to describe it. Since some of the people we were dealing with seemed to have a connection with both cases, I took the opportunity to do a bit of digging."

He paused, allowing his boss time to intervene, but Rees-Jones just sat scowling at him. "After the research we'd done during the course of the last few days, most of which was with a view to finding a motive for Amber Morgan's murder I have to stress, it seems there actually was a police officer who was involved in the Cwmberis fraud. Not Fabia Havard, but the then Assistant Chief Constable, Vivian Sligo."

At this the chief superintendent sat up and gripped the edge of his desk. "What?"

Before he could say anything else, Matt went on. "I've spoken to one of the other officers who was involved in the fraud case, apart from Fabia Havard, that is. He believes Sligo was aware the land at Cwmberis was toxic, but he was told, as was Superintendent Havard, that the case wouldn't be pursued. Neither of them was in a position to challenge that decision at the time, although the chap I spoke to yesterday did keep copies of some of the documentation, for his own protection, he says." Matt held up a hand as Rees-Jones began to protest. "I know, sir, but he felt he had to protect his back. Having seen these documents, and he's handed them over to me, I'm pretty sure Sligo had a financial interest in the scheme, which is why he turned a blind eye. I have a shrewd idea that the reason Breverton brought him in on it, and enabled him to make a great deal of money, was that the ACC had helped him wriggle out of a prosecution for sex with a minor, this was back when Breverton was a councillor in Cardiff. Perhaps this was his reward for that help."

"I really can't believe all this," but Rees-Jones didn't sound quite so sure of himself now. "I certainly hope you can back it all up. You'll be in very hot water if you can't."

"I realise that, sir. But Breverton and Sligo were, after all, very close friends, and their wives are related. I'm sure they felt they had good reason to stick together. I also have strong evidence Breverton was hand in glove with Tony Vasic and his fellow developers on the Cwmberis project, and they all ignored the fact the development was being built on poisoned land. I am not suggesting," Matt went on, looking across the desk at his boss who'd slumped back in his chair, mouth tight, saying nothing, "that you had any knowledge of this at all, sir, obviously not. All I'm asking is that it should be made known that Fabia Havard had no hand in it either, that she was well on the way to proving the fraud when she was forced out of her job – we all know that's what it amounted to – and that her name should be cleared and her full pension restored to her now that she's resigned from the force."

"Where is this evidence of yours?"

"I'm still processing it at the moment. I'll let you have it as soon as possible."

Rees-Jones stared across the desk at him, his jaw set and his eyes blank, his fingers drumming on the desk. Matt waited, but his boss said nothing.

"I hope you'll agree to opening up the Cwmberis case again. I think Breverton and Vasic, at least, have a lot of explaining to do, and Sligo if the truth were known." Matt got up from his chair. "I'm sure you agree with me that this has to be cleared up once and for all, if only for the good of the force. If we can, finally, prosecute Breverton and his pals, that would be a bonus. We definitely can't let this opportunity pass us by."

He waited and at last Rees-Jones cleared his throat and spoke. "Okay, Chief Inspector, leave it with me, I'll see what I can do."

Matt couldn't resist a smile before saying. "Thank you for your congratulations, sir, I'll pass them on to my team. And thank you for the coffee."

He left the room, closed the door quietly behind him and, just as quietly, punched the air with his fist.

* * *

Fabia came to and, very slowly, opened her eyes. For a second, she had no idea where she was; she frowned in concentration, then remembered, and her heart lurched. She remembered coming to a couple of times, people leaning over her, soft voices, pain, and then blissful oblivion. She closed her eyes tight for a second, then opened them and cautiously moved her head.

The painted white walls and paraphernalia of a hospital ward surrounded her, a white sheet and a pale blue Aertex blanket covered her, and low metal bars hedged her into the bed. The curtain that could be drawn round the bed, patterned with blue and mauve flowers, was pulled back, and she could see the other three beds in the room were all empty. She was on her own, except for several vases of flowers and, on the bedside table, an enormous basket of fruit. By squinting sideways, she could just about read the words written on a small card resting against a banana. "Get better soon, love Matt", it said. She felt a glow of warmth.

There was a blind let down over the window, but she could tell that outside the sun was shining. Somewhere in the building she could hear voices, footsteps, the rumble of trolleys being wheeled along corridors.

Very carefully she tried moving her legs, that wasn't too bad, she lifted her arms a little under the covers, pain jabbed in her side. Best not try that again. She moved her head on the pillow again, her head throbbed dully. But although she was uncomfortable, other than a rib, perhaps, she didn't think anything was actually broken.

Tentatively, her mind groped back. There was an urge to touch the wound, in spite of the fact she knew it would hurt like hell to do so. How long ago was it she'd been trapped in that awful room? Yesterday? The day before? She remembered Cole glowering over her, hitting her. Pain. Sick fear. She could feel herself flinching away from the memory, but she made herself face it. Better to do so now, when she was safe in this hospital bed.

She didn't remember anyone rescuing her, although there was a faint memory of banging at a door, and shouting. But someone must have got her out of there. Had it been Matt? And, where was he? He must know she was here, or he couldn't have sent the fruit. And what was happening about Cole? Had he confessed? Had he escaped? And Cecily, those bruises, the panic in the poor woman's eyes. Cole must have been drugging her. Please God don't let her be his third victim. Why hadn't someone come to tell her what had happened? Frustration mounted.

Fabia could see there was a red button dangling on a cord to her right. She lay there considering trying to move enough to press it, summon a nurse, anyone who could give her some answers. But before she'd plucked up the courage to do so, she heard voices near at hand. A moment later, the door opened, and an enormous bunch of daffodils appeared, followed by Cath, who smiled broadly immediately as she saw Fabia was awake.

"My dear," she said, coming forward and bending to kiss Fabia's cheek, "you're awake at last."

"What do you mean, at last?" Fabia asked, finding her voice was more a croak than anything else.

"Well, it's been a day and a half now."

"What day is it?"

"Friday," Cath glanced at her watch, "half past ten precisely."

"I'd lost all track of time. Yesterday – it was yesterday, wasn't it, that Murray–?"

"No love, the day before," Cath said gently.

"It's all a bit of a blur. How come you're here? It's not visiting time, is it?"

"No. That's one of the privileges that goes with this," Cath touched her clerical collar. "We vicars can come and go as we please, more or less. Tell me, how're you feeling?"

"My body is just one big ache. But other than that, I'm here, and safe." She took a deep, shuddering breath. It caused a stab of pain in her side. "Ouch. Must remember to breathe more carefully."

"That's the cracked rib. I made the charge nurse tell me all about your injuries. I wanted to know what you were up against."

"I'm not so bad. The biggest problem is the frustration of being stuck in this bed and not knowing what's going on. I've got so many questions that need answering."

Cath grinned. "That sounds more like you. Give me a moment to find a vase for these daffs, and then I'll sit down and answer as many questions as I can, although I don't know that much, I'm afraid." She disappeared out the door but was soon back carrying the daffodils in an ugly but capacious cut glass vase. She cleared a space on the bedside table and put them down.

"Can you sit me up?"

"Not completely, love, but I can lift the pillow end a bit." She searched around and came up with what looked a bit like a TV remote, pressed a button and Fabia felt herself lifted just a little. For some reason it made her feel more in control once she was propped up. Cath carefully straightened the pillows then pulled up a chair and sat down. "So, what do you want to know?" she asked.

"How's Cecily?"

Cath sighed. "Well, she's no longer out of it. Murray had been drugging her to keep her quiet."

"I thought as much."

"I think she'd guessed he was responsible for Amber's death, but she was too drugged up, and too scared to do anything about it. Did you know he'd been beating her?"

"I had my suspicions. The signs were there, and when I visited her yesterday, sorry, the day before, I saw the bruising. It was awful, all down her arm and over her back."

"Poor woman. It'll take a long time and a lot of care before she has any peace of mind. She keeps asking for you."

"The first thing I'll do when I get out of here is go and see her."

"She's blaming herself, of course."

"That hateful man," Fabia said forcefully. "I could never stand him, but when I first began to think he was Amber's killer I told myself it was because I was prejudiced, because of my dislike. And then, when I saw the photo of Neville in the newspaper, wearing that coat, just a black version of the one Murray Cole used to wear that was in the nearly-new-stuff bag, I realised I'd seen those lichen marks on it and I might be on the right track. Cole must have stuffed it into the bag thinking it was the

291

usual rubbish one. What a risk to take!"

"But he was probably counting on the bag being put out that night. And I think he's an incredibly arrogant man," said Cath, her expression hardening. "I dare say it would have never occurred to him that he'd be found out."

"You didn't like him either?"

"I used to. Whenever I had to go to the school, he was always rather charming, and he seemed to care a great deal about the students, particularly about their academic achievements. I suppose that should have rung warning bells, but I thought he cared as much about their welfare. It wasn't until he became so unreasonable about Amber that I began to change my mind."

"Everyone else seemed to like him, but I always had this niggling feeling it was one big performance. I don't know why."

"Probably because you're a very good judge of character."

"But why did he do it?" asked Fabia.

"That I can't answer, but I'm sure Matt Lambert will be able to tell you soon enough. I spoke to him late last night. Cecily's staying with me for a few days and he phoned to ask how she is, which I thought was very sweet of him. He's going to come and see you this morning."

Fabia's spirits lifted. She wanted to see Matt so much, and not just to have all her questions answered. She'd lived for over two years with the pain of their estrangement, and now she found it hard to believe it was no longer there.

"Anyway, I mustn't stay too long," Cath said. "You should rest." She got up to go, but before she did so, the door opened again. Matt appeared round it. His face lit up when he saw Fabia was awake, then became more guarded when he saw Cath.

"Talk of the devil. Hallo, Chief Inspector," Cath said, grinning at Fabia and then at Matt, a glint of mischief in her eyes. "I'll leave you two in peace, but I'll pop in again tomorrow, Fabia." And she bustled out of the room, giving them an approving smile as she left.

Matt came the rest of the way in and up to the bed. There was an anxious frown between his eyes and he pushed his hair back in a familiar gesture. He always does that when he's unsure of himself, Fabia thought.

"I told that terrifying charge nurse I had to speak to you about the case, so she let me in. How're you feeling?" he asked.

"As if I've been used as a punch bag."

He smiled. "That's a pretty good description I'd say, poor old girl."

"Less of the old, thanks very much." The feeble joke didn't really come off. There was an awkward little silence which neither seemed able to break. It lengthened until Fabia could bear it no longer.

"I'm so glad you're here," she said in a rush. "I'm desperate to know what's been happening." She tried to push herself up, but fell back, groaning.

"Don't start trying to sit up. That bastard did a lot of damage before we got to you." He bit his lower lip. "I just can't stop thinking – what if we'd arrived just a little later?"

Fabia, looking at him, realised there were tears in his eyes. For some reason, this took all the awkwardness away. She held a hand out to him. Very carefully Matt sat down on the edge of the bed, took her hand and kissed it lightly. "Fabia, I–"

"Don't think about it," she said. "I'm not Bethan. This time, Matt, you arrived in time. Remember that."

"Okay," he took a deep, shaking breath. "Okay, what do you want to know?"

"Everything," said Fabia.

Acknowledgements

A few thank-yous to my writing gurus, Jeannie and Dallas, and to all in the Guernsey Writers' Group, for their support and encouragement. To my fantastic editor, Arianna, for her eagle eye and quirky remarks, and to all at The Book Folks. And most of all, thank you to Niall for listening and contributing, for your unfailing encouragement, and for never grumbling when the potatoes boil dry.

If you enjoyed this book, please let others know by leaving a quick review on Amazon. Also, if you spot anything untoward in the paperback, get in touch. We strive for the best quality and appreciate reader feedback.

editor@thebookfolks.com

www.thebookfolks.com

Also by Pippa McCathie:

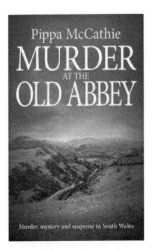

MURDER AT THE OLD ABBEY

The second book to feature Fabia Havard and Matt Lambert

When an overbearing patriarch and much begrudged ex-army officer is found dead in his home, there is no shortage of suspects. DCI Matt Lambert investigates, but struggles with a lack of evidence. He'll have to rely on his former boss, ex-detective Fabia Havard, to help him. But will their fractious relationship get in the way of solving the case?

Available in paperback, audio, and FREE with Kindle Unlimited.

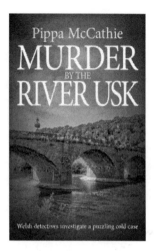

MURDER BY THE RIVER USK

The third book to feature Fabia Havard and Matt Lambert

Almost ten years after he went missing, a student's body is found. Forensics show that he was murdered and a cold case is reopened. But when detectives begin to investigate his background, many people he knew are found to be keeping a secret of sorts. Faced with subterfuge and deceit, rooting out the true killer will take all their detective skills.

Available in paperback, audio, and FREE with Kindle Unlimited.

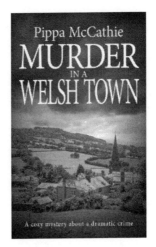

MURDER IN A WELSH TOWN

The fourth book to feature Fabia Havard and Matt Lambert

Hopes for a town pantomime are dashed when a participant is found murdered. The victim was the town gossip and there is no shortage of people who had a grudge to bear against him. Detective Matt Lambert leads the investigation but draws on the help of his girlfriend, ex-police officer Fabia Havard. Can they solve the crime together?

Available in paperback and FREE with Kindle Unlimited.

LIBERATION DAY

A standalone romantic thriller

Having become stranded in the English Channel after commandeering her cheating boyfriend's boat, Caro is rescued by a handsome stranger. But when the boat is impounded on suspicion of smuggling, she once again finds herself in deep water.

Available in paperback and FREE with Kindle Unlimited.

Made in the USA
Las Vegas, NV
03 March 2021

18925235R00178